MINT JULEP
MURDER

MINT JULEP
MURDER

Carolyn G. Hart

BANTAM BOOKS
New York Toronto London Sydney Auckland

To Phil,
who loves Hilton Head Island, too.

Author's Note

It was a pleasure to set a mystery on Hilton Head, the island that inspired the creation of Broward's Rock in *Death on Demand*. I hope I've provided enough of a glimpse of the island to bring happy memories to my readers who have vacationed there and to encourage others to discover its spacious beaches, moss-draped live oaks, and tranquil lagoons.

Everything in the book is true to the island except the Buccaneer Hotel, which I have placed just to the north of the Coligny Beach entrance, where the Breakers Villas stand, and Benedict Books, which is a composite of the several charming bookstores on the island.

The Dixie Book Festival is my own creation. It would be a tight fit on the Coligny Beach entrance plaza, but it could be done. And wouldn't it be fun!

MINT JULEP
MURDER

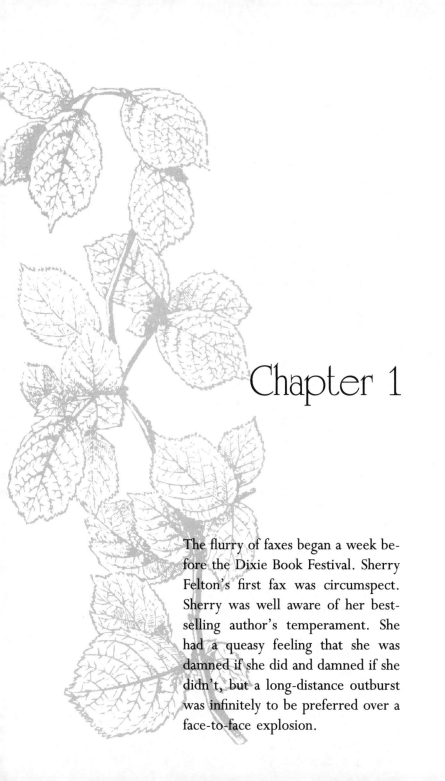

Chapter 1

The flurry of faxes began a week before the Dixie Book Festival. Sherry Felton's first fax was circumspect. Sherry was well aware of her best-selling author's temperament. She had a queasy feeling that she was damned if she did and damned if she didn't, but a long-distance outburst was infinitely to be preferred over a face-to-face explosion.

FAX 1 - FROM: Sherry Felton

TO: Leah Vixen Kirby

Dear Leah,

Biddy Maxwell tells me a Georgia publisher named Kenneth Hazlitt has approached her with an idea for a novel, a steamy sex-and-tell piece, all about some famous Southern writers and their indiscretions at a conference. He hinted to Biddy that it's a roman à clef. She's shopping the idea around.

Your latest sales figures are super. The paperback of *Love's Lost Splendour* is shipping like hotcakes.

See you at Hilton Head.

Best,

Sherry

It came as no surprise to Sherry when her fax machine signaled incoming material.

FAX 2 - FROM: Leah Kirby

TO: Sherry Felton

Dear Sherry,

Kenneth Hazlitt is a mediocre publisher and he couldn't write a decent novel if somebody handed him a mouse with an IQ of 200-plus. He's a buffoon who loves Dracula, Frankenstein, and Little Orphan Annie with the Statler Brothers bellowing in the background. But who gives a damn about quality? How much sex and who are the main characters?

If I could get a spot on *Oprah, Love's Lost Splendour* would sell five times what it's doing now. I must talk to you about publicity. And whose idea was it to schedule my Festival signing at four o'clock? They've got to be kidding. I want nine a.m. And I mean it.

As ever,

Leah

Sherry read as the fax paper oozed out. Damn. It was too late to change autographing times. The conference program was already printed. Leah knew that, of course. But who expected the world's most famous author of Civil War novels to give a damn about minor facts like printed programs? Sherry debated calling the Festival programmer. Maybe they could put up a sign announcing a time change at the information booth. . . . Oh, hell, what a bother. She didn't reach for the phone. Instead, her eyes glinting with malice, she waited thirty minutes, then dispatched a reply. As always, she used her author's full name. One had to take pleasure where one found it.

FAX 3 - FROM: Sherry Felton

TO: Leah Vixen Kirby

Dear Leah,

The programmer regrets being unable to change your autographing time. The committee wants the most famous author available at four p.m. The local TV promises a crew, and they feed to CBS.

Lots of sex, according to Biddy. And the cast of characters includes the most famous author of Civil War novels; the author of the latest male romance novel à la *Bridges* and *Love Story;* the author of Southern sojourns of the soul; the author of good-old-boy diatribes against blacks, Jews, feminists, and women in general; and the world's bestselling mystery writer.

Oh, and congratulations upon your receiving a Medallion at the Festival. I'll be sure and attend the ceremony.

Best,

Sherry

FAX 4 - FROM: Leah Kirby

    TO: Alan Blake

        Missy Sinclair

        Jimmy Jay Crabtree

        Emma Clyde

Dear Fellow Medallion Honorees,

FYI, Kenneth Hazlitt is shopping a proposal using thinly disguised (if disguised at all) characters patterned after all of us. Remember Wynnewood?

The sorry bastard.

Leah Kirby

FAX 5 - FROM: Emma Clyde

    TO: Leah Kirby

        Alan Blake

        Melissa Sinclair

        Jimmy Jay Crabtree

Dear Fellow Honorees,

I smell a Medallion-sized rat.

Best regards,

Emma

FAX 6 - FROM: Errol Beatty, publicist

    TO: Leah Kirby

        Emma Clyde

Dear Ms. Kirby and Ms. Clyde,

Mr. Crabtree is presently on a book tour. I will bring your faxes to his attention when I speak to him this evening.

Best wishes,

Errol Beatty

FAX 7 - FROM: Alan Blake

TO: Leah Kirby

Emma Clyde

Dear Leah and Emma:

Let's talk when we arrive at the Festival. They're putting me up at the Buccaneer.

Fondly,

Alan

FAX 8 - FROM: Melissa Sinclair

TO: Leah Kirby

Emma Clyde

Ladies,

I'll call Kenneth.

Ciao,

Missy

FAX 9 - FROM: Melissa Sinclair

TO: Leah Kirby

Emma Clyde

Dear Leah, Emma,

The dolt's excited out of his mind. He says Barker, Dunwoody & Kell is interested. This is all on the basis of a three-page proposal. I can't believe this!

By the way, who picked us as Medallion winners? Does anybody know? Kenneth swears the Medallions have *NO* connection with his book. And the Republican National Committee is proposing Clinton for the Nobel Peace Prize.

I am not a happy camper. Should we cancel?

Missy

On a separate sheet faxed solely to Leah Kirby, Missy appended the following:

P.S. The writer of Civil War novels is a redhead who always wears green—and there's a broad hint of sexual dalliance *NOT* with her spouse.

In her Belle Meade mansion in Nashville, Leah Kirby savagely crumpled the fax. She was a strikingly beautiful woman, tall and slender with hair as fiery as molten lava. Today's silk suit was a soft jade.

Footsteps sounded in the hallway.

Leah jammed the fax into her pocket as her husband, Carl, entered the room.

Carl Kirby was slender, sixty, with thinning gray hair. His face was pale and drawn, but when he saw Leah, his mouth curved into a cheerful smile. "It looks good on the interview with *People.* They'll focus on you as the greatest living writer of tender love stories." His voice was full of pride. For Leah. Of Leah. "The *People* crew wants to follow us around for a week or two. Maybe right after the Festival. They want to get the flavor of our true-life love story."

He stepped close, held out his arms.

Leah moved into his embrace, pressed against him.

The fax crackled in her pocket.

Chapter 2

"What do you mean, they want to give me less for the next contract?" Jimmy Jay Crabtree smacked the table and shifted the wad of chewing tobacco in his right cheek with his tongue. "That's a mother lode of crap, Harold. No way am I going to accept less than a half mil."

"You aren't selling, Jimmy Jay. That's the bottom line. The returns on your book are running around eighty percent. You're lucky they're even willing to talk a new contract. And Buzzy's not positive he can get it by the editorial board even if your advance is cut in half.'' A thoughtful pause. ''Truth is, things go in cycles in publishing, Jimmy Jay. Limbaugh. Grisham. Nobody could believe *their* sales figures. Outer space. So everybody started publishing down-home think pieces and lawyer books. Limbaugh and Grisham are still at the top of the charts.''

Jimmy Jay waited.

But his agent didn't go ahead to say the obvious: The clones weren't coming through. Readers wanted the real thing.

Jimmy Jay's mean little mouth closed in a tight hard line. He couldn't trust himself not to fire Harold on the spot.

But Harold was one of the best literary agents in New York.

If Harold couldn't get him a new contract . . .

''Talk to you later.'' Jimmy Jay slammed the phone down. It wasn't his fault. He was just as good as Limbaugh. Better. Because he *really* laid it on the line. He didn't bother to try and be cute. He told it straight out, and if people didn't like it, they could take a flying leap.

If his book wasn't selling, well, the asshole, knee-jerking liberals would laugh themselves silly if the word got out. Jimmy Jay knew they hated him for telling the good old unvarnished truth, like what a joke it was for the bleeding hearts to moan about poor little mamas on welfare. The bleeding hearts squealed like stuck pigs when he said it was time to cut those ladies off the dole if they kept on having babies. Look at it: If those sorry broads didn't want Uncle's check every month, they'd sure as hell figure out what made babies. It wasn't like it was a state secret. And all this crap about AIDS. As far as he was concerned, it was time to worry about ordinary, everyday Americans, not rejects who played Russian roulette in their sex lives.

But *The New York Times* had sure had it in for him ever since *Straighten Up and Fly Right* came out.

He'd mailed a copy of the bestseller list to *The NYT Book Review* for twenty-three weeks and circled his title on it.

No answer, of course.

Christ, he couldn't let those Yankees have the last laugh.

But he had an empty feeling in his gut. He aimed at the wastebasket. Tobacco juice splattered the side and dribbled onto the rug. So let the maid earn her salary.

Yeah, *Straighten Up* made the bestseller list for twenty-three weeks.

But that was based on titles shipped, not sold. His publishers had gambled that he could sell like Rush and Grizzard and Howard Stern. So the sales reps leaned on booksellers, gave special discounts to entice them to up their orders. The pub effort was great—radio spots across the country, a drive-by radio tour, signings in sixteen cities.

But none of that mattered if Harold was right. Returns around 80 percent. The book was not selling.

They'd toss him out like yesterday's headline.

Chapter 3

Alan Blake hummed as he shaved. ("Oh, What a Beautiful Morning.") Then he stopped and grinned. Green gel dripped from his chin. Sometimes he couldn't believe his own instincts. Jesus, that was *perfect*. Corny but lovable. The right touch for his upcoming *Parade* interview. He'd have to remember to tell the reporter in a half-chagrined way how he always hummed when he shaved. "A Day with Alan Blake." His readers would love it. He smiled at his reflection in the steamy mirror. An engaging smile. Good, white, even teeth. Steady blue eyes. Wavy chestnut hair. A manly chin with just the hint of a cleft. He carefully eased the razor over his upper lip. A few more strokes and he was done. He heard the telephone above the rush of water. He patted his face with a washcloth and reached for the bathroom extension.

His eyes admired the luxurious bathroom—a whirlpool, mirrors with lights that could brighten or dim, the heated towel rack—as he picked up the receiver.

"Hi, Alan. Long time no see."

He felt like a boxer hit in the kidneys.

"You there, Alan?"

"I'm sorry. I don't believe—"

"Come off it, man. We had a fun time in L.A. We'll have to get together. Talk about old times. I read in the paper you're gonna be at that book deal in Hilton Head. I'll look you up, man."

Chapter 4

Blue Benedict's back ached. Carefully, she bent her knees, keeping her lower back muscles straight, as she hefted another box of books into her Jeep Cherokee. She couldn't, absolutely could not, have back trouble now. She picked up another box. There were dozens more boxes yet to be transported to the booth. And more boxes for the signings at the hotel. Oh, Lord, had she remembered to call and see if the book room was open today? Okay, that was—

The startled half-scream brought Blue sharply around. The box thudded to the ground. Pain flared in her back.

"Mother!" Ginny's voice rose in a panicked squeal.

Blue Benedict scrambled through the open back door, skidded around stacks of boxes, plunged into the rear of the bookstore.

Ginny was blundering down the middle aisle, her hands held out in front on her. "Mother!" Her voice broke into a sob. "I can't see. I can't see! The box blew up."

White powder covered Ginny's face, speckled her black hair.

Blue reached her daughter. "This way. Into the john. Let's wash it off."

"I can't *see!*" Her daughter's voice shook with fear.

Blue didn't hesitate. She grabbed an empty vase and filled it with warm water. "Hold your breath, Ginny."

Blue splashed the whole of it into her daughter's face, then gently dabbed her eyes.

Ginny blinked. "I—it's smeary—but I can see. I can. I can."

Blue was trembling by the time she reached the front of the store and the pile of mail that Ginny had been opening. She looked grimly at the small ripped-open package. The still-hot flashcube inside it accounted for Ginny's sudden blindness. It was clever enough: The flashcube exploding as the lid was lifted. And the now uncoiled spring had flung up whitish powder.

Blue dampened a finger, touched it to the powder, gave a delicate lick.

Flour.

Flour pure and simple.

A practical joke.

But there was nothing funny about the message in all capital, cut-out letters:

THIS COULD HAVE BEEN A LETTER BOMB.
TRASH JIMMY JAY CRABTREE NOW.
OR LOOK FOR A BIGGER BANG.

Chapter 5

Annie nosed her Volvo behind the dumpmaster in the alley. She gazed at the back door to Death on Demand—the finest mystery bookstore this side of Atlanta—with wariness, trepidation, and deep yearning.

If she could survive this weekend, her store would once again be her pride, her joy, her refuge, and her delight.

But the Dixie Book Festival

would have to be history before Annie's life was once again predictable.

As predictable as life could ever be. . . .

She glanced at an ornately decorated square of shiny cardboard lying in the passenger seat atop a haphazard stack of files, packets, and notes to herself (*Tomorrow pick up the hotel keys FIRST, Stop by liquor store, GAS, Cleaners, Sugar? MAX?*), and sighed. In ornate script, the card held this legend:

❧

An Eagle Soars.
From Simplicity *by Laurel Darling Roethke. Page 2.*

Despite Annie's intense effort to discipline her mind, she immediately envisioned a majestic eagle, its imperious head held high, its magnificent wings spread wide.

And, dammit, it gave her a surge of energy.

Maybe her spacey mother-in-law was on to something.

"Come on," Annie muttered. "Don't lose it now." She absolutely was not going to get roped into the collective insanity on the part of Laurel and her fellow conspirators, Henny Brawley and Miss Dora Brevard. Just because Annie owned a bookstore and somehow had been persuaded to serve as an author liaison to this year's Medallion honorees at the Dixie Book Festival on Hilton Head Island, that did not —emphatically did NOT—mean that Annie had entree to the world of publishing, as in the ability to find publishers for the proud authors of three distinctly varied manuscripts.

Annie slid out of the car. "No," she said aloud. "No, no, no." She gave a hunted look over her shoulder. The three hopeful authors had bombarded her with ideas for finding publishers that ranged from the absurd (Miss Dora, imperiously: *Simply inform them our books* must *be published)* to the sensible (Henny, briskly: *I've surveyed the lists of publishers who are coming and Mint Julep Press is perfect. Extremely aggressive marketing.*)

Annie completed her survey of the alley. The coast was clear. Still, she ducked in the back door of Death on Demand like a fugitive. Jean Valjean had nothing on her.

Annie had learned to her dismay that entrapment could come so unexpectedly. Miss Dora didn't even live on Broward's Rock, but she'd turned up on the ferry that morning, and Annie had been trapped for a twenty-minute discourse on the originality and superiority of Miss Dora's cookbook.

Annie stood tensely in the storeroom. But there was no sound beyond the partially open door. She tiptoed across the floor, peered into the bookstore, her wonderful, dear store, full of fabulous mysteries from the newest (the delightful debut of Gar Anthony Haywood's Dottie and Joe Loudermilk series) to the oldest (leather-bound copies of the *Collected Edgar Allan Poe*). Reassured, she pushed the door wider.

"Dear Annie."

Annie froze.

Laurel Darling Roethke uncurled from the petit point sofa in front of the fireplace. It was a new acquisition to make readers feel quite at home. Just as cozy as the nooks and crannies in Denver's Tattered Cover bookstore. Though, of course, the Death on Demand hearth was cold now. South Carolina was much too balmy in May for a fire.

Agatha rose, too, stretching and hopping down to twine around Laurel's ankles.

Annie ignored a pang of jealousy. But it was irritating for her very own cat, the pampered prima donna of the store, to treat Laurel with such affection, especially since Agatha had ignored Annie for the past three days. That, of course, was why the sleek black cat was so ostentatiously pirouetting about Laurel. The message couldn't have been clearer.

To be fair, Annie understood. Nothing in the store was quite on schedule, despite Annie's best efforts. And nothing would be on schedule until the Festival was over. Agatha despised change. Or any other aspect of life that didn't suit. Too much wind. An unaccustomed frost. As far as Agatha was concerned, Annie was responsible. Period.

Annie crossed her arms and regarded her mother-in-law gravely. And tried hard not to let her mouth curve into a grin. She pressed her lips together. God, she mustn't *encourage* Laurel.

Laurel beamed. "Dear Annie," she caroled.

Annie's lips quivered. *Steady,* she warned herself. Laurel must not detect any softening of Annie's refusal to cooperate. No way did Annie intend be outmaneuvered by her silver-tongued, crafty, incredibly determined mother-in-law. Absolutely no way.

No matter how appealing Laurel looked in her simple white cotton blouse and beige linen skirt.

Anyone else would look like the class nerd in a Fifties movie. Laurel, of course, looked sublimely elegant and as gloriously and agelessly beautiful as ever, her hair as softly gold as moonlight, her patrician features touched with warmth, her vivid blue eyes merry with laughter and a hint of childlike expectation that bordered on the otherworldly. Bordered, hell. Crossed over, in Annie's opinion.

Laurel clasped a hand to her chest. "The Sun Shines."

Annie waited.

"Don't you think, my dear," Laurel's distinctive husky voice rose slightly, "that says it all?"

Now those beautifully manicured hands—shell-pink polish—were clasped soulfully to her chin.

A smooth, wrinkle-free chin, Annie noted acerbically. But Laurel insisted she'd never had cosmetic surgery.

Yeah.

Those deeply blue eyes continued to regard Annie patiently.

Annie realized a response was expected. "Uh . . . yes. Yes, I guess that sums it up pretty well."

Laurel darted to her, gave her a swift embrace. Annie felt the whisper of lips on her cheek, smelled a faint hint— Annie's nose wrinkled—rose? Hmm. Usually Laurel preferred the scent of lilac. Out of long experience, Annie wondered sharply what the change in fragrance augured. That it augured something, she didn't doubt. Oh, of course. Laurel's latest enthusiasm, the theme of her book: *Simplicity*. She was probably gathering up roses, drying them, squashing them, and making her own perfume. Were roses more easily obtained than lilac blooms? Who knew? Who *cared*? That was harmless enough. If only Laurel would confine her activities to similarly socially harmless pursuits. But, unfortunately—

Annie felt a piece of paper being tucked in her skirt pocket. Then Laurel wafted past her into the storeroom. "*Dear* Annie. Thank you, thank you, love. For everything. For your sweet nature. For your support. *The Sun Shines.* That shall be the opening truth. Page one. Oh, Annie, I can't wait until tomorrow."

The storeroom door closed.

Annie didn't retrieve the piece of paper.

Not now.

Maybe never.

As for tomorrow . . .

Tomorrow was the opening day of the Dixie Book Festival on the South's premier holiday island, Hilton Head. There would be more than seventy Southern authors to be wined and dined and showcased at breakfasts, luncheons, and dinners. Everybody from Carl Hiaasen to Celestine Sibley.

Booksellers from throughout the South.

Publishers and editors from small regional presses.

Plus a goodly number of booths from some of the big New York publishing houses.

Several thousand festivalgoers.

It should be a fabulous success, *would* be a fabulous success, and certainly Annie shouldn't let small embarrassments—

The storeroom door opened swiftly; her mother-in-law's golden head popped out. "One for All, All for One." Laurel's husky voice brimmed with confidence. A final beaming smile, then Laurel withdrew, and the door softly closed.

"Oh, God," Annie groaned, "that's what's driving me—" Annie felt a prick on her ankle. She looked down. "Dammit, Agatha, you could at least ask first."

The pressure from Agatha's two exceedingly sharp incisors increased, just a little.

"Okay, okay. I'll feed you." Annie moved fast. Once Agatha reached the incisor-to-the-ankle stage, bloodletting wasn't far off. As Annie pulled the tab on a can of savory salmon, she told the feline sternly, "I've about had enough of everybody. You, Laurel, Henny, Miss Dora, my authors." Actually, although she'd quite soon realized that dealing with authors meant handling very fragile egos accompanied by the ability to be *creatively* demanding, she still enjoyed—mostly—getting to know five very bright and gifted people. She'd even begun to think of them proprietorially. All except Jimmy Jay Crabtree, of course.

She picked up the coffee thermos, then turned behind the coffee bar to select a mug.

This was one of the great pleasures of Death on Demand.

Annie took pride in her collection of coffee mugs, each inscribed in red script with the name of a famous author and title. Usually, it put her in a good humor simply to pour a cup of special brew—sometimes Kona, sometimes Colombian, sometimes Kenya—into one of the mugs.

This afternoon, however, she eyed the mugs without enthusiasm. She considered *Phantom Lady* by William Irish. Maybe she could disappear. No. It wasn't quite that bad. She was tempted by Carolyn Wells's *Murder in the Bookshop* because that's what she felt like committing. First victim: Blue Benedict of Hilton Head's Benedict Books, who'd talked Annie into serving as an author liaison. "Annie, it won't take much time at all!" The memory of that hideously inaccurate prediction made Annie's lip curl. Annie had spent so much time on the telephone with her authors—and charming as most of them were (except, of course, Jimmy Jay Crabtree) —it had kept her up late at night and working weekends to get her ordering done and keep Death on Demand running smoothly, especially since Ingrid Jones, her wonderful assistant, had been out with foot surgery until this week.

But it *was* fascinating to get to know these very famous authors (except for Jimmy Jay Crabtree) and to try and make them feel comfortable and welcome. Annie had quickly read all their books, and now she felt she knew them very well indeed.

The phone rang. Death on Demand closed at five, and it was already past six o'clock.

The sharp peal sounded again.

Annie ignored the rings. She felt she could count on two verities. The call wasn't from the Georgia or Florida lotteries; the call was from one of her authors, and right now she absolutely couldn't handle one more task. Nada.

Annie poured coffee into *V as in Victim* by Lawrence

Treat, took a sip, and sighed. The coffee was tepid. She poured it out. Finally, the ringing stopped.

Annie swished out the sink, then moved around the coffee bar to the central aisle. She did take time to look up at the month's mystery paintings hanging over the fireplace. The first customer to correctly identify the author and title represented by each painting received a book and free coffee for a month.

Henny Brawley, her most knowledgeable customer, was the all-time champion. She had, in fact, won the past three months in a row.

But Henny hadn't visited Death on Demand even once this month. Definitely a financial loss, but maybe it would give someone else a chance to win.

Henny would know these five books, of course, because they were the start of something wonderful in mystery fiction, something that had changed the course of mystery publishing in the United States.

The first painting captured so beautifully the crowded, tatty splendor of an antique store. Furniture, vases, lamps, books, and artwork were jammed together. In the sharp, white glare from the floodlights set up by the police, the chalked outline of a corpse was starkly apparent against the Oriental rug. A golden chain dangled from the key still in the lock of the glass cabinet that contained small pieces of value, including a set of bone-handled knives. One knife was missing. A young woman, her black hair marked by a streak of gray, stood in a narrow aisle, staring at a mannequin of a small boy. The mannequin's feet had been fitted with an ornate pair of iron shoes.

In the second painting, the young woman on the temple stage was pinning a Berkeley police badge to her blouse. At

her feet, a knife protruding from his chest, sprawled a handsome Oriental man in a loose gold robe. His thin T-shirt and
pants were also gold. A crimson sash circled his waist. Behind
them rose an altar draped with gold, electric blue, and orange brocade. Prayer wheels flanked each side of the altar.
Overlooking the altar was a giant picture of the man who
now lay so still with the ugly weapon in his chest.

In the third painting, a good summer tan darkened the
face of the woman in the yellow cotton top and blue jeans.
She looked athletic. Her face was somber as she stared at the
decomposing body of a man slumped face forward over a
kitchen table. The back of his head was a mess from the
bullet's exit.

In the fourth painting, the woman in jeans knelt beside
the body in a kelly green bathrobe. The bullet hole was at the
base of the dead blonde's throat. The body lay straight back,
arms flung out, hips turned slightly. The green eyes were half
open. The living room carpet held no footprints.

In the fifth painting, the bathroom was Las Vegas style
with plenty of mirrors, pink marble, and gleaming white tile.
The only out-of-the-ordinary occupant of the sumptuous
room was the young girl lying on the red-and-white tile
floor. Her throat had been cut, and there was blood everywhere. On a nearby pink velvet couch, a middle-aged woman
sobbed. The house detective talked into his handheld radio.
An attractive young woman with brown hair and green eyes
stood to one side, taking everything in.

These books had made a difference in the mystery world.

Annie nodded in satisfaction.

Her good humor restored, she headed up the central
aisle, passing the Romantic Suspense. She paused at the Psychological Suspense section to put a Rochelle Majer Krich

title on the proper shelf. She took time to be sure she still had plenty of titles by Mary Higgins Clark and Patricia Highsmith and Judith Kelman.

Comedy mysteries—a whole shelf full of Joan Hess!—were on her right, and spy novels and thrillers to her left. She so enjoyed Eric Ambler and Manning Coles.

Annie reached the front desk. She looked thoughtfully at the answering machine. Blink. Blink. Blink. Blink. Blink.

Five red blinks.

Five messages.

Agatha flowed through the air, settled beside the answering machine, delicately began to wash her face.

"Want to bet it's the Gang of Five?" Her authors could be both charming and imperious. "Or another of the Three Musketeers?"

Agatha's cool green eyes looked through Annie as if she were indeed a phantom.

Annie reached out, gently stroked the shiny, sleek fur. "I'm sorry, Agatha. I know everything's topsy-turvy. But it won't be for much longer." Annie yanked her hand back just in time to escape the razor-sharp teeth. "Ingrid will be here all weekend. She loves you, too. And it *will* be a fun weekend."

That was for sure.

It was a great opportunity to see authors she'd admired and sold for so long: Lee Smith. Alexandra Ripley. Sharyn McCrumb. Louise Shivers. Ernest Gaines. Margaret Maron. And many, many more.

Although she did have a presentiment—no way were those the sole prerogative of damsels in distress—that she was going to be very busy with her own special charges. She could almost hear Blue Benedict's soft South Carolina accent:

"Annie honey, you're just *so* good with people, and it's *so* important to keep these *special* honorees happy . . ."

But enough was enough. Annie shook her head at the blinking lights, grabbed the notebook with the conference itineraries for her authors, and headed out the back door.

By the time she turned the car into the long, curving, dusty road leading home, she was humming. It increased her cheer that she no longer had to slow for the gated entry. Since the Burgers had moved to Australia, the Scarlet King Neighborhood Association, made up of the homeowners with houses around the lagoon, had agreed to remove the ugly gate. Annie was pleased. She pushed on the accelerator, and the car picked up speed.

Almost home. Sunshine glistened through the graceful swaths of Spanish moss. With the windows down, she could smell the sweet scent of blooming magnolias. She loved her island, the dusty unpaved roads, the palmetto palms and quick-growing ferns. Almost home.

As for her Festival duties, she would follow the example of the South's most famous literary heroine. "After all, tomorrow is another day," she murmured.

The gray road curved, and there was her beautiful house, hers and Max's.

As always, her heart lifted and her mouth curved into a smile. She loved the glistening expanses of glass that let streams and rivers of golden light pour into the sand-toned, two-story wooden house. Sometimes she couldn't believe her good fortune. Married to the most fun guy she'd ever known (and Max was undeniably as good-looking and sexy as a grown-up Joe Hardy), living on Broward's Rock, the most beautiful island off the coast of South Carolina, owner of the best little mystery bookstore east of Atlanta!

How could life get any better?

The thought was swift: When she was once again her own boss, the Dixie Book Festival successfully behind her . . .

Annie parked next to Max's red Maserati. Max! What had she promised? Oh, yes. The sugar. He'd left a message asking her to pick up sugar. Why sugar? She shrugged and picked up the five-pound sack. As she slammed the car door, she dropped the keys into her pocket and felt the square of paper Laurel had tucked there. Annie wanted to ignore it.

But delay would not make it more palatable.

She stood in the deep shadow from a live oak tree. The sun slanting through the branches cast a pattern on the paper, but it didn't mute the brilliant crimson of the letters—in script—or the bright blue foil border:

Cherish Good Humor.
From Simplicity *by Laurel Darling Roethke. Page 9.*

A yellow Post-it was stuck to the bottom. She read the note:

> *Dear Annie - This mock-up is just one of hundreds* (Annie didn't doubt it) *of possible formats. More anon. Laurel.*

Annie shoved the sheet back into her pocket. No matter what she said, Laurel refused to believe Annie had no clout in the world of publishing. Annie shook her head, then hurried up the oyster shell path. Of course, once the Festival was over, Laurel and Henny and Miss Dora would have to give up badgering Annie for introductions to publishers.

Annie skipped up the steps at the thought. And, despite the Three Musketeers, she was certain the Festival was going to be fabulous. She'd just have to be patient with Broward's Rock's publisher-obsessed wannabe authors.

She hurried up the steps and opened the front door.

''Max?''

She stopped in the entry hall, tilted her head, and, quite frankly, sniffed. Something was burning, something terribly sweet. . . .

''Annie!''

She doubted that Max had ever managed to put quite so much expression into the sound of her name.

She followed her nose toward the kitchen.

''Annie.'' Hope mingled with frustration.

She stopped in the doorway.

It was Max all right, blond hair that she always wanted to touch, eyes a darker blue than a Minnesota lake—vivid blue eyes usually shining with laughter, but not right now—an expressive mouth that could turn her resolve to jelly.

But Max with a difference. His face was bewildered, his polo shirt stained, his navy shorts—and he did look *so* good in shorts—dusted with flour. Actually, heavily splotched with flour.

There was flour on the floor, in his hair, dappled across the range, in interesting swirls and eddies atop the table. Dorothy L., too white for flour to show, sat on a countertop, gingerly licking her front paws. Annie could see dainty cat pawprints in the swirls and eddies.

''Uh—you're cooking.'' Annie said it with a straight face, without even a glimmer of sarcasm.

Max shot her a look of suspicion.

Perhaps being around Laurel had its recompenses. Annie smiled benignly. She did refrain from clasping her hands soulfully to her chin.

"Annie, I need help."

"Yes."

"You see, it's *Miss Dora's Delectables.*" Max pointed at the welter of cooking implements. "Apple Pan-Dowdy." He didn't say it with any conviction.

"Oh." Annie weighed her response. She knew what she *wanted* to announce. She wanted to shout: "*Miss Dora's Delectables* be damned."

But Max was talking as fast as she'd ever heard him.

". . . after all, Annie, my own mother. And she made a commitment. She and Henny and Miss Dora swore a blood oath—that's how Laurel put it—One for All—"

"All for One," Annie joined in.

Max's face brightened.

"You know about it?"

Annie knew. The impossible trio had probably met at high noon or on the stroke of midnight to plight their awesome pact: The three hopeful authors would together brave the cold world of publishing (the Dixie Book Festival), and they would not rest, they would not flag, they would not fail until each had found a publisher for her book. Three books, of course. Quite disparate in tone and content.

Laurel was offering a small volume filled with simple, quiet, pithy comments that celebrated simplicity. *The Sun Shines. Cherish Good Humor.* Annie was tempted to quote these excerpts to Max. But she did want to preserve her marriage.

Not to be outdone, Henny, Annie's most persistent customer, had decided to come up with her own small book of comments: *The Quotable Sleuth.*

And Miss Dora? A cookbook: *Miss Dora's Delectables.*

". . . Mother called this afternoon. They really needed help. She said it was easy, and she faxed me the recipe, but I wonder if I got something wrong?"

Annie's shoes scuffed up flour. Laurel, of course, waited comfortably at the bookstore to pounce on Annie, instead of cooking up a storm at her condo. Henny Brawley was probably cooking and writing at the same time. Henny excelled in efficiency.

Annie was grinning by the time she reached her husband. "You know something, Max? You look good enough to eat," and she slipped her arms around him.

"Oh—" Max brightened immediately. He tossed the wooden spoon toward the disaster in the sink. "Yeah, yeah, yeah." He murmured something indistinct about cooking later, and his mouth sought Annie's.

Neither paid any attention to the ringing of the telephone.

Chapter 6

The next morning, Annie stopped in the front hall on her way to the kitchen, yawned, and punched the play button on the answering machine. She could smell coffee—dear Max, who always arose first and made the best coffee in the world. But they'd ignored the phone the night before and really, as an author liaison, she wasn't supposed to be out of reach.

So—

Three calls of increasing petulance from Jimmy Jay Crabtree: ". . . has to be Wild Turkey. Two fifths . . ." ". . . won't eat any of that damn PC food. Make sure I get a steak at the brunch . . ." "So what's the deal on this Southern Medallion? What kind of honor is it?"

A slightly more politic, but no less sharply worded call from Melissa Sinclair: ". . . have some misgivings about the provenance of the Medallion Award. Please have the particulars available when I arrive tomorrow . . ." Gone was the honeycomb-smooth voice, the drawled "Annie, honey . . ." that had prefaced previous calls requesting various additions for the bestselling author's suite.

Emma Clyde's call was quite direct: "I won't be trifled with, Annie. Inform the 'committee'—made up of one odious Georgia publisher?—that I decline to be honored . . ."

Every vestige of sleepiness was gone by now.

Annie stared at the machine like a *Rolling Stone* editor handed a prayer tract.

Leah Kirby's soft drawl was sheathed in ice: ". . . find it difficult to understand how the Dixie Book Festival could be a party to such a tasteless exploitation of the honored authors. This book proposal by Kenneth Hazlitt is at the very least a breach of good manners. I would cancel my appearance, but my readers are expecting me, and I will not disappoint them . . ."

Alan Blake's aw-shucks tone didn't hide his uneasiness: ". . . just a country boy, I know. But how is it that the authors who've won the Medallions are the same ones Kenneth figures to write a book about? That seems kind of funny . . ."

Annie felt like she'd walked in on the second act without a program.

What the hell had got into her Gang of Five? What was wrong with the Medallions? What book? What was going on?

That's when Max yelled, "Annie, look at this!" and the volume of the television set in the kitchen trebled.

Annie bolted toward the kitchen, leaving the answering machine still playing and Henny's well-modulated voice exclaiming: ". . . don't want to be a bother, Annie. But I know my book's going to sell—and I'll give you credit in the foreword, if you'll just introduce me . . ."

Annie stopped and stared at the small TV that sat in the bookcase opposite the breakfast table.

". . . no one was injured. Detective Clarence Wheeler from the Southern Division of the Beaufort County Sheriff's Department said a postal inspector has arrived in Hilton Head to direct the investigation. Detective Wheeler said it is a violation of federal law to threaten harm through the United States mails even though the package which reached Benedict Books Thursday was a mock letter bomb. Booksellers are warned to be cautious of unexpected packages.

"Mrs. Benedict declined to talk with reporters"—the earnest young anchor here looked slightly aggrieved—"and refused to say whether the threat will cause her to cease selling books by Jimmy Jay Crabtree. Crabtree's first book, *Straighten Up and Fly Right,* was a bestseller."

Annie was shaking her head. Not in her store. In addition to mysteries, she carried a selection of Southern authors, who sold very well indeed, especially Dori Sanders and Bobbie Ann Mason. But she'd returned almost a full box of Crabtree's book. Having dealt with the man on the telephone, she'd made a mental note never to order another.

". . . reached by telephone at his hotel in New Orleans, Crabtree announced he refused to be intimidated and would continue his book tour. Crabtree believes the warning 'bomb' is in retaliation against his conservative views. He is expected to arrive at Hilton Head today to attend the Dixie Book Festival. Crabtree will hold a news conference at the Buccaneer Hotel at three o'clock this afternoon. Mrs. Benedict, the bookstore owner, is chairman of the Festival. Authorities believe the fake letter bomb might have been sent to Mrs. Benedict because of her prominence in Southern book circles. In other news . . .''

Max clicked the remote, and the picture faded to black. A frown creased his handsome face. ''Hey, Annie, isn't Crabtree one of the authors you're taking around?''

''Yes.'' Annie picked up the cordless phone and dialed Blue Benedict's home. The number was busy.

Max's expression was grim. ''I don't like it.''

''I know. He's a jerk. First class, certified—''

''No. If some nut's sending out letter bombs—''

''*Fake* letter bombs.''

''They might get real.''

''I won't open any strange packages.''

''Don't open *any* packages.''

''But Max—''

''I'm serious. And we need to warn Ingrid.'' He pushed back his plate. ''And I think I'll see about a dog.''

Annie reached for a coffee mug. Coffee, she needed coffee. ''A dog?''

''Sure. A bomb-sniffing dog.''

Annie grinned.

Max looked puzzled.

''Oh, Max, it reminds me of a story Susan Dunlap tells about what it's really like to live in Berkeley and why that makes it so easy for her to write her Detective Jill Smith books. A bomb-sniffing dog.'' Annie giggled.

''Is a bomb-sniffing dog a subject for levity in Berkeley?''

"Max, listen to this—and Susan Dunlap swears it's true —there was growing concern in Berkeley over drug deals down in the flatlands, so the city council discussed hiring a drug-sniffing dog. Dunlap says all the old liberals who'd gotten rich and moved up in the hills were simply appalled that their city would even consider hiring something like a ferocious German shepherd to sniff out drugs. The city council's compromise was to hire a drug-sniffing"—Annie choked with laughter—"cocker spaniel! Can't you just see it, Max? A ferocious, salivating, lop-eared, wiggle-butted *cocker*?"

Max refused to be deflected. "Shepherd. Spaniel. Dachshund. Who cares? I'll see to it. And I'll hang out with you today."

Annie was touched. "Max, that's sweet. But I'll be okay. I have to run all over the place, picking up the authors. And you need to buy something that can pass for one of Miss Dora's recipes. Why don't you try Signe's?" Signe's Heaven Bound Bakery was one of Hilton Head's most successful— and delicious.

But Max was looking unaccustomedly serious. "You'll be careful?"

"Of course." Annie felt warm and happy—until she remembered those odd phone messages from her Gang of Five. Lord, she had so much to do—and now she needed to find out what had, collectively, spooked her authors.

Annie always enjoyed going to Hilton Head. She and one million six hundred thousand other visitors every year. Not of course that the island was any finer than Broward's Rock, but it was truly a world-class resort, perfect for families, golfers, tennis players, joggers, and swimmers. And much more accessible, over its graceful swooping bridge, than her own small island, which could be reached only by boat.

There was a price to pay, of course, for Hilton Head's proliferation of magnificent golf courses and pine-shaded clay courts and private residential areas and ever-increasing variety of shops: TRAFFIC.

Indeed, the island's popularity had resulted in the election of a mayor whose chief goal was to limit growth. The hospitality industry was urgently reminding residents that Hilton Head's prosperity was a direct result of tourism. Annual payrolls amounted to more than $85 million.

As her Volvo crested the bridge with its spectacular view of the Sound and marshes, Annie sighed. Ahead it was bumper-to-bumper on Hilton Head's sole main artery, the William Hilton Parkway. She glanced impatiently at her watch. She had to be at the Savannah airport by eleven. Maybe she shouldn't have tried to squeeze in a stop here.

It was a long drive to the heart of the island, made much longer by the stop-and-go traffic more reminiscent of a big city than a vacation paradise. Finally, she reached the Wexford shopping area. Turning right, she drove up and down the rows and miraculously found a parking spot being vacated by a van. She swooped into it triumphantly.

The glass-paned windows of Benedict Books were filled with displays of books by authors attending the Festival. The latest by Anne Rivers Siddons was piled in a tempting face-out pyramid. A gorgeous cover.

It was only nine-fifteen, so Annie rattled the front door-knob.

A security guard came up behind the glass door. He pointed at the CLOSED sign.

"Blue," Annie said loudly. "I need to see her. The Festival. Tell her it's Annie Darling."

The middle-aged man turned away.

Even though most of the shops were just opening, Wexford Plaza teemed with vacationers. It was easy to spot them. Sunburned noses even though it was only May. Crisp new Salty Dog or Harbour Town T-shirts. A relaxed, good-humored, holiday air.

A young woman unlocked the door, held it open just an inch. "I'm sorry, we're closed and—"

"Please, I have to talk to Blue. About the Festival. I have five authors due in today, and they're all in a snit. These are the Medallion winners. I need to know—"

"Wait just a minute, please."

The door closed.

Annie moved restively from one foot to another. She must be at the airport in time. She had a clear sense that Leah Vixen Kirby would be distinctly unamused if Annie was late.

Finally, the door reopened. Blue poked her head out. "Annie, look, whatever it is, you're going to have to handle it." Blue stood just an inch over five feet. Her tight golden curls quivered as she talked. Blue always talked fast despite her thick South Carolina accent. Now the words shot out jackhammer quick. "The post office people are here, and more of those fake bombs have turned up—in Birmingham and two in Atlanta and one in Miami—and I'm just crazy! I don't know what's wrong with your authors, but it's your problem."

Annie stuck her foot in the door. "They want to know who picked the winners."

"How should I know?" Blue started to close the door.

Annie caught it with her palms. "Blue, you're in charge. Who picked the Medallion winners?"

"Oh, the Select Committee, of course." She looked around the veranda as if television cameras might lie in wait, and hissed, "That's me, if you want to know, but I'll deny it until the day I die, so don't repeat it. Good heavens, I couldn't dillydally with an awards committee with all I have to deal with. You know what it's like to have an *awards* committee. Everybody gets so damn *serious*. And these are good writers. Why shouldn't I pick them? So what's their problem? Winning a Dixie Book Festival Medallion is very prestigious. And you can tell them that's what I said. About the honor, not the selection. Annie, I've *got* to go." The door began to close.

Annie leaned against the door and was surprised to be on the losing side. Dammit, she was bigger than Blue. "Hazlitt," she yelled. "Kenneth Hazlitt. Who's he?"

"Annie, you're incoherent today. He's Mint Julep Press. If you need to see him, he's staying at the Buccaneer." Blue's face brightened. "Is that why you asked? Kenneth's really excited about the Medallions. He keeps calling and getting more details. I wish everyone was as supportive as he's been. Even if he does clown around too much. But he certainly keeps things hopping. And he's planning a cocktail party for the honorees, so I put him on the same floor with all of you. That will work out. A party. I wish I could come. I *love* Kenneth's parties." Her usually refined face twisted into a snicker. "Goldfish. Ask Kenneth about the goldfish. Got to go, Annie." And now the door moved in earnest. "As for the authors," (a last shout) "work it out, Annie, work it out."

The door slammed shut.

Annie found herself once again glaring at the locked door to Benedict Books.

Annie raised her hand to knock.

Someone pulled the shade, making the CLOSED sign even more prominent.

Okay, okay. Annie got the message. And, after all, she was capable, competent, cool—but she had to pick up Leah Vixen Kirby in just over an hour. And she'd better have some answers.

Annie almost sideswiped a cleaner's van when she neglected to yield at the Sea Pines traffic circle. Although she didn't know how anybody could be expected to master the intricate give-and-take of the circle, in her view as complex as the instructions for assembling a computer. In a word, the damn traffic circle wasn't user-friendly. Despite its evident problems, however, island residents tenaciously refused to approve a change to stoplights. Annie gritted her teeth and lifted her hands briefly from the wheel in a mea culpa apology to the indignant driver of the cleaner's van. If bumper-to-bumper cars weren't bad enough, the island's stubborn retention of the two traffic circles at the beginning and end of Pope Avenue hopelessly aggravated the problem.

But she managed to make the swing around and peel off onto Pope without smacking into another vehicle, even taking time to notice the ducks who inhabited the small pond and the sign cautioning traffic to watch for crossing ducks. She glanced at her watch and picked up speed.

She would be making this trip a lot today, each time with an author. She tried to see the landscape with a stranger's eye and smiled with almost proprietorial pride at the dense pockets of huge pines, the always appealing compact palmettos, the blooming oleanders in the grassy median, the carefully homogenized commercial buildings in shades of beige, tan, and lime.

She would have enjoyed taking her charges to Broward's Rock with its quiet lanes and equally gorgeous beach, but

Hilton Head, though bustling, was just as lovely. May was a perfect month on any of the Sea Islands. The air was balmy, the temperature in the seventies, and no humidity. Hilton Head's fourteen miles of beaches were never really crowded, even at the height of the tourist season.

Annie pulled into the Buccaneer's parking lot. The Festival Committee couldn't have assigned her charges to a nicer hotel. The Festival events were occurring at open-air, tented booths on the public entrance to Coligny Beach, just a short stroll from the Buccaneer. Authors were also quartered at the beachfront Holiday Inn and at several other luxurious beachfront hotels.

The Buccaneer was one of Annie's favorite hotels. Small, elegant, and charming, it was built like an Italian villa with dusky mauve stuccoed walls and arched windows.

She hurried up the oyster shell path between fragrant banana shrubs. Brilliantly flowering hibiscus flamed in clay pots by the side entrance.

She had a hand on the door when the six-foot-tall pittosporum bush quivered. Henny Brawley darted out into the path. "Annie, I'm so glad to see you."

Broward's Rock's most accomplished reader of mystery fiction wore a scarlet linen suit. A slender gold necklace supported an oblong ceramic likeness of Agatha Christie. Henny's gray hair was swept back in soft waves. Her expression of surprise mingled with delight would have done justice to Jessica Fletcher upon finding a corpse. Annie wondered how long Henny had lurked behind the bush, waiting.

"How'd you know I'd come in by the side door?"

Henny's eyes narrowed, then she capitulated. "You had to park," she said tersely. "Look, I wanted to give you this." She thrust a two-by-three-inch piece of cardboard into Annie's hand. "I know this will hit the bestseller list. I'm thinking a *little* book, with a single quote on each page. You know, like *Life's Little Instruction Book* or *Everything I Know I Learned from My Cat*. A book doesn't have to be big to succeed, just big in scope!'' She nodded in undisguised self-congratulation. "*The Quotable Sleuth* can't miss, Annie. You can leave a message for me at the desk. Room 403.'' She smiled brightly and turned away, paused, called back, "I plan to use Miss Marple on page one: 'The great thing to avoid is having in any way a trustful mind.'

"Then at the bottom of the page, it will say: Jane Marple, *A Pocket Full of Rye*. Isn't that wonderful? Annie, I'm so excited!''

With a wave of her hand, Henny disappeared behind the pittosporum bush.

Annie almost called out to tell Henny about a terrific collection, *The Mystery Lovers' Book of Quotations* by Jane Horning. Then, with a decided headshake, she dropped the piece of cardboard into her purse. No reason to deflate Death on Demand's indefatigable reader. Henny's book would have its own flavor. Still, Annie had other things to do than focus on her best customer's search for a publisher. Now all Annie needed to top off her morning would be for Miss Dora to be waiting inside.

A long, cool hallway with meeting rooms—Snowy Egret, White Ibis, Great Blue Heron, Brown Pelican—led to the central lobby and a rectangular reflecting pool. Whitewashed walls gave the lobby a bright, fresh aura. Brilliant scarlet bougainvillea bloomed in yellow terra-cotta urns.

Annie went directly to the desk. The assistant manager greeted her cheerfully. Jeff Garrett's carrot-hued hair sprigged in all directions. Freckles spattered his snub nose. His wide mouth spread in an infectious grin that

Annie returned despite her preoccupation. She felt she
and Jeff had forged a bond, she'd been there so often in
recent days.

"Everything's just as you ordered, Annie. Fruit baskets
and a magnum of champagne in each room. And, let's see, a
manicurist will be up to Ms. Sinclair's room at four, the six-
foot pine board's in place beneath Mrs. Kirby's mattress, the
foot massage appliance is in Mr. Crabtree's suite." Jeff
paused, leaned forward, and his voice dropped. "Got a call
this morning with a special request from Mr. Blake. I made a
special trip off-island to pick up three 'adult' videos for his
suite."

Annie merely nodded, but she felt a twinge of surprise.
Alan Blake's charming, boyish persona didn't square with the
X-rated video request. But as Miss Dora was wont to remark:
You can't always tell a package from its cover. In any event,
Annie was glad Blake hadn't asked her to get the videos.
There was a limit to how helpful she intended to be.

Jeff's eyes widened. "Do you know how much those
kind of movies cost? Wow. If my wife finds out I've been in
that place, I'm in deep trouble"—he glanced down at a
list—"and I've got the keys ready for you." He pulled out a
manila envelope from a drawer. "You'll find the room numbers inside with the keys. And do you want the key to your
suite?"

Annie took both the envelope and her own key and
thanked him. She opened the larger envelope. Five folders
with oblong cardboard electronic keys were enclosed. She
handed the folder for Room 506 to Garrett. "Emma Clyde
will pick her key up at the desk." At least, Emma should—if
she would. Annie added calling Emma to her mental list of
responsibilities. She tucked the other four folders back into

the envelope. "I understand Kenneth Hazlitt is staying here. Has he checked in?"

Jeff stepped to a computer, punched in the name. "Yes. Could I call for you?"

She felt a tiny spurt of irritation. For heaven's sake, she was hardly a security risk. Jeff knew who she was. He had just handed her the oblong cardboard room keys for five expected guests. To be fair to Jeff, that was different. The Festival was paying for the accommodations for the honorees. And it was contrary to hotel policy to provide inquirers with the room numbers of guests. So okay, Jeff was just following the rules.

"Yes, please."

Jeff nodded toward an alcove. "The house phones are over there, Annie."

"Thanks." She crossed to the alcove, picked up a receiver.

The desk rang the room.

"Hello." The deep drawl was instantly attractive.

"May I speak to Mr. Hazlitt, please?"

"Which one?"

"Mr. Kenneth Hazlitt."

"Ken's not in. This is Willie. Can I help you?"

Damn. Annie looked again at her watch. "I need to speak with Mr. Hazlitt. Do you know when he will return?"

"Who knows? If he's found a good party, it may be a while. But we've got our own little party this afternoon, and a book open house all day tomorrow. You can count on catching him one time or the other. Ken never misses a party, especially not his own."

"Do you know anything about the book he's writing?" She had reached that level of desperation.

"Not much," Willie replied cheerfully. "But I can paw through the stuff we brought. See if I find anything. I think maybe there're some flyers he's going to have at the booth. Kind of a teaser, you know? For the open house. Are you press?"

Annie would have claimed membership in the Mafia if she thought it would help. She gave it some consideration (she credited a vicious second-grade teacher with helping her shed any compunction always to tell the truth), but in this instance, she didn't see any advantage to be gained. "No. I'm a bookseller, and I'm serving as an author liaison." It sounded official even if it didn't have a thing to do with Mr. Kenneth Hazlitt's literary aspirations. "Could I have a flyer?"

"Sure. Come on up. Room 500."

Annie was halfway across the lobby when she remembered Emma. She scooted back to the alcove, found a pay phone, and dialed Emma's number. The answering machine picked up. Of course. But Annie knew damn well Broward's Rock's most famous author was in her office because Emma's routine was invariable—a half-hour walk on the beach in front of her palatial home, then three hours at her computer. Neither war nor storms (excepting electrical failures) nor holidays nor celebrations nor illness (unless major surgery) varied Emma's writing schedule.

Annie enunciated loudly and clearly. "Emma, the Medallions are strictly on the up-and-up. I've got the word straight—"

Emma picked up her phone. "From whom?"

"Blue Benedict. She swears that Hazlitt guy had nothing to do with your selection. So you'll come, won't you?"

The silence was frosty—and thoughtful. Emma's voice

was as cool and sharp as a dueling sword. "If that's true, it makes Kenneth's novel even more interesting."

And she hung up.

Annie glared at the phone. The public might adore dear Marigold Rembrandt (". . . America's sweetest and canniest sleuth," *The New York Times*. ". . . delights readers with her warmth and charisma," *Chicago Sun-Times*. ". . . won the hearts of readers from coast to coast," the *Los Angeles Times*), but her creator had about as much charm for Annie as the seven-foot alligator that lived in the pond behind Annie's home. Annie knew dangerous beasts when she saw them.

Annie slammed the receiver into its cradle, jolting her fingers. "Ouch."

All the way up in the elevator, Annie tried to figure it out. Why did it make Hazlitt's novel more interesting? Or was Emma being supercilious?

And did Annie really give a damn?

Well, yes. She was responsible for the care and feeding of the honorees and their mental well-being throughout the Festival. So, yes. But she didn't understand what Emma meant. . . .

The elevator doors opened, and Annie confronted her own image in a huge mirror with a gilt baroque frame.

She had that instant of surprise that always came when seeing her reflection. Sandy hair. Gray eyes. Slim, athletic figure.

Annie paused.

Laurel always urged Annie to relax, to imbibe more deeply from Life's Fountain of Joy.

Annie thought the message was clear. She frowned. Dammit, did she really look harried and intense?

She forced her shoulders to relax. Actually, she looked

stylishly resortish, her smooth cotton top crisply white, her light blue chambray skirt long enough to swirl. Annie smoothed her hair and tried a casual smile. Okay.

The door to Room 500 opened immediately.

Annie looked into amused green eyes that widened with perceptible pleasure as they surveyed her.

"*Do* come in, said the lonely guy to the good-looking girl." His voice was a pleasant baritone, and he used it to matinee-idol perfection. He thrust out his hand. "Hi, I'm Willie Hazlitt, and my crystal ball tells me you're the author liaison who just called. I had no idea author liaisons were beautiful. What a delightful surprise."

Willie's hand was warm, his grin seductive.

Annie smiled, but with definite reserve. She knew all about the Willie Hazlitts of the world. Good-looking, charming, playful. And not to be trusted with either the household silver or a woman's reputation.

"Hello, Mr. Hazlitt. I appreciate your help." The room behind him was nice. Lots of white wicker and brightly striped pillows and a seashell motif in the sand-shaded wallpaper. If all the suites were this attractive, her authors should at least be pleased with their accommodations.

"Anything I can do, anything at all. And my name's Willie." He looked at her expectantly.

"Annie Darling. Now, this flyer—"

"Sure, sure, Annie." He led the way into the living area. "Let me take a look in these boxes."

Willie Hazlitt made it look easy to heft four big cartons onto a table near the wet bar. He was about six feet tall, with broad shoulders and muscular arms. He was also so spectacularly handsome—thick, smooth black hair, regular features, a smile that combined charm with a hint of wickedness—that not even his vivid sport shirt—emerald-beaked, crimson-feathered toucans against a bright fuschia background—could compete with his looks. And it would take a man inordinately confident of both his appearance and his masculinity to wear that particular shirt.

He kept up a nonstop chatter as he poked through the boxes. ". . . more than you ever wanted to know about the fall list from Mint Julep Press: *Red Hot Tips from Hot Rod Hal, Blue Grass in My Old Kentucky Home, Press the Pedal to the Metal* —huh, now that sounds like fun, the memoirs of a long-haul trucker—*Sea Island Reverie*—oh, poems. I thought it might be a primer on how to have your very own little grass shack, which I could relate to, ma'am"—here he favored Annie with a bright, not too suggestive glance—"*Root Hog or Die,* which I do *not* relate to. Well, not this box, I guess. Let's see." He pushed the first box away, pulled the second one close. "Nope. This one's got party stuff in it, nuts—the house-brand peanuts from a discount store—you can count on Ken to cut corners wherever, oh yeah," Annie heard a remnant of a southern drawl, but she guessed Willie had spent some years elsewhere, "and paper plates, that kind of stuff. Now here's a box that's taped shut. That's special for the open house. Can't get into those yet. But I know there's a bunch of other flyers. Unless he's already taken them to the booth. He's really on a high about his book." A shrug. "My brother publishes books—I mean, we do. You'd think it would just be another day at the office. But no, Ken's beside himself."

Willie delved into the last box and, triumphantly, yanked up a stack of sheets so electrically pink that Annie blinked.

"Here we go." He handed one to Annie.

Annie took the sheet.

All Day Saturday, the White Ibis Room,
the Buccaneer Hotel

Come to Mint Julep Press's
GRAND CELEBRATION
SEE MINT JULEP'S FALL LIST
and
Discover how much TRUTH there can be in fiction.
Kenneth Hazlitt will reveal the inspiration for his
forthcoming novel:
SONG OF THE SOUTH
The story of five famous Southern novelists and the
passions (some illicit!) that have dominated their lives
and changed their fiction.
SONG OF THE SOUTH
will be the talk of the South. Come find out more.
And take advantage of deep discounts available
only during the Festival in ordering
Mint Julep Press Fall Titles.

Annie took a deep breath. Oh, Lordy.

''Would you like extra copies?'' Willie asked helpfully.

''Five.''

Before pulling the brochures from the box, she saw him glance at her wedding ring.

Annie took the flyers. ''Thanks so much.''

''Oh, we've got hundreds. We'll have a stack of them here this afternoon at the cocktail party.''

''Who's coming to the cocktail party?''

''Ken sent out invitations to booksellers. But you're definitely invited. Five o'clock. Here in the suite. And feel free, take some extra copies of the flyer.''

Willie smiled happily, obviously unaware his offering was as welcome as the Bud Light truck at a Baptist church social.

Annie accepted another handful. Should she give flyers to her authors as they arrived? Or should she await a propitious moment?

She turned toward the door.

Willie didn't exactly block her way, but he was right there, an eager hand on her elbow. ''How about a drink tonight?''

''I'm not sure,'' she replied vaguely, ''but thanks.''

''Anytime. Just give me a ring.''

He leaned against the doorjamb and watched as she walked toward the elevators.

As Annie punched the button, she gave him a final, non-committal smile. Willie probably preferred married women. She stepped into the elevator, the pink sheets in her hand, and wished that she had nothing else to do that day but fend off Willie's advances. That she could do. Duck soup. Instead, she had a horrid premonition that her Gang of Five might make mincemeat out of her. She opened her purse and absently dredged up a partially squashed mint.

No, stress didn't make her hungry, fill her mind with images of food.

Of course not.

Chapter 7

Drop-dead gorgeous.

That was Annie's first thought as she welcomed Leah Vixen Kirby.

The famed author was much better-looking than her publicity stills. Masses of fiery red hair, brilliant green eyes, and an elegant, narrow face. Today she wore an emerald-green blazer and cream skirt with a hint of lime. It was an unusual but effective combination.

Drop-dead gorgeous and seething.

That was Annie's second thought.

She almost wondered that the author didn't crackle as she walked, Annie's sense of psychic trauma was so great.

Yet Leah Kirby managed to flash a take-charge smile, even though there wasn't a particle of warmth in those clever, searching, combative eyes.

"Hello, Annie. It's good of you to meet us. And this is my husband, Carl." Leah started down the airport hallway. She took two steps, then paused.

Her husband reached out for her carry-on. "I'll take it, Leah."

"No, no. It's all right."

"But if your back . . ."

"It's all right, Carl." Leah moved on, but she walked stiffly.

Annie slowed her pace. "Mrs. Kirby, I enjoy your books so much. *Love's Lost Splendour* is one of the most exciting novels I've ever read, and the end just broke my heart." Surprisingly, Annie felt a sting of tears as she recalled the weary Confederate soldier limping up a dusty red Georgia road to find the ashes of his home, and beneath a towering pine, a grave with a wilted wreath and his wife's locket hanging from the simple wooden cross.

Carl Kirby nodded in agreement. He was tall, thin, and pale, and his weary face crooked in a sudden, warm smile. "It is wonderful, isn't it?"

"Please call me Leah." That was all the author said.

At the luggage carousel, the author directed Annie to get a luggage cart. As Annie loaded it, Carl kept up a running commentary. ". . . such an attractive new airport, but small enough to still be pleasant. It's always a pleasure to come to Savannah . . ." while he darted anxious looks at his wife's stony face.

Leah Kirby didn't say another word until she was seated in the front passenger seat of Annie's Volvo. Then she pressed scarlet nails briefly to her temple. "I have a dreadful headache." She closed her eyes and leaned back in the seat.

Carl immediately began to search in her carry-on. "Leah, all I find is aspirin." He looked hopefully at Annie. "Do you happen to have any ibuprofen? Leah's allergic to aspirin."

"No, but there's a Quick Stop right outside the airport. We can stop there."

Carl accepted her suggestion gratefully; Leah remained mute.

At the gas station, Carl got out of the car very slowly. Annie wondered if he, too, suffered from back trouble or arthritis.

The minute the door closed behind him, Leah Kirby faced Annie. Her eyes were clear and sharp. There was no trace of a headache in them. "I want to know the truth. Have I been set up? Is the Medallion award simply an excuse to bring—"

Annie cut in swiftly. "Absolutely not. Kenneth Hazlitt had nothing whatsoever to do with choosing the Medallion winners. I promise you. I have that from the chair of the Select Committee." Chair and sole member, but Annie didn't intend to tell everything she knew. "After I received the phone messages from you and the other authors, I went to Hilton Head this morning and talked to Blue Benedict, the chairman of the Festival. Whatever Kenneth Hazlitt is doing —his book—it has no connection to the awards at all."

The skin of Leah Kirby's face was pulled tight against the bones. Her green eyes bored into Annie's. "I have to know what's in Kenneth's proposal. I *have* to know. I want you to find out for me as soon as we get to the hotel.''

Annie hesitated, then reached into her purse and pulled out one of the pink sheets. It wasn't the kind of thing she liked to do. It was right on a level with telling your best friend her husband was running around on her. In Annie's view, that wasn't a friendly thing to do.

But Leah Kirby should be forewarned.

''I got this from Kenneth Hazlitt's suite at the Buccaneer. He wasn't there, but his brother gave it to me. I'm afraid—''

Annie stopped because Leah Kirby wasn't listening.

The author's eyes sped down the sheet. When she looked at Annie, her face was grim and white. ''I have to know what he's going to write. I *have*—''

The car door opened.

Leah Kirby's head jerked up. ''Carl, I'll need some water—''

''I have it, sweetheart.''

Smoothly, Leah folded the sheet of paper, as if it were of no moment, and slipped it in her purse. Then she reached out for the bottle of water and the pills. Her hand was trembling.

It was a long, quiet drive to Hilton Head.

Annie didn't even try to provide small talk.

After all, there was an excuse, a passenger with a headache.

Annie glanced in her rearview mirror. A worried frown creased Carl Kirby's pale face. Several times he almost spoke, then he slumped silently back against the seat. His eyes never left his wife.

Leah Kirby relaxed against the headrest, her eyes closed.

But her hands gripped her purse so tightly her fingers blanched.

·   ·   ·

As soon as the door to the Kirbys' suite closed, Annie stalked the few feet to Room 500. Something had to be done about Kenneth Hazlitt, and she was just the person to do it. What right did he have to cause this kind of misery? And what was it going to do to the Festival if the honored authors were distraught? Certainly, distraught put it mildly, so far as Leah Kirby was concerned. Yes, it was up to her to do something.

The door to the Hazlitt suite was propped open.

Knocking briskly, Annie called out, "Willie? Mr. Hazlitt?"

No answer.

She pushed the door wider, stepped into the foyer.

The boxes still sat on the table near the wet bar.

Annie hesitated, then walked to the table. She called out again. Loudly.

No answer.

So she had the suite to herself.

Annie thought swiftly. Certainly Perry Mason wouldn't pass up an opportunity like this.

Annie darted to the wet bar and grabbed a tumbler from the glass shelf. She took the wastebasket near the desk, up-ended it, placed it on the floor directly behind the partially open door, and set the glass on it.

That should give her at least a moment's warning.

She returned to the table. It only took a moment to rifle through the open boxes, but she found nothing that mentioned Hazlitt's proposed book except the pink flyers. She glanced at the sealed box. SONG OF THE SOUTH was scrawled in bright orange marker on its lid. Beneath that, a card was taped. On it was the notation: *Bright red chalk footprints through bookroom? Place these sheets on table by* <u>BACK</u> *wall.*

Annie's fingers itched to open the box. But she didn't have any sealing tape with her, and it would be very obvious if she tampered with the lid. Even Perry Mason might think twice here.

Regretfully, she moved away from the table, glancing around the living room area. No more boxes, no loose sheets of paper.

She glanced toward the partially open door, then impulsively ducked into the first bedroom. A beach towel hung over a chair back; damp swim trunks were lying on the floor. An open suitcase rested on a luggage rack.

Annie checked the suitcase and the closet. Nothing book-related at all.

In the second bedroom—the larger one—she found a pile of Festival material addressed to Kenneth Hazlitt. "Bingo," she said softly. She went through the open luggage and the chest of drawers and closet in a flash.

But she didn't find a manuscript entitled *Song of the South*.

And she didn't find any other promotion material mentioning the book, although she found plenty of pamphlets and flyers on the autumn titles from Mint Julep Press.

Annie returned to the living area.

That's when she saw the Limoges platter on the coffee table in front of the sofa.

Annie skirted the sofa, stared down at the platter. A card lay propped against it. She would know that spidery handwriting anywhere, curlicues and furbelows and many words heavily underlined:

Dear Mr. Hazlitt,
Please enjoy the <u>delicious</u> candies, provided courtesy

of Miss Dora Brevard of Chastain, South Carolina, and author of <u>Miss Dora's Delectables,</u> a cookbook of <u>authentic</u> South Carolina receipts. This manuscript is <u>available</u> for <u>purchase.</u> Just some of the wonderful receipts: Hoppin' John, Divinity (samples included here), Apple Pan Dowdy, and She Crab Soup. All are <u>authentic culinary masterpieces.</u>

Annie looked around the room, half-expecting Miss Dora to materialize in her black silk dress with her coal-black, frighteningly intelligent eyes, her shaggy silver hair, and her wizened, parchment-pale face.

But there was only the platter with its note.

The postscript looked like an inebriated spider had decided to dance a polka:

This is not only your opportunity to achieve <u>last-ing</u> success with the <u>finest</u> Southern cookbook ever proffered, it is a day of <u>glorious</u> opportunity, to wit, YOU have offered to you here (see either end of the platter) two exquisitely <u>tasteful</u> and <u>brilliant</u> manuscripts:

Simplicity by Laurel Darling Roethke
and
The Quotable Sleuth by Henrietta Brawley

You will find excerpts from these fine works on the platter.

It was the P.P.S. that made Annie shake her head in wonder.

P.P.S. We will be <u>available</u> to sign contracts <u>at your</u> <u>convenience</u> (Room 405). And, though we know you have many tasks to accomplish after we have executed our agreements, we three (authors) would appreciate notification prior to the appearance of our books on the bestseller lists.

Annie lifted the plastic wrap from the platter. Hmm. She picked up a piece of Divinity from the middle. It wouldn't be missed.

The candy melted in her mouth. She licked her fingers. Unable to resist temptation, she scooped up a second piece, then, shrugging, picked up a foil-decorated square. A mock-up of a page from Laurel's book, of course.

Call Home.
Simplicity *by Laurel Darling Roethke. Page 11.*

Annie gave it a 2 out of 10. She edged out a third piece of candy. What the hey. She'd *earned* it.

Then she picked up Henny's excerpt:

Pfui.

She didn't even bother to glance at the identifying line. "Right on, Nero," she said aloud.

Pfui, indeed.

On the ground floor, Annie hurried out of the elevator. She was halfway down the hall by the meeting rooms when

Willie Hazlitt came in the side door, lugging a hefty box. He stopped in front of the open doors to the White Ibis Room and beamed. And blocked her way.

"I knew if I was a good boy I'd be rewarded. And I am—the prettiest author liaison in publishing history. Come on in and note my good work." He walked into the White Ibis Room, calling out over his shoulder, "Come look."

He was so proud of himself, in such good humor, that Annie smiled and followed him into the room.

And yes, there were books everywhere.

"I unpacked all the boxes. God, you wouldn't think there could be that many boxes! Everything's set up for the open house tomorrow, all the new books from Mint Julep Press, sure to impress everybody." He leaned forward and whispered conspiratorially, "Booksellers, that's the ticket. Kenneth's invited hundreds of them!"

Annie knew that was an exaggeration. There were maybe a hundred and twenty bookstore people registered for the book fair.

"Ken was torn. He wanted books upstairs, he wanted books here. I've still got some to scatter about in the suite for our little gathering this afternoon. Not, of course, a gathering for *hoi polloi*. Just the cream of the crop. The Medallion winners and a few select others. Including you." He sighed. "Of course, then I have to pack all those books up and haul them to the booth."

Annie gave it a try. "Kenneth?" she asked crisply.

Willie shook his head in mock sorrow. "I can't imagine why you'd want Ken instead of me. I'm much better looking. Don't you agree?" He strolled to a six-foot-tall cutout next to the first table and draped his arm over the shoulders. "Ken's latest promo effort. I asked him what he's trying to sell, his body or his books?"

Annie walked over to the cutout.

By this time, Kenneth Hazlitt had taken shape in her mind as a leering, hateful creature practically endowed with horns.

She said, as she so often did, the first thing that came to mind.

"You don't look a bit alike."

"Nope. My mama married his papa. We're step-buds."

The cardboard Kenneth was a big man, bigger than Willie, with thick curly blond hair and a round face. A huge grin stretched his wide mouth. Dimples creased his plump cheeks. A big Panama hat tilted jauntily on the back of his head. A pink carnation poked from the lapel of his artistically crumpled white suit. In his hands, he held a book.

With a sense of shock, Annie read the title: *Song of the South.*

"It's not out, is it?"

Willie looked blank.

"The book." She pointed.

Willie shrugged. "I don't know. I get confused. I've only been with the company for two weeks. All I know is, brother Ken's having a blast. But hey, I know lots more fun things to talk about. Like me. Why don't we find the bar . . ."

Annie nimbly sidestepped the arm Willie tried to drape over her shoulder. "Sorry." Her smile was blithe. "I've got to run."

Annie watched the small plane roll to a stop.

The Hilton Head airport handled commuter flights. She'd just have time to get Alan Blake to the hotel and return to pick up Missy Sinclair, then head back for Jimmy Jay Crabtree. At least she didn't have to trek to the Savannah airport again today. Leah Kirby was the only author who had refused to fly on a small plane. Not that Annie thought that an unreasonable decision.

Blake was the third passenger out. He paused for just an instant on the top step before starting down.

Full of himself, Annie immediately decided. Though perhaps he couldn't be faulted. Blake's kind of all-American good looks—wavy chestnut hair, blue eyes, regular features —would have invited adulation throughout his life. And she thought she recalled from his bio sheet that he was an accomplished tennis player. Of course, football was the route to hero status in the South, but any letter jacket would be a plus.

He ran lightly down the steps. He stopped on the runway, his eyes swiftly scanning the welcomers behind the fence.

Annie waved and called, ''Mr. Blake.''

He returned her wave, but his eyes kept right on looking. His smile was automatic, meaningless. Then he was through the gate, shaking her hand. There was a little more effort to charm.

''Annie, this is a real pleasure. I've heard about your wonderful bookstore—no, this is all the luggage I have— So you just sell mysteries. Who are your favorite writers in the genre? I really enjoy Tony Hillerman.''

This conversation Annie could do. ''He's one of my biggest sellers. If you like his books, you'd enjoy the Cherokee mysteries by Jean Hager. And Judith Van Gieson's New Mexico books.''

They talked mysteries—Caroline Graham and Betty Rowlands, Max Allan Collins and Ed Gorman, Barbara D'Amato and Maxine O'Callaghan, Marilyn Wallace and Jeffery Deaver—all the way to the parking lot.

Blake continued to scan his surroundings.

It wasn't the eager gaze of a tourist.

It was wary, defensive—and very alert.

Even when they were in the car, he continued to look around the parking area.

Annie reached into her carryall. "Mr. Blake—"

"Alan," he interrupted immediately, "by all means."

Annie smiled. "All right, Alan. Here's your packet. It has your schedule, including your panel and book-signing times." She gave him a few minutes to look it over, then, with a deep breath, she retrieved a pink sheet from her purse. "This brochure is being distributed by Mr. Kenneth Hazlitt."

And she handed it to Blake.

As he read it, Annie quickly repeated her defense of the Medallion selection process, concluding, "The Festival is outraged on behalf of its honorees, and we're doing everything we can to prevent Mr. Hazlitt from continuing his harassment."

The Volvo segued into the proper lanes as she curved around the Sea Pines Circle. Smoothly. She was so busy congratulating herself on this success that she was startled and almost swerved into the lagoon when Blake demanded sharply: "What *are* you doing?"

In mysteries, Annie especially admired the nimble-witted protagonist never at a loss for an answer. Tommy Hambledon never sputtered in a reply.

Unprepared, she blurted, "I'm going to tell Hazlitt he has to stop harassing our honorees or I'll bar him from the Festival."

"That won't do anything about the book." Blake's voice was bleak.

"No one can do anything about that." She concentrated on negotiating Coligny Circle. As she turned into the hotel parking lot, she asked briskly, "Is there anything you need for this evening?"

Alan Blake rubbed the bridge of his nose. He looked suddenly older, not quite so pretty. "Where's Kenneth Hazlitt staying?"

There was an undercurrent to his question.

But that, as far as Annie was concerned, was solely the problem of Mr. Kenneth Hazlitt.

"This hotel. Room 500."

As they rode up in the elevator, he glanced at his folder with the electronic cardboard key. "Same floor as Kenneth?" He gave her a swift, suspicious look. Now his tone was hostile.

Annie told the truth. "Hazlitt engineered that. He convinced the director of the Festival that he was very excited about the honorees and wanted to have a party in their honor, so she put him on the same floor."

Blake didn't say anything until they stood in the living room of his suite. "So Kenneth conned the Festival, huh?"

"Mr. Blake, I've never met Kenneth Hazlitt. I don't have any idea what he's doing. I've told you all I know about it."

But Blake wasn't listening. Abruptly, he plunged past her, his face hard and tight. He reached the coffee table and grabbed up three videocassettes, knocking over the fruit basket in his haste.

He held the cassettes in his hands like they were snakes, then, his face convulsed with rage, he turned on Annie.

"What the hell's this stuff doing here?"

Annie carefully ignored the sexually explicit vinyl covers and said stiffly, "Those are the videos you ordered—"

"I ordered nothing. Get this crap out of here. And you get the hell out!"

.   .   .

Annie, her face flushed, returned the videos to Jeff Garrett at the desk. "There's been a mistake. Mr. Blake said he didn't order these."

Garrett shrugged. "Somebody did. And so who's going to pay for them? I'd put them on Blake's bill."

Annie shrugged in turn. "Jeff, I've got a lot of problems today, and that one's not on my list. Oh, and please leave a message from me for Kenneth Hazlitt. 'Mr. Hazlitt, I must speak to you, ASAP. Annie Darling, Room 508.' Thanks, Jeff."

"Annie, honey." The drawl was sugar-sweet, but it coated a core of steel. "What does the Festival intend to do?" Spiky black hair framed a smooth, round face.

At first glance, Missy Sinclair looked like a little dumpling of a woman with an unlined, placid face.

In a second glance, a perceptive viewer might note that her bright dark eyes had a hypnotic quality and her rosebud mouth curved in a blend of guile and willfulness.

Annie eyed her carefully. She might not have given Missy Sinclair that second, careful glance except that she had read Missy's books.

In *Corinne's Passion,* when the heroine discovered that her husband was unfaithful, she bided her time until he and his lover planned a weekend tryst at a secluded cabin. Then she quite skillfully arranged for the woman's husband to find them. The scorned husband was hard-drinking, high-tempered—and he always carried a rifle in his car. At her husband's funeral, the grieving Corinne touched a black lace handkerchief to her lips—to hide her smile.

In *Midnight Answer,* Mary Ann walked to the end of the pier. An unshaven, haggard young man swung to meet her. She held up both hands. ''Don't touch me.'' He stared at her in disbelief. ''I can't imagine why you want to see me, Derek. But I've brought you some cash and a recommendation—''

''Mary Ann, I don't want money. I didn't do it for money.''

''Do what?'' she asked.

''Mary Ann, you know. You know.'' Her elderly husband had been found floating, drowned, in their pool.

''Why, Derek, I've no idea what you're talking about.''

Now Annie looked into those hypnotic eyes. ''We shall bar Mr. Hazlitt from participating in the Festival.'' Annie said it firmly.

Those bright dark eyes blinked slowly. ''I don't reckon that will faze Kenneth. I wonder . . .''

Annie wondered, too. She had an inkling that the thoughts behind that pudding-soft face might put Edgar Allan Poe to shame.

''I will certainly insist that he refrain from any further linkage of his novel to the Medallion honorees.''

''Oh, honey, bless your heart.'' Missy splashed two fingers of scotch in a tumbler. ''Do you know, I doubt if that will just scare old Kenneth out of his pants. I think maybe it will take a little more than that. Why don't you tell him—''

''Miss Sinclair—''

''Call me Missy, honey. Everybody does.''

Annie thought to do so was rather on a par with naming an anaconda Buffy. But Missy Sinclair's plump face was so genial.

"Uh, thank you. Missy, perhaps it would be more effective if you spoke to Mr. Hazlitt yourself. He's in Room 500."

Missy downed half the glass of liquor. She did it smoothly, easily. Her mouth curved into an enigmatic smile. "Honey, I just might do that." It was the same sugar-sweet drawl.

But there was nothing sweet about those dark, hypnotic eyes.

"Who's gonna carry my stuff?" Jimmy Jay Crabtree demanded. He pointed at a huge plaid duffel bag.

Annie eyed him with distaste. She hadn't liked his picture on the back of his dust jacket, squinty little eyes, weak chin, sour mouth. On the telephone, his whiny voice had grated, and he wasn't any better in person. Moreover, he was scrawny. She loathed scrawny men. She had an instant image of Max—solid, muscular, and sexy—and that made Crabtree look even weedier. And somebody should have told him that his blue polka-dot shirt clashed with his striped seersucker trousers. And his pants sagged over his bony butt.

Without a word, she reached down, hefted the bag, and started for the parking lot.

The lout followed, complaining. "Where are the reporters? Didn't you get the word out when I was arriving?"

Annie snapped, "I'm not your publicist, Mr. Crabtree."

"You're supposed to set things up, aren't you?" He scrambled to keep up.

Annie opened the trunk, dumped in the bag, slammed it shut, stalked around the automobile, not bothering to reply.

She unlocked the Volvo, slid behind the wheel.

Crabtree opened the passenger door.

And Annie saw the cigarette in his hand.

And smelled it, noisome, nasty, and rank.

"If you don't mind, Mr. Crabtree, I don't permit smoking in my car."

He slumped in the seat, took a deep drag, and blew the smoke toward her. "Look, broad, I smoke where and when I want to."

"Out."

He looked at her angrily.

"Out."

And she was out herself and whirling to the trunk. Seconds later, the plaid duffel bag hit the asphalt.

He charged around the car. "Wait a minute. You can't do this."

"The hell I can't."

And Annie was in the driver's seat and punching the door lock.

Crabtree pounded on the side of the car.

Annie gunned the motor; the Volvo leapt forward.

Let him walk. Let him *crawl*. Hopefully, he'd stumble into a lagoon and be eaten by a 'gator.

She was halfway to the hotel when she realized she hadn't given Crabtree his Festival packet or his key.

No problem.

She stopped at the desk. "Jeff, when Mr. Crabtree arrives, please give him this packet. It includes the key to his room."

It also included, right on top, the first item in the packet, one of the bright pink flyers. Annie printed at the top: *Kenneth Hazlitt is in Room 500.*

It was the most satisfactory moment in a profoundly unsatisfactory day.

Annie delicately edged out yet another Oyster Rockefeller. Okay, so they were a little rich for lunch. So?

Max speared a melon ball. "Ingrid's alerted. She'll be very cautious about packages."

"I can certainly understand why somebody would be tempted to blow *him* up. So why don't they send the letter bombs to Crabtree? Why bother perfectly innocent booksellers?"

"Obviously someone wants to damage his sales." Max sipped his chardonnay.

"He doesn't sell all that well," Annie said absently. She savored her last oyster. "But he's not the problem right now." As much as she would like to luxuriate in lunch and Max, her Puritan nature prevailed. "The problem is this Hazlitt guy and his book. I tried to call Blue, but she's still in a tizzy, and all I got back was a message saying, 'Work it out, work it out.' And he's still not in the suite, or at least not answering the phone, and he's not in the White Ibis Room. So, I've got to get over to the booths and find him."

Max replenished her wineglass. "What good will that do?"

Annie grinned. "I don't know, but at least I can go look at the booths and get outside. It's a beautiful day," she said wistfully. She brightened. "I can say you're the Festival's legal counsel and—"

Max shook his head. "Let's keep the fiction in the books —and me out of jail." Max's law degree hung in his office, but he always made it very clear to the clients of Confidential Commissions, his rather unusual business, which provided services to those in need of information, that he had never taken the South Carolina bar and wasn't licensed to practice law. Max was also quick to make it clear to clients that Confidential Commissions wasn't a private inquiry firm. The State of South Carolina had extremely particular requirements that had to be fulfilled to obtain a private investigator's license, requirements Max had no intention of meeting. The county's most odious assistant circuit solicitor, Brice Willard Posey, longed to charge Max with impersonating a private detective.

"Well, at the very least you can stand there and fold your arms in a macho way and glower."

Max grinned at the thought and immediately crossed his arms in practice and glowered.

Annie loved the glower. Very Michael Douglas. Very sexy. And she managed to catch the wine bottle before it toppled.

She wasn't a Puritan in all regards. She was opening her mouth to suggest they check out their suite before she went in search of Hazlitt when brisk steps stopped beside them and a glossy invitation was flung to the center of the table.

"What do you know about this?" Emma Clyde demanded.

When the world's most successful mystery writer demanded, the world—including Annie—snapped to attention.

The big square invitation was quite tony, embossed with a silver glass spouting a sprig of mint, the logo of Mint Julep Press.

> *You are invited to cocktails in Suite 500 to honor this
> year's Dixie Book Festival Medallion Winners*
> *Alan Blake*
> *Emma Clyde*
> *Jimmy Jay Crabtree*
> *Leah Vixen Kirby*
> *Melissa Sinclair*
> 5 P.M.   Friday   May 13
> *MINT JULEP PRESS*

"So what gives? It sounds like a Festival event." Emma's fictional detective, Marigold Rembrandt, exuded a bright charm that bewitched critics. The charm did not extend to Emma. She stood there, her square face creased with suspicion, her pale blue eyes cold and searching, her broad, capable hands firmly planted on her substantial hips.

Annie knew that Emma wouldn't budge until she received an answer.

"Emma, Kenneth Hazlitt's his own show. The Festival didn't authorize the party. We have absolutely nothing to do with it."

Max was on his feet and pulling out a chair for Emma.

Annie knew her role. "Won't you join us?" And she did try to sound cordial. She really did.

Emma shook her head, which made her blue-gray hair quiver. It was a new color and style, still short but with crisp waves instead of spikes. Emma wore her customary caftan, this one with alternating broad vertical stripes of violet and black.

Annie stood, too, and smiled, and thought the writer looked like an ambulatory awning.

Those pale blue eyes touched Annie, and she instantly felt a chill. Dammit, Emma couldn't know what she was thinking. Uncomfortable, Annie plunged into speech.

"Emma, have you heard anything about what happens in Hazlitt's novel?"

It wasn't a dumb question. Emma knew everybody in the book business: editors, agents, bookstore owners, book buyers, publishing reps, critics, publicists. So if word of the plot of Hazlitt's book had trickled through this small and gossipy community, Emma would know.

The minute the words were out, Annie would have given the world to have them back. It was one of those watershed moments. Like asking your host at a cocktail party, "Who's that unpleasant-looking woman in the red dress?" only to learn that it is the host's beloved cousin.

Dear God, Emma was one of the authors Hazlitt claimed he was writing about!

And Annie knew why. At least, she knew of one skeleton in Emma's closet. Several years earlier, Emma's much younger, philandering second husband had fallen (was pushed?) from the stern of *Marigold's Pleasure,* Emma's luxurious yacht. Late at night. Emma claimed she was sleeping soundly. The death was officially ruled an accident.

Those cool blue eyes probed Annie's.

Annie swallowed and once again hurtled into speech. "Of course, it's probably not true what everyone's saying."

"And what is everyone saying?"

Annie would have sworn that Emma's broad mouth twitched.

"That . . ." Annie looked at Max for inspiration.

His face was sympathetic, but he didn't say a word.

Annie knew she only had one hope, a diversionary tactic.

"Emma, what was the deal with Kenneth Hazlitt and gold-fish?"

Amusement flickered briefly in Emma's cool blue eyes. "Oh, yes. The famous goldfish caper. Kenneth was throwing a party for a Mint Julep book on Indonesia. And don't ask me why a Georgia press would buy that title. Anyway, the author had arranged for Indonesian delicacies to be delivered by air freight from Los Angeles. For some reason, the stuff didn't show up. So an hour before the party started, Kenneth scooped up eight goldfish—the big ones—out of a pond in his backyard, smoked them in his barbecue, chopped them up, and served them at the party on wheat thins. People raved about the great taste. Of course, Kenneth waited until every scrap was gone, then, ho ho ho, he announced what he'd done. It became the most famous book party of the year."

For just an instant, a faint smile touched Emma's square face. Then she leaned forward and picked up the invitation. Slowly, she crushed it in that strong, capable hand. *(Did he fall? Was he pushed?)* She stared at the crumpled invitation for a moment. "Kenneth always likes to top himself. I'm afraid that's what he has in mind for today. But I don't like the idea of being served up like cubed carp."

"Don't go," Annie said briskly.

Emma's chilly eyes moved from the invitation to Annie.

Annie nodded emphatically. "It's like, What if they had a war and nobody came? If the authors don't come, his party will be a flop."

"I'd like to think so." Her gruff voice was thoughtful. "But, Annie, what if it isn't?"

Chapter 8

"Oh, Max, isn't it gorgeous!" Annie spread her arms wide as if to encompass all of the Dixie Book Festival.

Red-and-white-striped awnings projected over the booths that dotted the broad wooden plaza leading to the public beach. Every booth was crammed with books. Country music blared from loudspeakers. An area near the boardwalk offered delicacies from island restaurants, and a large poster announced signing and reading times. The air was as silky and soft as cat fur. A gentle sea breeze fluttered the awnings. Sand gritted underfoot on the gray wooden planking. The tangy smell of the ocean competed with the sour and sweet scents wafting from the hot dog vendor and the cotton candy stand. And the books!

Annie stopped in front of the poster. "Max, look! Marilyn Schwartz is speaking at four. She is *so* funny. We can't miss that."

People swarmed and thronged and milled. It was a sight guaranteed to delight the Chamber of Commerce and annoy the growth-curbing mayor.

Annie spotted Leah Kirby deep in conversation with a slim blond woman, who stood with her hands jammed in the pockets of her dirndl skirt. Leah gestured emphatically. The author's face was flushed with anger. Her companion shook her head vigorously.

Annie glanced around. Carl Kirby wasn't there.

A fan shyly stepped up, holding out a copy of Kirby's latest book. The author looked blank for a moment, then she forced a smile. She nodded, reached out for the book.

Annie tugged on Max's arm. "There, Max. Over by the third booth. That's Leah Kirby." Annie's grip tightened. "And look, coming up behind them, that good-looking guy in the orange polo shirt, the one who looks like he's spoiling for a fight, that's Alan Blake." Quickly she told Max about the videos. "I wonder if he's hunting for Kenneth Hazlitt? Maybe I should let Blake take him on."

But she'd promised Blue Benedict she'd handle it.

Annie headed for the information booth and a large map indicating exhibitors' stalls. She nodded in approval. Blue had done a great job. The book booths were easily accessible.

Reading and autograph sessions were set up at intervals on the beach. How was that for a resort atmosphere? (As long as it didn't rain, but the gods usually smiled on Hilton Head in May.) The panels were spread among the meeting rooms in nearby hotels.

Annie already knew which author talks she wanted to attend, in addition, of course, to the appearances by her five. (Four, actually. Somehow she could pass up the pleasure of seeing Jimmy Jay Crabtree here or anywhere.) But tomorrow she definitely would catch Robert Olen Butler and Jane Roberts Wood.

As for now—

Mint Julep Press was in Booth 16.

Despite her best intentions, Annie had to stop at several booths to greet local booksellers and then, of course, she ran into bookstore friends from Birmingham and Tallahassee and Columbia and Augusta and Raleigh and Memphis and Charleston . . .

"Max, isn't this fun!" She took a little sideways dance in sheer exuberance.

He gave her a fond, amused, *nice* smile, and she thought how lucky she was. Then his face changed and he reached out to grab her. "Careful, Annie . . ." but she was already toppling, along with the cardboard cutout she'd sideswiped.

Ignoring her scraped knee, she bounced back to her feet, hastily assuring a small crowd she was just fine, thank you.

"Sweetheart, I'd fall down with you anywhere, anytime," a huge voice boomed.

It could have been sexist, it could have been offensive, but the big man's light tone robbed the words of offense, and the hand on her elbow was gentle.

Without warning, Annie stood face-to-face with Kenneth Hazlitt, who was setting the cutout on its stand and was, in fact, even larger and blonder with a bigger smile than his replica.

"You!" she exclaimed.

"Me, in the flesh and in cardboard." He laughed so hard his chest wobbled. "Don't know when I've had so much fun. Here, come to our open house tomorrow. See the Mint Julep Press fall list and get the best discounts in the business. And get a great preview at our cocktail party this afternoon. Fifth floor of the Buccaneer Hotel."

"That's what I want to talk to you about."

"Sweetheart, you won't want to miss it! Today or tomorrow. We'll have the most exciting book bash in the history of Southern books all day tomorrow. And this afternoon, we're having a super preview, and guess who'll be there? The Medallion authors themselves! Because they're the inspiration for the book I'm writing. Listen, New York's hot for my book. Everybody's excited. Isn't that great?"

"No."

It was like watching a fast freeze in a film. The huge grin locked in place; the china-blue eyes widened. "No?" Kenneth Hazlitt repeated. The little word quivered with amusement and curiosity. "Sweetheart, are you a book grinch? Aren't you interested in the life experiences that create great literature?"

Annie thought fleetingly of Jimmy Jay Crabtree. Great literature?

"Look—"

But Hazlitt was riding his horse hard. "Honey, you won't believe the exciting possibilities I'm exploring. What heartbreak fuels the passion and power of Southern stories? What is the truth of the lives behind these works?"

A crowd was gathering, to Hazlitt's obvious delight. He beamed at the eager faces surrounding them.

"How better to understand their greatness than to create a grand and passionate novel about writers like Alan Blake, Leah Vixen Kirby, Emma Clyde, Jimmy Jay Crabtree, and Melissa Sinclair, the Festival's brilliant and fascinating Medallion winners."

No one within fifty feet could have missed hearing him. He grabbed up a sheaf of pink flyers. "Don't miss the open house tomorrow, folks. That's when we give you a sneak preview of the contents of the book the whole South's gonna be wild about. We'll honor these fine authors and realize how their lives can inspire and educate us. We'll look behind their public masks. How does Leah Vixen Kirby know so much about love, about men and women torn by doubt and jealousy and desire? Does Jimmy Jay Crabtree struggle with the old devil rum? How much real-life experience does Emma Clyde have with murder? Alan Blake is as handsome as his heroes. How have his looks always put him in a starring role? Melissa Sinclair describes the dark struggles of the soul in old Southern families. What about *her* family?"

People reaching for flyers jostled Annie.

She stood on tiptoe, trying to get his attention. "Mr. Hazlitt, wait a minute, wait a minute!"

Hazlitt leaned around her, shoving flyers toward grasping hands. His face flushed with excitement, he boomed, "Come one, come all. The most exciting book bash—"

Annie's eyes narrowed. She stood with her arms akimbo.

Recognizing the warning signs, Max tugged on her elbow. "Annie, he's—"

"Mr. Hazlitt, the Festival demands that you immediately cease coupling your name with those of the Medallion winners."

The publisher of Mint Julep Press paused and looked down at Annie, his big face stricken with incredulity.

"My goodness gracious. That's a most upsetting piece of news." He grinned hugely. "Why, sweetie, I'm just sorry as I can be if the Festival has its nose out of joint, but, sugar, the Festival isn't my daddy. At least, if it is, my momma never told me."

Annie glowered. "If we have to close down your booth—"

Kenneth Hazlitt's eyes widened in mock horror. "Think of it, a poor ol' publisher thrown out into the street. Why, I suppose I'd just have to get my lawyer to talk to your lawyer, and, honey, you know how that goes. This Festival will be over before they've cleared their throats twice at a couple hundred dollars an hour, and you know what? I'll be right here at my booth the whole time. Except for when I'm at the party this afternoon and the open house tomorrow." He held up another fistful of flyers, waggled them at the crowd. "Come on, all you folks, come to Mint Julep's open house and find out why the Festival's trying to snub me. Find out what's going on behind the scenes. I promise a book bash you'll never forget, the best bash—"

"Bash. That's what it is all right!" Annie shouted. "This is lousy, cheap exploitation. What right do you have to embarrass—"

"Embarrass?" Astonishment wreathed his big, amused face. "Why, honey, you do me a disservice." He bowed from the waist, while still handing out flyers. "I am the first and foremost admirer of these fine writers. It is my humble hope to catch even a reflection of their greatness in my own novel. But I know that we can learn much from their lives, and it is my privilege to join in the fine tradition of the roman à clef. Why, sweetheart, we're talking *Literature*." And then he brushed past Annie, reaching out to offer his flyers. "Come one, come all. Don't miss the open house that will

be the most talked-about book event this year. All day tomorrow in the White Ibis Room of the Buccaneer Hotel!''

"Annie, it's not your problem."

"Max, I could kill that man! That's the most—"

"Shh, we're filming."

A crush of television cameramen clogged the hotel lobby.
Annie peered around film crews.

Jimmy Jay Crabtree gestured with his fist. "I'm telling
you right now. Nobody scares Jimmy Jay Crabtree. It's a
liberal plot, trying to scare booksellers into dropping my
book. But it ain't going to work. And I've got news for the
lousy, chickenhearted scum who're sending those letter
bombs—Jimmy Jay Crabtree doesn't scare." His eyes narrowed. His skinny chin jutted forward. "I'm here at the
Festival, and here I'll stay. And threats don't mean birdshit to
me. I'll accept my Medallion, and I'm going to go right on
carrying the word to the American people. We don't have to
put up with the sick, muddleheaded liberals who want to
make country clubs out of our prisons. We can take this
country back and make it a country Daniel Boone and Robert
E. Lee would be proud of.''

Annie paced the floor.

"Annie," Max said once again, "it's not your problem."
He added a final fizz to the mug of cappuccino.

Annie was torn between appreciation of a husband who
had brought to the hotel their small cappuccino machine plus
a box of Godiva raspberry truffles, and her still bubbling fury
at Kenneth Hazlitt.

"Max—thank you." Her eyes told him that she appreciated more than just a cup of coffee.

Max grinned and flung himself comfortably on the couch. His eyes told her he foresaw more than book discussions in this hotel suite, which just happened to be the Honeymoon Suite. Max had booked it. Max liked honeymoon suites.

So did she, of course.

But right now, she had to think. Later—

"Max, I'm the author liaison. I represent the Festival."

He sipped his cappuccino. "Maybe a little more cinnamon?"

He found the cinnamon in the picnic hamper and sprinkled the froth.

Annie took a gulp of cappuccino. Oh, yes. Good, good, good. Suddenly, as smoothly as Laurel engaging in automatic writing, Annie retrieved a truffle. That was better, better, better.

But her eyes kept returning to the glossy square invitation they'd found slipped beneath the door to their room. "Max, I don't get it. Why a small party in his suite for the Medallion honorees? He's got the open house bash"—she snapped it out—"set for the White Ibis Room tomorrow." Absently, she finished the truffle, scarcely even noticing the mellow, dark chocolate and the succulent raspberry. "You don't suppose he's idiot enough to think the Medallion honorees approve of his plans for the novel?"

Max returned to the couch. His face was pensive. "I don't think Kenneth Hazlitt is any kind of an idiot."

"So, why—"

"Annie," he said again gently, "it isn't your problem. You've made it clear the Festival opposes what Hazlitt is doing. But he's right. There's nothing at all you can do to stop him.''

''I just wish—''

There was a brisk knock at the door.

''I'll get it.'' Annie put down her coffee mug. It was probably one of her authors, and what could she say?

But she didn't know the stocky man standing in her hallway. In his mid-forties, he had a weathered, sensible face, short brown hair flecked with gray, and cool gray eyes. He looked neither pleasant nor unpleasant. He looked capable, the kind of man who could fix a car, coach a team, chair a meeting. He wore a light tan cotton suit, a blue shirt, a tie. Not, obviously, a tourist.

''Mrs. Darling?'' His voice was soft, southern, confident: *Miz Darlin'*. ''I'd like to visit with you for a moment. I'm Detective Clarence Wheeler from the Southern Division of the Beaufort County Sheriff's Department.'' He held open his billfold.

She glanced down at the identification.

No frog could jump to a lily pad faster than Annie could jump to a conclusion.

''Has someone sent a letter bomb to my store? Come in, Detective Wheeler.'' She held the door. ''Detective Wheeler, this is my husband Max. I can't believe what's happening! Fake letter bombs to bookstores all over the place. It's insane. Although I can certainly understand how Jimmy Jay Crabtree might make a few enemies . . .''

The men shook hands. Detective Wheeler accepted a chair, but he sat as crisply as a Parris Island drill sergeant.

Annie joined Max on the couch, still holding forth. ''. . . he's just obnoxious. Odious. Right on a level with a 'gator. He has the same kind of eyes, dangerous and shiny and—''

''You don't much care for Mr. Crabtree, Mrs. Darling?''

Annie nodded, ready to launch into a further description of the origin and habits of Jimmy Jay Crabtree, but Max cut her off.

''Annie, let's see what Detective Wheeler wants.''

Annie's mouth closed. There was the faintest edge of warning in Max's voice. She looked at her husband and read the message in his eyes: *Careful*.

''Detective Wheeler?'' she asked.

Those cool gray eyes gave nothing away. He smiled, but the smile didn't reach his eyes. ''Mrs. Darling, I understand you had access to Mr. Crabtree's suite today.''

''I certainly did not—'' She broke off. ''Oh, well, yes, I did pick up the keys for all the authors. To have them ready when they arrived.''

Detective Wheeler's voice was smooth as Tennessee sippin' whiskey. ''You didn't give Mr. Crabtree his key.''

Annie's eyes flashed. ''If he hadn't been such a butt—''

Max's voice was crisp. ''Detective Wheeler, why does it matter?''

''We're investigating a death threat found on the table in Mr. Crabtree's suite, and Mrs. Darling is among those who could have—''

Annie jumped to her feet. ''Did that sorry little jerk suggest I put it there? I'll death-threat him the next time I—''

Wheeler rose, too. ''Mrs. Darling, you were observed quarreling with Mr. Crabtree at the airport.''

''I wasn't quarreling. I simply kicked him—and his nasty cigarette—out of my car. Then I drove straight to the hotel and left his packet—key included—at the desk. I never set foot in his suite then or ever. And—you can put it in the bank—I never will.''

Annie dived into a wave. She came up in the foam, welcoming the taste of brine on her lips, the kiss of the sun on her face. Max came up beside her with a float.

They clung to its side and kicked their way out past the first wave.

The water was milky warm, the sunshine soft as a caress, the sky a Monet blue. And they had this stretch of ocean all to themselves, another pleasure of Hilton Head.

Annie smacked the water. ''You're right. I feel a lot better.'' The water washed away all of the day's frustrations. Who cared what Jimmy Jay Crabtree said? Not she.

Max's arm slipped around her waist.

And yes, when they got back to the room—

Max looked gorgeous in his striped cotton shirt and cream slacks. Annie glanced in the hall mirror. Her crisp new floral print dress was fine, too.

''We,'' she said determinedly, ''are going to have a good time. After all, everybody says he gives great parties.''

''Are you sure—''

She touched his lips with her finger. They'd been over it and over it.

No, she hadn't taken the authors to raise.

Yes, these were savvy, sophisticated people who should be able to handle themselves in a clinch.

No, she couldn't duck the party. No matter what happened, she had to represent the Festival. Blue had said, ''Work it out.''

Yes, they were going to be fashionably late. They hadn't hurried when they'd come in from their swim. There was the Jacuzzi and a king-size bed and matters of much more import and delight than arriving at the Mint Julep Press cocktail party at the stroke of five.

As they stepped out of their suite—and they could hear the rumble of voices down the hall and see the open doors to 500—Annie said, "We'll just stay for a little while, then grab my authors and go to Harbour Town for dinner."

Kenneth Hazlitt welcomed them with hearty handshakes and a friendly smile. "Come right on in. Pick up our fall catalog, right by the snacks." Beads of sweat glistened on his big face. A touch of too much sun had turned his cheeks pink. His planter's white suit was heavily wrinkled. "See, honey, I told you this would be fun." His smile was friendly. "And the Medallion winners are here. I knew they wouldn't want to miss it." He gulped from the tumbler in his hand. Annie caught the sweet whiff of bourbon. The sprig of mint was probably at the bottom of the glass.

The suite was jammed. Despite the open doors to the balcony, it was getting hot. Annie looked over her shoulder, then pointed toward the balconies. Max nodded.

As they wove their way across the room, Annie caught snatches of book talk:

". . . free freight's the ticket, believe . . ."

". . . Marilou Awiakta's poetry is the most lyrical . . ."

". . . mark my words, Tina McElroy Ansa is a writer to . . ."

". . . actually talked to Jesse Hill Ford!"

". . . when she was interviewed on Rebecca Bain's show last . . ."

Annie scooted past two women in identical crimson

dresses and reached the wet bar. Several trays contained glasses already filled with wine. There were alternating trays of white or red. Annie remembered Willie's revelation about cheap peanuts. Probably this was fairly cheap wine provided by Kenneth Hazlitt. It would certainly cut the cost of entertaining if you did it without waiters and brought your own alcohol and snacks. She wondered if the hotel knew. Annie picked a glass of red, took a sip, and looked for a spot to put her glass down. She edged to the side of the wet bar and tucked the glass behind the counter.

And saw a fifth of bourbon.

A warm arm slid around her shoulders. Willie Hazlitt bent close and yelled in her ear. ''Sweetie, if you want the real stuff, just say so. You've got friends in high places.''

Annie refused to be rattled. So she was caught discarding her wine; hadn't Kenneth Hazlitt been revealed as a niggardly and self-gratifying host? She slipped free of Willie's arm.

''Thanks, Willie. I'm not thirsty. Willie, I want you to meet my husband, Max.''

The two men shook hands. And eyed each other pleasantly, but with an undertone.

Ah, the male animal. Annie enjoyed it thoroughly. Really, this was turning out not to be such a downer day, after all. ''Great party, Willie,'' she called over the increasing din. ''Got to find my authors.''

She turned away and scanned the crowd.

Leah Vixen Kirby stood only a few feet away, holding an almost-full glass of red wine. Annie wondered if she, too, had tasted the wine and found it wanting. Leah looked cool and fresh in a pale green organdy dress. Her titian hair cascaded to bare, creamy shoulders. She stood with her head bent, her narrow face attentive, then her mouth curved in a triumphant, victorious smile. She lifted her glass in a toast.

The woman facing her didn't look the least bit triumphant. She looked nervous, uncertain, and edgy. It was the same blonde Annie had seen Leah talking to earlier at the Festival booths. But as Leah lifted her glass, the woman's plain, worried face relaxed.

Leah sipped, made a face at the wine's taste, then laughed.

The blonde managed a wan smile.

Leah leaned close, her face conspiratorial, and whispered in her companion's ear.

A hand touched Annie's elbow. "My, my, I wonder what Leah's up to?" Missy Sinclair's drawl was cool and amused.

Annie looked down.

The plump little author's mouth curved in a sly smile. Her unwinking dark eyes glistened. "When Leah gets that look, you know she's up to something. And the marvelous Carl's not handy to keep her in line."

Annie felt a flicker of distaste. "I don't know what you mean."

Those hypnotic eyes briefly moved toward Annie, then back to Leah. "Don't you? Oh, I think you do. But there are none so blind as those who choose not to see."

"Janet. To her sister. In *Playing the Fool*."

"Very, very good, my dear. So you did your homework. One of my best books." Another sly, amused smile. "Ciao."

And she slipped away.

Annie realized she hadn't invited Missy to join them for dinner. Annie took one step after the author, then stopped. She wasn't at all sure she cared to spend an entire evening with Melissa Sinclair.

Max murmured, "Don't turn your back on Ms. Sinclair."

"Don't worry." But Annie said it absently. Her eyes

were on Alan Blake. He stood half in, half out of the room on a nearby balcony. His scowl made him look older and ill-tempered. Annie could only see the back of Blake's companion. Long, curly dark hair. Broad shoulders in a short-sleeve, campesino-style white cotton shirt. Blake looked over his companion's shoulder. The author's eyes darted nervously around the room.

His gaze caught hers.

Blake stared at Annie blankly for a moment, still scowling, then abruptly, he forced a smile, nodded.

Annie lifted her hand in acknowledgment.

Well, if she gave out dinner invitations, she'd better wait until Mr. Blake was in a bit better frame of mind.

She knew one invitation she definitely wouldn't extend.

Jimmy Jay Crabtree's petulant rasp rose behind her. ". . . should of grabbed me some bourbon. This wine shit's enough to make me puke. Listen, I told it like it is at my press conference. Dirty commie liberals are out to crucify me. The bleeding hearts don't like it when you talk about Medicare fraud. And all this whining about people without insurance. Hell, let 'em get jobs and earn some insurance. And if they can't get a job with insurance or keep it, why should the rest of us have to bail 'em out? We don't have a health-care crisis in this country, we have a whiny baby crisis. How about some old-fashioned work ethic? That's why they're threatening to blow me up, and the latest thing is a death threat. Yeah. Sure as hell . . ."

Max glanced over Annie's shoulder. "Going strong."

"Dandy little fellow, isn't he?"

"I believe I'll kill him in my next book." Emma Clyde's voice was meditative. "Hi, Annie. Max."

Annie turned and grinned at the imposing author. It wasn't actually that Emma was tall. But she *seemed* tall.

And her cornflower-blue eyes were shrewdly calculating.

Annie felt quite sure Emma was indeed, at that moment, considering methods of disposing of Jimmy Jay Crabtree.

"How?" Annie asked.

"A cobra in his suitcase would be rather fun."

"Wouldn't the cobra smother?"

"All right. A gift box with some strategic holes. Have it delivered to his hotel room late enough that he'd be too drunk to notice." Emma's square face was grimly amused. "Opening the package would frighten the cobra, and I picture the cobra as already being highly irritated. Yes, I like it."

Perhaps Annie was too literal ever to try her hand at writing. She frowned. "Emma, where would you get a cobra?"

The detective novelist waved her hand airily. "Snake house at a zoo. Most zoos wouldn't have enough money for an alarm system. Or one of those places that milk vipers for their venom to make antivenom." Her eyes narrowed. "Have to find out if they milk cobras. Be rather a challenge to cop one, wouldn't it?"

Those detached blue eyes swung toward the front door and their host. Thoughtfully.

Annie felt a chill.

Surely Emma wasn't seriously considering a true-life cobra-in-a-box?

No, of course not.

Emma's broad mouth quivered with amusement.

She was simply enjoying the idea.

Which was harmless enough.

Kenneth Hazlitt mopped his face with a sodden handkerchief and downed the rest of his drink. He looked at the empty glass and turned toward the wet bar.

Halfway there, he ran into a roadblock made up of three determined authors.

Annie foresaw the contest. "Be interesting to see what prevails, Kenneth's thirst or our trio's sales pitch."

Max smiled fondly. "The old girls are giving it a real try, aren't they?"

Miss Dora scarcely came to Hazlitt's elbow. She was holding up a plate.

Annie licked her lips. She hoped there was some Divinity left. It was simply divine. She had a sudden picture of cookbook editors across the land. Were they all roly-poly? Did authors share samples of their best recipes? Mysteries with recipes sold at an incredible pace. Diane Mott Davidson, whose sleuth was caterer Goldy Bear, always came to signings with morsels to die for. And a Sisters in Crime potluck in Anchorage, Alaska, once featured the chili from Nancy Pickard's *The 27 Ingredient Chili Con Carne Murders* mystery. Hey, how about a party at Death on Demand, with readers each bringing a dish from their favorite culinary mystery? Annie made a mental note. Oh, it could be great. There were the dishes Spenser fixed, and how about the best from Nero Wolfe's kitchen?

"Bourbon over Divinity," Annie wagered, eyes still on Hazlitt.

The publisher moved doggedly forward. But the importuning authors, if not attached to his coattails, were hanging in, like tails to a comet. Kenneth reached the wet bar; the wannabes were in close pursuit.

Annie reached out and snagged a piece of candy.

Miss Dora didn't even notice. The old lady's dark eyes were riveted on the publisher's ruddy face. "It's time for a cookbook with collard greens and grits. And *real* key lime pie." Her tiny nose wrinkled. "Not green!" Miss Dora stood on tiptoe to raise the plate close to Hazlitt's face.

Hazlitt reached out and took two pieces of Divinity.

Miss Dora beamed.

Henny moved in as smoothly as Frances and Richard Lockridge's Jerry North mixing a martini. "Mr. Hazlitt, *everyone* wants it."

Hazlitt popped the candies in his mouth. "Ma'am?" he mumbled. He edged toward the wet bar.

Henny matched him step for step. "Quick fixes. Think *Life's Little Instruction Book.* Think *Everything I Know I Learned from My Cat.* Publishing history. And I've got the next sure bestseller, *The Quotable Sleuth.* 'Eliminate all other factors, and the one which remains must be the truth.' "

Hazlitt slid around the corner of the bar. "Holmes." He grinned at Henny. His hands were hidden by the bar, but from the happy look on his face, Annie felt certain he was pouring bourbon into his empty glass.

"To the heart of the matter." Laurel's husky voice rose in admiration. "Mr. Hazlitt—may I call you Kenneth?—I am so impressed by your perspicacity, your unerring instinct, your knowledge, all the qualities so essential to successful publishing. I feel confident you are the man."

Hazlitt's eyes widened in delight.

Of course, Annie thought. Why not? Laurel was her usual gorgeous self. No man under eighty could resist her. It was not so much a wonder that Max's mother had been married five times, but that she hadn't been married ten. And now the full force of those deep blue eyes were turned on the publisher.

"Betcha he buys her book," Max murmured, his voice brimming with pride.

Annie privately thought Hazlitt might be a little disappointed when he realized he was only being offered a publishing opportunity, but she decided it wouldn't be tactful to share this insight with her husband.

Laurel lifted her slender hands, clasped them together. "Fly Like a Dove."

Like a moth to the flame, Hazlitt leaned on the bar. "Ma'am, that's music to my ears."

Annie couldn't resist the impulse to mutter, "Beam me up, Scotty, before I gag."

Hazlitt raised his glass in a toast to Laurel, then upended the tumbler.

It happened so swiftly.

The big man wavered. His face contorted until every feature was transformed. A bubbling, anguished cry of agony hung in the air. His whiskey tumbler bounced on top of the bar. Hazlitt clawed at his throat. That terrible keen of pain wavered, then ceased. His chest heaved. A glottal rasp signaled the desperate, final struggle for breath. His body arched, his arms flailed. He crashed into the shelving behind the bar. Glasses scattered; the mirror shattered. Hazlitt caromed against the bar, then dropped to the floor only a few feet from where Annie and Max were standing.

Willie Hazlitt pushed past a clot of abruptly silenced partygoers and dropped to his knees beside the thrashing, heaving body. "Ken, Ken! Oh, Christ, help me, someone. Help me!"

Emma Clyde pushed past Annie to join Willie.

Henny's voice rang out. "I've called 911 for medics and the emergency squad. Please, ladies and gentlemen, let's clear the area in an orderly fashion. As you pass through the front door, sign the tally sheet—"

Annie's head jerked toward Henny.

"—and list your hotel and room number. The authorities will wish a record of everyone who was here, but there is no reason to detain you.''

Annie stared at Henny. Why the list? For heaven's sake, this was—what was it?

A seizure? An accident?

Henny's face was stern and grim.

A hideously public suicide?

Attempted murder?

Annie grabbed Max's arm. Henny was simply taking the thousands of mysteries she'd devoured too much to heart.

But Annie found herself and Max moving in the orderly line toward the door, where Henny waited.

One by one those filing out signed as Henny directed.

As the hushed partygoers inched slowly toward the door, they could still hear the hideous sounds behind them. Annie clung tighter to Max. It seemed so wrong to leave, but they could do nothing to help. If there was anything that could be done, Emma would know. Funny to remember that Emma had once been a nurse. Once a nurse, always a nurse? Annie concentrated on what she knew about Emma, a nurse in World War II in North Africa.

The sounds stopped.

In the stark silence, a woman's voice carried clearly, ''But he just took a drink, then he died? My God, why?''

Chapter 9

Emma Clyde speared a succulent shrimp and dipped it in the thick red cocktail sauce. Every face at the table was turned toward the self-possessed mystery writer.

The setting sun splashed through the windows overlooking Calibogue Sound. The rosy light emphasized the dark hollows beneath Leah Kirby's eyes.

Carl Kirby's glance flickered from his wife to Emma and back again.

Alan Blake's cheeks were freshly shaven, but his determinedly charming smile appeared frozen in place. He no longer looked angry. His eyes were thoughtful.

Jimmy Jay Crabtree poked another caviar-laden cracker into his already bulging cheek. He was not freshly shaven.

Missy Sinclair smiled her satisfied, sly, frightening smile.

Emma bit the shrimp in half. ". . . poison, of course, something that caused respiratory arrest . . ."

Annie's fingers closed on a packet of crackers, crushed them. "Emma, couldn't it have been some kind of seizure?"

Cornflower-blue eyes flicked toward her. "Annie, that was not a natural death. Trust me."

Annie determinedly refused to remember those desperate, labored, whistling efforts to breathe. She pushed back her bowl of seafood gumbo. How could anyone eat?

Emma munched the rest of the shrimp with every evidence of enjoyment. "The laboratory tests will determine what kind of poison. Since the onset came immediately after he drank the bourbon, the whiskey probably contained the poison. If it did, the first question has to be, 'When was the bourbon poisoned?' "

"The first question?" Leah smoothed back a strand of titian hair. Her green eyes narrowed. "Surely the first question is, 'Who put the poison in the bottle? Kenneth? Or someone else?' "

Carl Kirby nodded in agreement.

Annie shook her head. Absently, she pulled the bowl of soup closer. Questions of time she understood—and they weren't disturbing to consider. "I see what Emma means. It makes all the difference as to who could have done it." Time could mean everything, if this were indeed murder. Think of the time element in *Have His Carcase,* one of Dorothy L. Sayers's finer efforts.

Missy Sinclair sipped her Chardonnay. "Honey, you put your finger on it. If that bottle was poisoned before it got to the hotel room"—her sleepy eyes moved from face to face—"why, it lets all of us out, sure enough." Her soft, throaty voice was as complacent as a cat's purr.

Alan Blake looked at her sharply. "Wait a minute, Missy. Why should any of us be suspected?"

Jimmy Jay Crabtree snickered.

Annie gritted her teeth. Okay, he'd come upon their group in the lobby and simply assumed he was invited to join them for dinner. What could she do?

Jimmy Jay's thin little mouth twisted in derision. "Alan baby, even your choirboy looks can't carry that off."

Leah frowned. "Jimmy Jay, don't be a fool," she said sharply. "If you're by any chance talking about Kenneth's wonderful book proposal, why, I know all of us felt so *honored* that he wanted to include us, to talk about our books and what makes them great."

There was an instant of quiet.

Jimmy Jay opened his mouth. Then he closed it without saying a word.

Annie knew he was tempted. It was a moment ready-made for an abrasive, gouging comment.

But she had to hand it to Jimmy Jay. He might be a butt, but nobody could call him stupid. He nodded slowly, his usually sneering face thoughtful, his pale eyes absorbed. He lifted his drink, brought it to his mouth, paused, looked down into the glass, and put it down again.

Missy Sinclair watched as the tumbler clicked decisively against the table. She shook with silent laughter.

The faintest suggestion of sorrow touched Leah's lovely,

porcelain-smooth, weary face. "It's such a shame that Kenneth's wonderful book will never see light of day."

Annie's omelet was untouched. She poured a second cup of coffee. Max had brought Kona from home and brewed it. She never took her eyes off the morning newspaper clutched in her hand. ". . . and it says Hazlitt is believed to have died from nicotine poisoning." She frowned. "Max, why does it say 'believed'? I mean, wouldn't the laboratory results be definite? Oh, but wait a minute. Here it says 'an autopsy is scheduled today.' Hmm. Anyway, the Sheriff's Department is 'pursuing leads discovered at the death scene.' " She lowered the newspaper. "Hey, is that double-talk or did they really find something there? I don't know what it could have been. It's just a hotel room. Unless it was some kind of note."

Max took his last bite of cantaloupe. "Note from whom?"

"Well, it's always possible that Hazlitt picked a spectacular way to commit suicide."

Annie averted her eyes as Max spread apple butter on a bran muffin. Honestly, didn't he ever get bored with eating so damn correctly? She propped the newspaper against the orange juice carafe and reached defiantly past the margarine for the butter. After all, Elsie the Cow couldn't have led generations of Americans down the garden path. Could she?

Annie spread a minute portion of the butter on her toasted English muffin, knowing that she'd been brainwashed by the health police. She plumped a mound of marmalade on top. So okay, maybe it even tasted better than in the days of yore when she'd drenched toast with butter. So okay, she could learn, adapt, relinquish, accept, evolve. Someday maybe she'd even prefer a pale slab of fish to filet mignon, rice cakes to raspberry truffles, fruit gelatin to apple pie. Sure, when cats took up square dancing!

Oblivious to his wife's internal nutrition soliloquy, Max munched on his muffin. "Suicide? Not likely. If Hazlitt was depressed, it certainly didn't show. And that was a pretty tough way to die."

Annie put down her English muffin, smudged marmalade from her fingers. "He must have hurt so much." Her fingers slipped up to touch her throat, and she scarcely noticed their faint stickiness. "Oh, Max, poison is dreadful." She reached out for her juice glass, stared at the gently swirling contents. "You have to have food to live. And food means hospitality, people giving to each other. It would be so dreadful to think you are among friends and to drink something—then to feel pain that doesn't stop, pain that tears at your throat and your chest and your stomach, and, finally, your throat closes and you know you are going to die and you don't even know who did this to you—and you'll never know! Max, it's awful!" She set the glass down. "That's why Christie used poison so often. It wasn't simply that she had trained as a pharmacist. It was much more than that; it was her knowledge that the worst kind of betrayal comes when someone you know—perhaps someone you love—wears a false face. That's the most dreadful thing that can happen to anyone." Annie took a deep, shaky breath. "At least he didn't die at home."

Max looked puzzled just for an instant, then he nodded.

Annie picked up her juice, absently sipped. "It could have been anyone at the party. Unless the bourbon was poisoned before the party started. Then it could be anyone who had access to the suite. But if the whiskey was poisoned before he came to the hotel, it would have to be someone who could get into his house. Of course, we don't know when the bottle was bought. Or where. But I imagine the police know that by now." She lifted the newspaper. "I wonder what they mean about leads discovered at the scene." She read quietly for a moment. "No mention about my Famous Five. Except it says the party was to honor the Medallion winners. But there's nothing in here about Hazlitt's book proposal. Who knows? Maybe he had wall-to-wall enemies at the party. Maybe somebody he'd cheated was there, or a jealous husband or a bookseller who owed Mint Julep Press money and couldn't pay it. Though certainly a bookstore in that shape would owe lots of publishers, and only Hazlitt got poisoned. So far. Oh, Max, I wonder if he was married—" She flipped over to the page where the story continued. "Let's see, that'd be at the bottom. It says 'services are pending'—of course, they have to wait until the autopsy's done, and that can take several days for all the poison tests to come back." She lowered the paper, frowning again. "I don't understand why they think it's nicotine and the autopsy hasn't been done." She shrugged and turned back to the paper. "Oh, here we go. 'Hazlitt is survived by a son, Michael, and a daughter, Jennifer, Calabasas, California.' No mention of a wife, so I guess they were divorced. And he's survived 'by his brother, William.' That must be Willie. Actually, they were stepbrothers, but it doesn't say so. Hmm. So his wife—ex-wife—couldn't have been at the party. Unless she was in disguise."

"Disguise?" Max looked bewildered.

"Well, you know," Annie murmured, "anything's possible. Remember *The Mousetrap*. But I'll bet Henny got everyone's name as they left. You know Henny. And the police can check and make certain everyone's who they say they are." She sprinkled some picante sauce on her omelet. She was, after all, Texas-born and Texas-bred. For good measure, she added a splash to her grits, which Texans enjoy as much as do South Carolinians.

"The problem won't be finding out who was there. The problem will be that so many were there," Max predicted. "Unless the police come up with some good physical evidence, they're going to have a hard time charging anyone."

Annie nudged onions and peppers atop the portion of omelet. "Do you suppose anyone's going to tell them about the infamous book proposal?"

Max refilled their coffee cups. "Physical evidence counts for a lot more than motive. Who's to say what suffices for a motive? The police will be looking for reasons someone might want Hazlitt dead, but their main focus will be on opportunity and physical evidence."

Annie nodded. Motives could often be surprising. The morning newspaper also contained a story about a slaying in West Virginia where one neighbor shot another over the volume of the victim's stereo system. She grinned. "You can bet our Famous Five have their stories down pat by now. They've had all night to think about how thrilled they were to be portrayed in Hazlitt's novel. You have to hand it to Leah Kirby. It's brilliant, absolutely brilliant, and I'll have to say it will certainly make my job easier. Can you imagine how frantic the authors would be if the police started hounding them?" Annie tossed down her napkin and checked her watch. "And speaking of the Gang of Five, I'd better check on them, be sure everything's in order for their appearances." Pens, surely they'd all brought pens. Alan Blake's panel was at ten o'clock. Better call him first.

As Annie pushed back her chair, a brisk knock sounded on their door.

"I'll bet it's one of them," she murmured.

But when she opened the door, Detective Wheeler inclined his head politely. A younger, stocky man in a blue suit stood impassively beside him.

This morning, Wheeler looked like a tired, capable coach. He wore the same tan cotton suit, but today his shirt was white. He said softly, "Good morning, ma'am. I'd like to speak with you for a moment. Along with Sergeant Kennedy here."

Annie glanced again at her watch. "I need to escort an author in half an hour. But I can talk to you until then."

"Thank you, ma'am." He followed Annie into the suite and said good morning to Max. Sergeant Kennedy followed. He said nothing.

When they settled at the table, Wheeler courteously declined the offer of coffee. Instead, he rested his hands—broad, sturdy hands with blunt nails—on the table. His cool, unreadable gray eyes fastened on Annie.

Sergeant Kennedy pulled a notebook from his pocket. He had a round, earnest face and wore thick glasses. He held a blue pen in stubby fingers.

Max's air of sleepy relaxation vanished. He looked from Kennedy to Wheeler.

"Mrs. Darling, are you a gardener?" the detective began.

Kennedy was poised to write.

Annie simply stared at Wheeler.

Max leaned forward. "Detective Wheeler, I'd like to know why you are here."

"For information, Mr. Darling."

"In regard to?"

"Murder, Mr. Darling. The murder of Kenneth Hazlitt."

"My wife scarcely knew Mr. Hazlitt, and I can see no reason why you should wish to interview her in any greater depth than the sixty-some-odd people who were also present when Hazlitt died yesterday.''

"Mr. Darling, she can answer questions here or she can come—under arrest as a material witness—to the Sheriff's Department in Beaufort.''

"Now, wait a minute,'' Annie stormed, "what's going on here? Are you jumping on me because that jerk Jimmy Jay Crabtree says somebody put a death threat in his room? I think—''

"Excuse me, Mrs. Darling. The Crabtree matter has no relation—except it seems to be another indication of your very excitable temper. It was your public altercation yesterday with Mr. Hazlitt that led us to you. And led us to obtain information about you from the Broward's Rock Police Department.''

That had an ominous ring. Though surely Chief Saulter had explained that the murder in her bookstore some years earlier had been solved largely because of her own efforts?

Detective Wheeler pointed at his sergeant.

Sergeant Kennedy, his face bland, flipped back several pages. He began to read in a pleasant tenor. "Statement from Jessie Beal: *'A really pretty young lady, short blond hair and a nice figure, athletic. She was furious. She threatened to close down his booth, but Kenneth came right back at her. She ended up yelling at him, something about a bash.'* Statement from Laetitia Hess: *'I couldn't make out what they were fighting about, but this young woman was absolutely livid. I think it had something to do with the cocktail party where he dropped dead. No, I don't know who she was.'* Statement from—''

Max held up his hand. "Lieutenant, there is a simple explanation.''

Annie jumped right in. "I'll say there is.'' In a few swift

sentences, she described Hazlitt's intention to write a roman
à clef based on the Famous Five. She was glad to note that
Sergeant Kennedy diligently took down everything she said.
She concluded triumphantly, "So, the problem was between
Hazlitt and the authors. I was trying to protect the authors.
I'm their liaison with the Festival. I had no reason whatsoever
to wish Hazlitt dead." The combativeness seeped out of her
face. "God, it was awful. Actually, he was kind of likable.
He was causing a lot of trouble but, you know, he didn't
seem like a mean person. Maybe he just didn't understand
how upsetting the idea of his book was to the authors."

Detective Wheeler's face remained impassive. Politely,
he asked her to explain what a roman à clef was.

"So, Hazlitt was talking about doing a book based on
their lives?"

"That's it exactly." Annie felt like she'd reached the top
of a mountain. Finally.

"But he was just talking about a book. Right?" Detective
Wheeler was polite, but his tone was dismissive.

Annie bristled. Wheeler didn't understand. "He had a
big New York publisher interested. And he was going to let
everyone know about the novel at the Mint Julep open house
today."

"Those folks he was going to write about, they all came
to his party?"

"Yes. They did. Don't you see—"

"Yes, ma'am. You've raised some interesting points. But
right now, I'd like to talk about what you did yesterday.
Right from the start."

It went easily until she got to the hotel for the first time.

Detective Wheeler really straightened up—shoulders
back, chest out—hey, he had to be a former Marine—when
she described going upstairs to the Hazlitt suite. His colorless

eyes never left her face. He took her through a laborious step-by-step description of that visit.

Max looked like John J. Malone waiting for his client to be arrested.

Annie felt hot and uncomfortable.

So, when she came to the part about her second visit upstairs, she compressed it. "After I got back from Savannah, I went up looking for Kenneth Hazlitt, but nobody answered the door." Which was, literally, true. She didn't want to be grilled about every step she'd taken during that second, face it, surreptitious exploration of Hazlitt's suite. "On my way out," she continued smoothly, "I talked to Willie—his brother—his stepbrother, I mean—downstairs in the White Ibis Room, and then I went to the airport . . ."

Wheeler nodded. Kennedy scribbled.

When she stopped, she glanced at her watch. It had only been ten minutes, but it felt like an hour. "Detective Wheeler, I have to meet Alan Blake before his panel."

"I'd like to accommodate you, Mrs. Darling, but there are a few more points to cover."

Abruptly, Annie felt like Eliza on her ice floe, colder than hell and scared.

"There's nothing in what you've said this morning that explains one fact, Mrs. Darling."

Annie looked into his cold, suspicious eyes. In the instant before he spoke, she knew that she was in trouble. Big time.

But she never expected the words that came, measured, inexorable, devastating.

"How did your fingerprints get on the glass containing the poison that killed Kenneth Hazlitt?"

"My fingerprints! *My* fingerprints?"

It honestly took her a pulsing, difficult, seemingly interminable interval, when those probing eyes never wavered from her face, to make the connection, the connection that had to be the answer. "You mean *that* glass was the one he was drinking from? *That* glass?"

"What glass, Mrs. Darling?"

"Annie." Max shoved back his chair. "I believe we'll call for legal counsel."

"No, no. There's nothing to it. Let me explain." But, as she spoke, Wheeler watching her with the avidity of a cougar stalking a deer, the words came haltingly, the open door, the empty suite, the impulse to look for a manuscript, the glass lifted from behind the wet bar and balanced on the upended wastebasket.

"That," she said firmly, "is the only glass I touched. When I finished looking, I put the glass back behind the wet bar."

Annie knew that if she were a deer and the officer a cougar, she would be dead meat.

"You didn't say anything about picking up a glass when you described that visit."

Annie deliberately didn't look toward Max, but she could feel his reproachful glance. So, okay, she'd condensed her first version a little. Was that a crime?

"I didn't see a soul. So I didn't think it mattered."

There were no Hamilton Burger antics. Detective Wheeler didn't stand and yell and point an accusatory finger, but in a quiet, steely way the effect was the same. "Mrs. Darling: You didn't think it mattered that you had access to that suite, uninterrupted, unobserved access, to do whatever you wanted to do?"

Annie could hear the ice crackling. She wondered if Eliza had endured the same sinking feeling. Annie took a deep breath, but Max spoke first.

"Detective Wheeler, was that bottle of whiskey unopened when it was brought to the suite?"

The detective looked steadily at Max for a moment, then slowly nodded.

"At least," Max amended, "that's what you've been told. You can't be certain."

"The bourbon was purchased at a package store in Atlanta, Georgia, three days ago. Mr. Hazlitt—Mr. William Hazlitt—told us the bottle was one of several bought for this trip and that he carried them unopened up to the suite Friday morning."

"He could be lying," Max said mildly.

"He could."

"You're questioning Mr. William Hazlitt?"

"We're questioning everybody." Those implacable eyes turned again to Annie. "But Mrs. Darling's fingerprints are on the glass."

"And what other prints are on that glass?" Max demanded.

Wheeler nodded. "The victim's. Mr. William Hazlitt's. The maid's."

Annie wanted to cheer. She knew this was no reprieve, but at least she wasn't the only person to have touched the glass except for the murdered man. "So it isn't just me."

Wheeler stared at her.

She shoved a hand through her hair. "Are you sure that glass is the one he was drinking from when he died?"

"Positive. Traces of his saliva are on the glass."

"And the poison was in there?" she pressed.

"Yes."

"How did you know it was nicotine?" It had been worrying her all morning. "They haven't done the autopsy yet."

The detective's eyes narrowed.

"I read all about it this morning." She pointed at the open newspaper.

"Do you garden, Mrs. Darling?"

"That's the second time you've asked me that. No, Detective Wheeler, I do not. Why?"

"Do you have roses?" the detective persisted.

Max lounged back in his chair. "Yes. We do. And yes, we probably have nicotine in the garden shed." He smiled at Wheeler's sharp glance. "My mother gardens. Sometimes."

When she wasn't busy, Annie thought, penning great books, or mountain climbing in Peru, or driving her daughter-in-law mad.

The ice floe felt a trifle more secure. "So anybody could get that kind of poison at the local garden shop," Annie said happily. "Am I right?"

Wheeler's answer was grudging. "That's correct."

Max abruptly leaned forward, a confident smile lighting his face.

Annie looked at him in surprise. She could practically hear the tumblers turning. So what was making Max so happy?

"Detective Wheeler, it will be easy to prove that my wife is telling you the truth and that her fingerprints on that glass can be accounted for just as she says."

"Yes?"

Detective Wheeler didn't appear to be hanging on Max's every word, but Annie was.

"Let's go down the hall and let Annie show us the places she recalls touching when she searched the suite. If her fingerprints are there, she's telling the truth."

Wheeler considered it. At least Annie honestly thought he did. Finally, he shook his head. "We'll see where her prints are. We don't need a guided tour."

Max's tone sharpened. "But you have to admit that if you find her prints throughout the suite, it will certainly support her story."

"Maybe." Wheeler cocked his head. "But your story isn't quite complete, is it, Mrs. Darling?"

Annie stared at him blankly.

"What did you take from the suite?"

Annie looked at him in surprise. "Nothing, Mr. Wheeler. Absolutely nothing."

"I advise you to tell the truth, Mrs. Darling."

Annie's face flamed. "I don't like your attitude, Detective Wheeler. I am telling you the truth, and I give you my word I took absolutely nothing from that suite."

Once again Wheeler nodded toward his sergeant.

Kennedy flipped through his book. "Statement from Judy Fleet, fifth-floor maid: *'I was at the far end of the hall. I saw a woman come out of Suite 500 yesterday afternoon carrying a big box. I couldn't see her face, but she was blond and young. She lugged it to the elevator and went downstairs.'*"

Annie had an eerie feeling, like the woman who returned to her hotel room to find no trace of it.

"No." She cleared her throat, tried for a more robust tone. "Absolutely not. It wasn't me."

Max folded his arms on the table. His gaze was combative. "I was with my wife from lunchtime until the start of the cocktail party."

"So you say, Mr. Darling."

"I do say. Moreover, Detective Wheeler, the fact that my wife was in that suite has to be irrelevant to the poisoning of the bottle."

Annie frowned, then, suddenly, she understood. It was enlightenment right on a *Eureka!* level. She felt a twinge of chagrin. She hated being Mrs. Latham to Max's Colonel

Primrose. *She* was the mystery expert, and she should have spotted the flaw.

"Of course!" She was too excited even to be scared. "Hazlitt was drinking bourbon when we came to the party. Were his fingerprints on top of mine on that glass?"

Max beamed.

Annie charged ahead despite the unchanged coldness in Detective Wheeler's eyes. "Yes," she said eagerly, "they had to be. And if he was drinking bourbon out of that glass, why wasn't he already dead? I mean, look at it, if the poison was put in the bottle of bourbon ahead of time, he would have keeled over when he drank the drink in his hand. And I know he'd been drinking bourbon, I could smell it."

The detective's hard gaze didn't falter. "Right, Mrs. Darling. From a bottle that he'd just finished. The bottle was in the wastebasket. The drink he poured out of the bottle behind the wet bar—the drink everyone saw him pour—was the first from a fresh bottle." Wheeler's smile was wintry. "So you see, Mr. Darling, Mrs. Darling"—he gave them each a deliberate, measured glance—"it *does* matter that Mrs. Darling visited the suite beforehand. Because that bottle, the new bottle, could have been poisoned at any time after it was purchased, and that includes the period in the hotel room before the party began." He paused, then added without expression, "It also, of course, could have been poisoned during the party. But that isn't as likely. Is it?"

Why, Annie wondered disconsolately, did the bon mot, the perfect rejoinder, the ultimate putdown, never occur to her until it was too late?

Her eyes were on the elevated podium where Alan Blake

smiled winningly at his audience, but her mind was still in their hotel suite in combat with Detective Wheeler.

Okay. Wheeler, for obvious reasons, thought it was much more likely that the second bottle was poisoned before the party.

That made all kinds of sense. It would take a murderer with incredible nerve to sidle up to the wet bar, pick up the bottle of bourbon, and pour nicotine into it.

Her mind skewed off into a fresh field. She pawed through her purse, found a program, and wrote on it:

1. WHOSE FINGERPRINTS ARE ON THE BOTTLE?

2. WAS THE NICOTINE LIQUID? DOES IT COME IN ANY OTHER FORM?

3. HOW DID THE POISONER CARRY THE NICOTINE?

She chewed on the pencil, then added:

4. HOW LONG WAS THE DOOR TO HAZLITT'S SUITE UN-LOCKED?

From her own knowledge, it was open at a few minutes past noon. She tapped the pencil on her chin, then continued:

5. CHECK WITH HENNY, LAUREL, AND MISS DORA.

6. WHO KNEW HAZLITT'S SUITE NUMBER?

7. WHAT BOX WAS TAKEN?

She focused on Number 6. So, okay, the world. Well, almost. She'd had no reason not to tell the authors, and she'd let all of them know, one way or another, how to find Hazlitt. And all five were on the fifth floor.

She put a check mark by Number 6 and wrote: *The Famous 5.*

After a moment's thought, she added, more reluctantly: *The Three Musketeers.*

She knew Broward's Rock's wannabe authors had visited

the suite, although it was absurd to think they'd poison Hazlitt. Miss Dora, Henny, and Laurel wanted a publisher, alive and thriving.

But the authors—any one of the five could have slipped down the hall to the Hazlitt suite.

With nicotine in hand?

Annie nodded. Sure. Somebody came prepared. These people all knew Hazlitt. They would know he drank bourbon.

Wasn't it a terrible gamble to lace a bottle of bourbon and assume only Kenneth Hazlitt would drink from it?

Sure. But the mind that consigned Kenneth Hazlitt to a hideous death probably wouldn't be concerned about danger to bystanders. This was not a warm-hearted killer. If any ever were.

But for heaven's sake—

8. WAS IT CERTAIN THAT KENNETH HAZLITT WAS THE IN-TENDED VICTIM?????

Had that even occurred to Detective Wheeler?

Probably.

Although he wasn't impressed by literary motives, Annie didn't doubt Wheeler was as industrious and thorough as Inspector Slack ever thought about being. More charming, though. Captain Heimrich with a Southern accent.

How could she make Wheeler understand it wasn't simply a matter of information in a novel? Who knew what Hazlitt intended to write? If the stuff were fiery enough, it could destroy reputations.

Annie wrote quickly:

9. TRY TO GET A COPY OF HAZLITT'S PROPOSAL.

10. HOW DID THE FAMOUS 5 KNOW ABOUT THE BOOK?

They definitely knew, because they'd all called her *before* they arrived on the island. That meant any one of them could have dropped into a garden center and arrived prepared to kill.

Applause erupted.

Annie looked blankly around the room.

"Isn't he just wonderful!" the woman next to her breathed, her voice soft and tremulous, her eyes shining.

Alan Blake leaned on the podium, his smile diffident and endearing. "Thanks. Thanks, folks. God, it's my pleasure. Thanks so much."

Annie suppressed a desire to stand and shout, "Come off it!" Blake autographed books and grinned and charmed. But finally, every book was signed, and the last adoring straggler departed.

He was gathering up his papers when Annie approached.

"Mr. Blake, could I visit with you for a moment?"

His face still held a vestige of down-home shyness. But he shed it faster than Vidocq changing disguises. "That was great. Thank God for little old ladies. And call me Alan, okay?"

Annie hesitated, but only for a second. This morning she'd told Detective Wheeler she was simply trying to protect the authors. Protection she was willing to provide, but serving as a sacrificial lamb wasn't in her job description. Not now. Not ever.

"Alan, I'd like to try and help you with the police."

"Help me do what?" His face was puzzled, but his eyes were abruptly wary.

"Explain the stuff Kenneth was putting in his novel."

Every semblance of charm seeped out of his handsome face. His features were still quite perfect—smooth cheeks, wide-spaced eyes, firm chin—but the skin was stretched tight, the eyes flint hard, the mouth tense. "Are you threatening me?" The words dropped like icy pellets between them.

Blake didn't move.

But Annie took a step back.

"Of course not." She glanced toward the doors. They were closed. There were just the two of them.

She took another step back.

He followed. "What stuff? What stuff are you talking about?"

Blake was so close she could smell his aftershave, see a tiny nick from shaving on his neck.

"You know," she improvised swiftly. "All that old stuff."

Abruptly, the sense of menace lifted. Blake smiled. It was not a nice smile. "Trying me on, aren't you?" He smoothed back a lock of chestnut hair. "You got into it hot and heavy with Kenneth yesterday. By his booth. Are the cops making you uncomfortable?" His grin expanded. "Gee, that's a shame." His voice was light and smooth and pleased. "Hope everything turns out okay for you." Then he brushed past her and pushed through the doors.

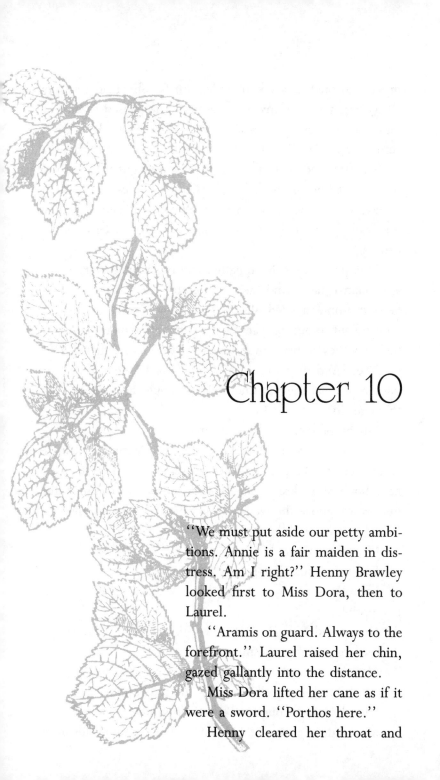

Chapter 10

"We must put aside our petty ambitions. Annie is a fair maiden in distress. Am I right?" Henny Brawley looked first to Miss Dora, then to Laurel.

"Aramis on guard. Always to the forefront." Laurel raised her chin, gazed gallantly into the distance.

Miss Dora lifted her cane as if it were a sword. "Porthos here."

Henny cleared her throat and

flipped through a stack of index cards. She held one up. "Page nineteen. Of my manuscript." She paused to be certain she had everyone's attention. "Sergeant Hemingway sums it up so well in Georgette Heyer's *A Blunt Instrument:* 'When fate's got it in for you there's no limit to what you may have to put up with.'" She slapped the cards together. "Max, we are here, we three, ready to dedicate our lives, our souls, and our fortunes to Annie's defense. Give us our orders."

Max pressed his lips together and maintained a grave and appreciative face. And tried desperately to think. Certainly he and Annie needed all the help they could get. But he didn't want to put this game threesome into danger, although he knew they'd shrug away any effort to relegate them to the sidelines. And they were canny and capable, no matter how unconventional their attitudes. What could he—safely—ask them to do?

But he pondered a bit too long.

"Perhaps," Miss Dora suggested ruminatively, "Annie would feel better if I fixed her a dish of butter beans with ham bone and okra." She looked across the room at the microwave above the wet bar, appraisal mixed with disdain. "Page twenty-two."

"Troubles Grow Us."

Everyone looked at Laurel and waited.

Laurel's smile was serene, her headshake almost imperceptible.

Henny and Miss Dora shared a glance of chagrin. Was it déclassé to specify page numbers?

Max intervened. A gentle reminder apparently was in order. "One for all, all for one," he murmured.

Laurel came through. "Page twenty-nine."

Max didn't glance at his watch. But he knew he must

hurry. He looked at his guests, sitting so patiently—so im-movably?—on the couch.

A rush of pride suffused him. Laurel was unmatchable. No one had a mother quite like his. Although sometimes . . . Max concentrated on the positive. This morning, as usual, her hair shone like spun gold, her face was camellia smooth, her dark blue eyes glowed with good humor—and perhaps just a touch of otherworldliness. He certainly didn't accept Annie's description of Laurel as "spacey." Not at all.

There was nothing spacey about Miss Dora's raisin-dark eyes. They glistened with a sharp, cold intelligence. Right now her parchment-colored, wizened face was scrunched in thought. Occasionally, she lifted her cane and made a thrust and parry.

Henny wore a crisp seersucker suit and looked like a director on many boards. As she was.

Max and Henny spoke together.

"Why don't you three—"

"The people at the party—"

Each stopped. Max nodded politely.

"The party," Henny said again. "I made a copy of the list of names before I gave it to the police."

Her cohorts smiled in approval.

Max thumped his hand with his fist. "Great! Here's what I suggest—"

They listened, making various sounds of agreement, then departed, stepping briskly.

Max watched them go down the hall. There were only three of them. So why did he keep thinking of a Roman phalanx?

But they would now be well occupied, and surely they would be safe. This legwork needed to be done. But how long would it take for them to contact everyone who had attended the fatal party and try to chart each person's movements within the Hazlitt suite? It would take mounds of graph paper. Actually, a three-dimensional approach might be required.

And the possibility that this task would also provide the wannabe authors with a reason to chat with the many book publishers among the party attendees—well, Max dismissed that from his mind as unworthy.

His smile slipped away. He closed the door, crossed to the telephone, and punched the number of his office on Broward's Rock.

Annie wiped beads of sweat from her face. She longed to crack the door to the telephone booth, but even with the door closed, she could barely hear above the country music twanging from the nearby stage.

A rush of static blitzed the phone.

Annie held the receiver away from her ear until the crackling stopped.

"What did you say, Chief?"

". . . damn mobile phones are more trouble than they're worth." Frank Saulter, police chief of Broward's Rock, had been a close friend of Annie's late uncle, Ambrose, the original owner of the Death on Demand bookstore. Now Saulter was a staunch friend of both Annie and Max. "I said what the heck have you gotten mixed up in?"

"Murder," she replied drearily. And she quickly brought him up to date, including the infamous glass.

"So that's"—crackle, crackle—"your prints—"

Annie had no trouble filling in the missing words.

"Yes. Listen, Chief, the detective in charge of the investigation thinks I might have done it! Have you talked to any-body in the Sheriff's Department about this case?''

''Just got off the phone. They won't know for sure until the autopsy reports are in, but they found a small bottle with nicotine in it—you know, the kind you buy at garden stores —on the floor of the suite. And there were traces of nicotine in the glass.''

That explained why the police believed nicotine to be the poison, but the presence of the little bottle meant even more to her. Relief lifted her voice. ''Well, I know my fingerprints weren't on *that* container!''

Then she fought a swift, sharp fear. It would be in the realm of nightmares if somehow, some way, her fingerprints appeared there. But, obviously they hadn't. If they had, she'd be languishing right that moment in the Beaufort County jail.

Static.

''. . . wiped clean. Not a print on it.''

So, she might be in a mess, but it didn't yet have the dimensions of a nightmare.

''How about the whiskey bottle?''

''The victim's prints, plus his brother's, plus some as yet unidentified.''

But not hers. Annie felt another surge of relief, but she didn't harbor a hope that the murderer had conveniently forgotten to wipe the whiskey bottle, thereby leaving his or her incriminating fingerprints behind.

But why polish the nicotine bottle and *not* the whiskey bottle?

She propped open her purse, fumbled for her pen.

''Have you heard anything about the direction of the investigation?'' She added the query about bottles and prints to her list of questions, checking off Numbers 1–3.

The line was suddenly clear, but Saulter didn't say a word. The silence was ominous.

"Chief, who do they suspect?"

Saulter's tone was weary. "Young lady, how the *hell* do you manage to get into so much trouble?"

She was too hot and worried to take exception. She ignored the implied criticism of Max (Chief Saulter expected husbands to keep their wives occupied with more salutary matters than homicide) and the sexist judgment (only a damn fool woman would search through someone else's suite even if the door *was* open). Because she also heard the unmistakable uneasiness in his voice.

And that was really scary.

Annie didn't try to defend herself. Chief Saulter wouldn't understand how concern for the authors assigned to her put her in this pickle.

Instead she wiped her face, wriggled against her sticky blouse, and said quietly, "Chief, I promise. I'll never—" She paused. Ransack somebody's hotel room? That was a peculiar promise to make. And maybe it begged the question. She started over. "Chief, you know I wouldn't kill anybody."

"Not with poison." His voice was quiet and grave.

His utter certainty made her feel like a million dollars. She blinked back a tear. Maybe sometimes it was almost worth panic and fear to discover how someone close to you saw you. "Thank you, Frank." She took a deep breath. "Chief, I need your help . . ."

In the hotel business center, Max signed for the fax pages, then used the copy machine. He made three sets. He left one at the front desk for Annie and one in the suite. The third he took with him.

The silky sea breeze ruffled the candy-striped awnings. The plaza was jammed with festival-goers this morning. Annie struggled through the holiday crowds.

". . . Waldron's such an insightful writer. She . . ."

". . . don't want to miss the panel on Southern food."

"Arthur Flowers is one of my favorite . . ."

". . . from Yoknapatawpha County to . . ."

"Did you attend Madison Smartt Bell's panel?"

Damn, damn, damn. She was missing everything! And she only had an hour before she needed to escort Leah Kirby to her panel. By then, Annie had to figure out a way to break through Kirby's defenses. She'd tried the old Everything-Is-Known-Flee-At-Once ploy with Alan Blake, and it had failed. Miserably. As far as she was concerned, Jimmy Jay Crabtree and Alan Blake were now in a dead heat for her least favorite author.

She reached the Mint Julep Press booth.

The life-size poster of Kenneth Hazlitt still stood, panama hat buoyantly tilted, grin ebullient enough for Fat Tuesday, the merry blue eyes cocky and unseeing.

Willie Hazlitt wasn't there.

The phone in his suite hadn't been answered. The doors to the White Ibis Room were locked. God, what if Willie'd loaded up and gone back to Atlanta? But, no: The booth was still here, though the somber-faced woman slumped forlornly in a metal chair didn't look like she could sell the original manuscript of *Sanctuary* with Faulkner's handwritten corrections.

A roar of laughter rolled up from a Festival session on the beach. A trombone wailed and a trumpet soared as a Dixieland jazz band snaked by the booths.

Annie leaned across the counter. "Willie!" she shouted. "Do you know where he is?"

The woman in the metal chair pushed gold-rimmed glasses higher on a narrow nose. She had a white rabbit face and weak blue eyes that avoided Annie's gaze. She pointed toward the beach. "Mr. Hazlitt's gone for a walk. May I help you?" The offer was made without enthusiasm.

"Thanks, but I need to see him. Do you know when he will be back?"

Bony shoulders rose and fell.

Annie looked at her watch, then plunged into the swirling mass of festival-goers.

Sand gritted beneath her sandals as she quickly crossed the boardwalk over the dunes to the beach.

A cool breeze fluttered her skirt. Whitecaps glittered on the choppy green water. She breathed deeply, relishing the salty tang, and looked up and down the beach.

Umbrellas rustled in the wind. Only a few were up, and beachgoers nestled in blankets and towels. It would warm to the low seventies by afternoon, but right now, with the breeze off the water, it was chilly.

Right or left?

Either way, a brisk walk would lead to almost empty beaches within a hundred yards.

A wedge formation of brown pelicans skimmed the wave tops heading south.

It was as good an omen as any.

Annie turned right. She walked on the firm sand still damp from the outgoing tide. Shading her eyes, she checked every blanket, every chair, and then she was past the beachgoers clumped near the boardwalk.

Million-dollar homes with two and three levels of balconies and shining expanses of glass rose behind the dunes.

Two joggers loped past, a family on bikes wheeled by, a woman walked an Irish setter.

Annie squinted. Fifty yards ahead, a man in blue sweats leaned against a half-buried bone-white log long ago tossed up on the beach by a storm.

Annie picked up speed.

Willie Hazlitt stared somberly at the horizon, his arms folded across his chest. The wind tousled his dark hair, but Annie thought that perhaps for the first time in his life, Willie Hazlitt wasn't even aware of his appearance. His eyes were red-rimmed; his mouth set in a grim line.

Overhead a laughing gull rode a wind current, and its strange, cackling call hung in the air. The unceasing curl and crash of breaking waves boomed like a faraway cannon. The breeze rustled the sea oats on the dunes like ghostly fingers plucking the strings of a mandolin.

Annie stepped closer.

''Willie, I'm so sorry.''

He tried to smile, but it came out lopsided. ''I never thought I'd see a beautiful girl on a beach—and not even care.'' His eyes were dark with pain. ''I've never felt so lost in my whole life. Not even when my mom died. Ken was there. He's always been there. Ever since I was five and my mom married his dad. The big guy. My big bud. And now—'' He swiped a hand roughly across his face. ''And now I don't know what the hell to do about everything. About anything. I called Mike and Jenny. God, that was awful. And it's all up in the air. When the funeral will be.

And where. Then I tried to decide about the stuff here. I mean, what the hell does it matter now? But it mattered to Ken. What do you think? Should I pack it all up? Forget about the Festival? But Ken was hoping for big orders. Maybe I should have the open house just like he'd planned.''

Annie knew something about grief. It was better to be busy. Much better. Firmly, she said, ''I'd carry on. Have the open house. Get the orders.'' She hesitated, then made the plunge. ''But first, Willie, I want to ask for your help.'' She didn't feel her request was totally self-serving. Surely it would begin to ease Willie's pain to try and discover his brother's murderer. She started with the easy question first. ''Is there anyone who can tell me more about the novel Kenneth was going to write?''

''That book?'' He shot her an odd, almost angry look. ''What difference does it make now?''

''It may make all the difference—in finding out who poisoned him.''

Willie's eyes searched her face. ''You're serious, aren't you? You really think one of those authors did it?'' He didn't wait for her answer. He pushed off the log, stood stiff and straight, his hands clenched into fists. He was too angry, too absorbed in her suggestion to wonder, even so, why she should care.

Maybe that thought wouldn't occur to him until long after today. Maybe never.

Obviously, Willie didn't know about her fingerprints on the fatal glass. Which proved Detective Wheeler was closemouthed. That was good. But Willie's shock at her suggestion also proved Detective Wheeler hadn't mentioned the famous authors as possible suspects. That was not so good.

"That stupid book? Who'd kill somebody over stuff in a book?"

"It depends upon what kind of stuff it was going to be, Willie. I know the authors he said he was going to put in it were upset and scared. And these are people who live and die because of words. I tried to tell your brother, but he wouldn't listen."

Some of the tension eased out of his body. Now the smile was stronger, genuine. "Ken was on a roll. He was having a hell of a time."

Annie remembered Kenneth Hazlitt's booming voice, his undisguised elation. A man who loved parties. A man who had planned one party too many where the fun was at someone else's expense.

"The authors weren't," she said grimly.

Willie rubbed his chin. "But that's silly, you know, to think somebody'd kill him over a book. Though . . ." He looked puzzled.

Annie pounced. "What, Willie?"

"The box for the open house is gone. I noticed it this morning. It had some stuff about the book. Kenneth was going to put these announcements about the book right at the back of the open house. He said people would be curious as hell and that would move them through the whole Mint Julep display."

The missing box.

Taken by a young blond woman who looked so like her.

"Willie, did Kenneth know any blondes?"

"Blondes? Sure."

"Are any of them here this weekend?"

"Maybe. I don't know. Why?"

Annie hesitated. She didn't want to make Wheeler mad,

but what harm could it do? "The maid saw a blond woman take that box from your suite yesterday afternoon."

"Oh. Well, I guess the police will find out. Though I can't see how it could matter."

Nobody, not the victim's brother nor the police, seemed to take the threat of a tell-all novel seriously.

Annie said sharply, "Well, if one of the authors didn't poison Kenneth, then who did? Who would want to kill him?"

Willie hunched his shoulders; he stared out at the murky green water. "It's nuts. Nobody. No way. Never. Not Ken." His face creased in bewilderment. "He was a fun guy. Oh, I'm not saying he couldn't rile people. I mean, Ken always had to be in charge, the main man. That's the way he was. Always. From the time we were kids. He rode his bike faster. He ate more pizza. His hot rod beat everybody's. He screwed more girls. He drank more beer. He made more money. He sold more books." He paused, laughed softly. "I'm guessing there. I'll bet he sold more books. I don't know a lot about what he's done the last couple of years. I just came back a few weeks ago."

"Came back?"

Willie reached down, picked up a broken shell, bounced it in his palm. In his rueful smile, there was a touch of yesterday's insouciant Willie. "Sweetheart, you don't want to know. I've lived more places, had more jobs, made and lost more money—God, that's fun—than a television evangelist. Bartended. Ran a bungee-jumping outfit. Prospected for gold. Sold vacuum cleaners. Taught ballroom dancing." His eyes rolled. "But there comes a day when you realize you don't have any roots." His thumb flicked at the tiny barnacles on the shell. "Ken had been after me for years to come back and work with him. So, one morning I looked in the mirror when I started to shave—and I saw flecks of gray. So . . . I came home." His hand closed around the shell. He lifted his arm and threw. The shell skipped across the water, then sank. "I came home," he repeated heavily.

Annie's heart sank just like the shell. "So you don't know who might have been angry at Kenneth? Or afraid of him? Or jealous of him?"

"Mad enough to make him hurt like that?" Willie's face twisted. "Jesus, no. Oh, he was a little crossways with some folks. There was a printer who wanted to be paid, and Kenneth was behind. He said sometimes you had to get a new printer, start over, if the money just wasn't there. But he told the guy he'd make it good when he could. And Ken was mad at his distributor. Ken said the fellow hadn't gotten the books out like he promised."

Annie nodded. Small presses sometimes came up short with printers. It wasn't good, it wasn't fair, but it happened. And poisoning Kenneth wouldn't pay the bill.

Or would it?

"The printer. Where's he located?"

Willie frowned. "Illinois, I think. Gustafson Printers."

Annie pulled out her heavily marked program and jotted down the name.

"And the distributor?"

"Hmm. Wherry Brothers. Out of Tampa."

"Willie, does Mint Julep Press have any kind of insurance on your brother?"

"I don't know. You'd have to talk to Wanda. She handles everything. Wanda Dillon. She's been with Ken forever."

Annie wrote down the name.

"But you don't know of any violent quarrels?"

"No."

"Who profits from his death?"

"Ask Wanda. Like I said, I've only been back a couple of weeks."

"You don't know the contents of his will?"

"Honey, I don't even know if he *had* a will. My guess would be that everything goes to his kids. Who else? He hadn't remarried. He hung out with this gal, Cheryl. A babe. Sells makeup at a Lord and Taylor. But she's in the Bahamas this week with a girlfriend. Oh, God, I've got to call her." His shoulders slumped.

"Willie, why was Kenneth drinking bourbon instead of the wine?"

Willie rubbed his cheek. "Money, sweetheart. I mean, Ken was a great guy, but he always cut corners. You know: bought store brands, shopped around for a bindery that'd make him the best deal, paid Wanda just enough to keep her from leaving, and he never met a raise he liked. So, he wasn't going to spring for whiskey for the party. That whiskey was for us. He figured he was putting on the show, he could call the tune, and he liked bourbon."

"Do you drink bourbon?"

"Sure." His answer was casual, unconcerned.

Annie stared at him. An ugly thought had just occurred to her.

"Willie, could the poisoned bourbon have been meant for *you*?"

His eyes widened. His lips parted, but no sound came. He gnawed at his underlip, dragged in a ragged breath. "Christ. I almost poured a drink, but I had some scotch in my suitcase. I like scotch better." He shook his head violently. "Hell, why would anybody want to kill me?"

"Why would anyone want to kill Kenneth?"

"Nobody. Like I told you, nobody. Unless—" Anger

flickered in his eyes. "These writers. You think it could have mattered that much to them?"

"To *one* of them," Annie amended. "That's why I need to know more about the book. Willie, would Kenneth's secretary know about the proposal?"

"Proposal?"

"That's a description of what will be in a book. The rumor is that Kenneth was trying to sell the book to a publisher on the basis of a proposal. Would Wanda know?"

"Yeah. I guess. If anybody would. Yeah, Wanda will probably know."

"I'll call her."

"Tell her I gave you her name."

"Thanks. And, Willie? About the whiskey—did you open the bottle that held the poison?"

"No." Then he frowned. "Hey, that's funny. I mean, that's kind of weird. There were three bottles. The third one's still sitting there, unopened. Before the party started, I poured Ken a drink and tossed the first bottle in the trash. Then there was the second bottle, the one that last drink came from. Who opened it?"

"You didn't?"

"No. Ken could have." But he said it doubtfully. "No, no, no, I don't think so. He didn't come up to the suite until maybe ten minutes before the party started. I don't remember him even going near the bar. He flopped on the couch. I went over to the wet bar and fixed us a drink, his from that almost empty bottle of bourbon. Mine from my bottle of scotch." He stopped. His face tightened in concentration. "That second bottle! Who opened it? When?"

She had one answer. She needed the second. "The murderer opened it. What we have to figure out is when he had the opportunity to do so."

"But I don't see—" Willie broke off.

So, she didn't have to ask the second question, the most crucial question.

Shock slackened the muscles of his face, draining his handsome features of life and animation.

"Those writers—"

"Yes."

"They're all on the fifth floor, on our floor?"

"Yes."

He swallowed jerkily. "I got tired shoving that damn cardboard key in the slot, so I—" He lifted a shaking hand to rub against his temple. "I propped the doors to the suite open while I was setting up down in the White Ibis Room."

She knew it, of course.

But for how long?

She said, "When did you start working down there?"

"Just after you came up looking for Ken."

So, maybe a quarter after ten.

"Somebody got in our suite while I was downstairs?" His eyes were stricken.

"I think so, yes."

His face crumpled. He folded his arms tight across his chest.

She kept her voice gentle. "How long were the doors open?"

"I came up at three."

Between ten A.M. and three P.M., a poisoner walked softly down the hall.

"I made it easy, didn't I?" Willie cried. "I sure as hell made it easy to murder my brother." He buried his face in his hands.

.   .   .

The bellman stood with his feet apart, his arms folded behind him. He was tall and thin and wore his maroon-colored uniform with pride. He nodded shrewdly. "Yeah. You mean the suite where the guy croaked. Sure. I remember taking their stuff up. Took me four trips to get the luggage and all them boxes up there. Good tip."

Max smiled encouragingly. "What time of day was it?"

"About nine. Yesterday morning."

"Friday?" Max pinned it down.

"That's right."

"Did one of the boxes have liquor bottles in it?"

"Yeah. Ten, twelve bottles of wine, some bourbon. I unpacked that box, set the stuff on the wet bar."

Max kept his voice casual. "Did you happen to notice the seals on the whiskey bottles?"

The bellman's eyes narrowed in thought. "Yeah, I remember. One bottle was almost empty. The other two hadn't been opened."

Annie skidded by the desk.

"Yes, ma'am. Here's a folder for you."

Annie saw Max's bold handwriting on the outside.

"Thank you." She tucked the folder under her arm, then turned toward the reflecting pond in the center of the lobby.

Leah Kirby waited near a terra-cotta vase. Her hair was a richer, deeper red than the trailing bougainvillea. She wore an emerald-green linen suit this morning. The face she turned to Annie was quite lovely. And untroubled. "Good morning, Annie."

Annie felt a spurt of irritation. She knew she looked frazzled. It was definitely frazzling to be suspected of murder and maddening to know the police weren't even interested in the likeliest suspects.

Annie managed a tight smile. "Good morning, Leah. You look very well this morning."

"Thank you. It's a spectacular day. And I've met so many wonderful readers already. Now, where is our panel?" She held up a program, opened to the Saturday schedule.

"It's in the hotel next door. We can either walk or I can drive you."

"By all means, let's walk."

Annie led the way. Once outside, she lengthened her stride to keep up with the long-legged author. "I saw you and Mr. Kirby over by the booths yesterday afternoon."

Leah slipped on her sunglasses. "Wonderful exhibits. As soon as my panel and signing are done, I want to go back. Carl's gone to the Red Piano art gallery."

Annie tried to keep her voice light. "What did Carl do yesterday?"

"Oh, he stayed in the room, rested. I think he took a walk on the beach in the afternoon."

Annie decided to gamble. "What time did you go to Kenneth Hazlitt's suite?"

Leah Vixen Kirby didn't break stride, but the good-humored smile slipped away. Slowly, her head turned toward Annie. "I beg your pardon?" The mirrored sunglasses hid the author's eyes, but her mouth was a thin, tight line.

She was buying time with that question.

Annie said, "Did you go to the suite when your husband went for a walk?"

Leah's face was smooth, impervious, but tiny lines splayed on either side of her mouth. "I didn't go to Kenneth's suite. I only left my room once. To get some ice."

Annie longed to shout *Bingo!* Leah was covering her

tracks. If anyone had seen her out in the hall yesterday afternoon, she had an excuse.

"Someone saw you at the door to the Hazlitt suite."

"Someone is mistaken." A light, strained laugh. "But it doesn't really matter."

It mattered. Annie had known that Leah was on the fifth floor, that she could have gone into the Hazlitt suite.

Now, she was confident the author had done just that.

Had she carried a small vial of nicotine with her?

"Do you garden?" Annie asked. They were almost to the hotel. Annie pointed toward the north wing. "The meeting rooms are through that door."

"Garden? Oh, yes." Now a genuine smile touched that lovely mouth. "I'm quite famous for my azaleas."

They walked into the broad hallway. Leah's panel was in the Dolphin Room.

The author looked at Annie. The dark lenses hid her eyes. "I'll be fine now that I know my way. Thanks so much for walking over with me."

She turned away.

It was a dismissal.

Eager readers surrounded Leah, surged down the aisle around her.

Annie felt not only frazzled, but thwarted. Leah Kirby had won that round.

But the fight wasn't over.

In one hour, Leah Kirby would walk out of that room.

Annie would be there.

Whether Leah liked it or not.

Chapter 11

"You got my packet."

Annie turned, her frown curving upward into a smile. "Max, what are you doing here?"

"Looking for you." He waggled the Festival program. "Come on, let's get something to drink by the pool."

They settled beneath an umbrella and ordered ice tea. Unsweetened.

Annie clutched her folder. "I haven't looked at it yet."

Max was quite pleased with himself. "It's good stuff. Personal essays by the authors."

It wasn't, of course, that she felt competitive with her handsome husband. But *she* was the specialist in crime. Quickly, she described her talk on the beach with Willie Hazlitt.

Max's face was skeptical, but he admitted reluctantly, "Willie did steer you in the right direction. That was one of the first calls I made. Kenneth's secretary is very competent. If Wanda doesn't know the answer, she knows where to look. She knew Kenneth was talking about writing a novel, but she hadn't seen any notes for a book or a proposal for one. She nosed around in his computer. Here's what she found." Max dug in his briefcase and pulled out a flimsy fax sheet.

It was a copy of a letter, dated May 2.

Biddy Maxwell

Maxwell and Associates

New York, NY 10103

Dear Biddy:

You're going to be nuts over my proposal for *Song of the South*. It's going to be the hottest seller since the sequel to *GWTW:*

Annie cringed. Surely, Hazlitt couldn't hope to compete with Margaret Mitchell or Alexandra Ripley?

A 125,000-word novel set in Atlanta in the high-rolling eighties, interweaving the lives of five famous Southern writers. They're so Southern, they eat black-eyed peas all year round, blow off firecrackers on New Year's Eve, call their mothers Mama, their poppas Sir, their aunts Maybelle, and never try to open the attic door to poor Sister Sue's room.

You'll be fascinated by the trauma and sexual escapades of these five authors:

Aristocratic and elegant Lesa Hurby is a gorgeous redhead. Her Civil War novels top the charts every year. An unfortunate first marriage (hardly even whispered about, but we'll titillate readers with a blow-by-blow) ended with a mental breakdown. She enjoys a late great passion with marriage to Tarl, a gentle titan of industry. However, rumors are swirling that she is involved with a much younger male writer, unbeknownst, of course, to her present cuckolded husband. Who is this lady's love, and what does it mean to her fiction?

Handsome Lake Allen is America's sweetheart novelist. His latest books put Madison County's bridges in the shade. But he didn't always write books. His career started in Hollywood, and there are whispers that some of his scripts wouldn't fit in with today's wholesome image. Allen's stonewalling the past, but an intrepid writer for a Southern literary magazine (my book's hero, macho writer Buds Hanagin) is hot on the scent. Hanagin is sure there's a raunchy story behind Allen's facade of super Southern gentleman.

Lily St. Mair dwells on the menace behind the magnolia. Her stories are creepy. St. Mair's a plump little woman with a full figure and sloe eyes. When she laughs, you can hear the shake of bones and the slither of scorpions. Hanagin reads her life story and decides it sounds like fiction.

Billy Bob Appleton's dumped three wives, refused to marry a college girl he seduced (she committed suicide), and he's two years behind on child support. And there's the kid who was killed when a car driven by Appleton's secretary went out of control and rammed the school-bus stop. Hanagin's intrigued by the way Billy Bob handled it. He behaved like a real gent and didn't fire her.

Said it was because she was running errands for him. Of course, the insurance covered it, but it's the first time in recorded history this guy's ever shown a heart of gold. Hanagin really wants to chat with Billy Bob's secretary.

Ada Pride is America's Agatha Christie. She is immensely wealthy and somewhat reclusive. A gifted public speaker, she comes across in media presentations as genial and good-humored. Her sleuth, Petunia Monet, is adored by legions of fans. Hanagin wants to describe Pride's personality—tough, cold, incisive—and he wants to know if there is any truth to the rumor that Pride shoved her second husband off her yacht when she discovered he was involved with another woman.

When these five authors come together one haunting week at a writers' conference on a fog-shrouded campus, their lives will never be the same.

And neither will ours, Biddy. I'll make a bet: Forty weeks straight on the *PW* Bestseller list. Wanna take me up on it?

Novelist-to-be,

K. H.

His initials were scrawled in huge letters.

Annie smoothed the curling sheet. She'd never before felt that she was touching dynamite. ''Wow!''

''You know what Wanda Dillon said?''

Annie shook her head, took a big gulp of tea.

''She said, 'That proposal's pure Kenneth. I swear the man never had any brains. He dealt with authors! He knew what they're like! Brilliant, fractious, volatile. That proposal was like handing a five-year-old a loaded gun. He probably hadn't looked past the party at the Festival. Of course, nobody—but nobody—would have skipped that party. And Kenneth always wanted each party to be bigger than the last one.' ''

"So Wanda wasn't in love with her boss."

"Willie indicate she was?" Max was surprised.

"No. Not at all. But when a man gets murdered, you have to wonder. About everything."

"Including Willie." Max's lip didn't exactly curl when he mentioned the younger Hazlitt, but it came close.

Annie lifted her glass to hide her quick smile. "Frank Saulter's going to slip me some information about Willie."

Max had the satisfied look of Poirot at the scene of a crime. "I'm already there. The guy's a flake. Wanda said Handsome Willie has never been able to hold a job and he's always in debt. Kenneth refused to bail him out of his latest money problem. He insisted Willie come home and go to work."

Annie noted the discrepancy in Willie's version and Wanda's. But a man had to save face. Especially a man like Willie.

Max continued, his voice neutral. "Wanda said Willie was dancing around trying to fit in. He didn't even complain when Kenneth refused to okay Willie coming into the principal of a trust left by his mother. Apparently, Kenneth was the trustee."

Annie recalled Willie's quiet words on the beach. Sometimes people liked limits. Maybe Willie had gone his own way as long as he wanted to. And then . . .

"It's too bad he hasn't been back long enough to know everybody his brother might have quarreled with."

Max was unconcerned. "Don't worry, Wanda Dillon knows where the bodies are buried. Kenneth's wife left him because he was running around on her. He was dating this gal who's in the Caribbean, but he kept trying to pick up a waitress at the café across the street. He was always in trouble with the IRS, and he wanted a dime's worth of stuff for every nickel. And I got the lowdown on everybody he was crossways with. Look at the last three pages of his bio.''

Annie took the sheaf of papers. She turned to page five. The heading was succinct:

ALIBIED

Sue Ellen Hazlitt Peters   (former wife)—Works Friday afternoons at a Waldenbooks in Fountain Valley, California. Was there yesterday.

Michael and Jennifer Hazlitt   (children)— Competing in a swim meet in Santa Barbara, California.

Wanda Dillon   (KH's secretary)—At the offices of M. J. Press in Atlanta, Georgia.

Jason Gustafson of Gustafason Printers—Having his hair cut in Peoria.

Cheryl Holt—Swimming at hotel pool in the Bahamas.

Ed Wherry—Deep-sea fishing in the Gulf of Mexico.

And there were names that were new to Annie:

Thomas Brinson   (M. J. Press employee fired last week)—On a Greyhound bus en route to Tuscaloosa, Alabama.

Harry Lowell   (former boyfriend of Cheryl Holt) —In an Atlanta bar with his new girlfriend.

Venita Jones   (local zealot who'd picketed Mint Julep P over the publication of *Black Voices in Today's South*)—Being interviewed on a local talk-radio program. (She advocated stamping all library books with a G or E.)

Annie looked at Max. "G or E?"

"Good or Evil."

"My, my," Annie said mildly. "How generous of Ms. Jones to wish to share her moral discernment with the world."

Annie didn't bother to read the rest of the list. She looked at Max gravely. "You're saying nobody with any kind of motive—likely or absurd—could have been at the party yesterday?"

"Yes." Max lifted his glass. "Of course, this isn't to say I might not have missed somebody who managed to harbor a grudge without anyone else ever knowing about it. But, Annie, I don't think so. Wanda Dillon's known Kenneth since they were in grade school. She liked him, but she wasn't an adoring secretary. It was a job, a pleasant one, that's all. And, her alibi's rock solid. An insurance salesman was there talking to her until after five o'clock Friday. So, unless the killer was a mad poisoner who picked that bottle of whiskey at random, we have to look at the people with access to that hotel suite between nine A.M. Friday when the bellman placed the whiskey bottles on top of the wet bar and half-past five when Kenneth poured that drink."

Annie nodded, but absently. She closed the file on Kenneth Hazlitt and put it on the table. "This isn't going to help us, Max. Not this time."

Max scowled. "I know it isn't good news, but now we know we have to look here."

Annie reopened the file and smoothed the top sheet. "I don't mean that. I mean I don't think it matters"—she flipped through the single-spaced sheets, dense with facts about the life, loves, interests, pursuits, and despairs of Kenneth Alvin Hazlitt, late resident of Atlanta, Georgia—"what we find out about him. That's the conventional wisdom, that the reason for a victim's death can be found in his life. But not this time.'' She picked up her tea, welcomed the sharp fresh taste, and thought again how dreadful to lift a glass, then die. ''Oh, sure. Who he was mattered. It mattered that he didn't mind trampling on other people's feelings.'' She picked out the sprig of mint, nipped it between her teeth. ''Probably he didn't have a lot of imagination, even if he was a publisher. Anyone with even a shred of sensitivity would have realized how appalled those five authors would be by his book idea. Maybe more than appalled. Maybe dangerously angry. Kenneth thought it was wonderful. It mattered that he liked to entertain on the cheap, but he pampered himself. It mattered that he liked to show off. But what really matters now is what's in here,'' and she picked up the packet Max had prepared about the authors.

''We have to find out every scrap we can about our Famous Five, Max. One of them's a murderer.''

Henny Brawley hung up the house phone. Busy signal. Should she take her materials up to Annie and Max's suite? Or leave it at the desk? Hmm. It was critical that they be apprised of the tentative conclusions she, Miss Dora, and Laurel had drawn. Decisively, Henny patted the poster board covered with encircled numbers and pulled a hotel notepad closer.

In their fifth-floor suite, Max sprawled comfortably on the couch, the phone cradled between his ear and shoulder. ''Miss Perkins, this is Theobald Fortune of Amalgamated

Insurances. We have received some new information about the automobile-pedestrian accident on September 7, 1990, which leads us to question—''

Max broke off, listening to the dial tone in his ear.

He raised an eyebrow.

Miss Perkins didn't want to talk.

Max sat up, returned the receiver to the base. He pushed up from the couch and crossed to the circular table near the wet bar. It was covered with papers. He glanced from pile to pile, then picked up a fax copy of the petition filed in the wrongful death suit naming Regina Perkins as the defendant.

The case had been settled out of court.

It was over and done with.

So why did Jimmy Jay Crabtree's estimable Miss Perkins slam down her phone?

It could be as simple as continuing distress at accidentally having killed a child.

But it takes a special person to refuse to hear about ''new information.''

Or a person to whom ''new information'' might be very bad news indeed.

Max thumbed through the petition. The investigating officer was Jed Robert MacDougal of Marietta, Georgia.

Max returned to the telephone and punched information in Atlanta.

Annie peeked into the Dolphin Room. Leah Kirby had a full house. All of the listening faces were rapt. Gently, Annie closed the door. She settled on a bench facing the room and opened Max's packet. As he'd indicated, there were copies of five autobiographies taken from the entries in *Contemporary*

Authors. The copies were in alphabetical order. She found Leah Kirby's essay next to the last.

She studied the photograph. It was a close-up. Leah had looked directly into the lens. Her eyes were filled with intelligence, sensitivity, and a hint of sadness. She was, quite simply, a breathtakingly lovely woman.

Leah Vixen Kirby: I look back on my childhood as a time of enchantment, a time of perfection, a time of magnificence. I remember my father as a booming voice and a hearty laugh. He died when I was seven, so his face is misty in my memory. I have photos. Now, even the pictures from the end of his life are younger than I am. His face is so unlined. I wonder what he would have been had he lived to be old? He was a lawyer. Does that tell me much? Does it tell me anything? The last time I was home, I met one of his contemporaries, a man now graying and thin, with a drooping mouth and a raspy voice. He said that my father was a brilliant lawyer, who could make cogent, compelling arguments, that my father was absolutely honest, ''straight as a string,'' that he was competitive, argumentative, clever, amusing, that he was a good companion.

I only know that he was and then he was not, that I lived in a circle of safety until one day my mother wept and said Daddy had gone to heaven to be with the angels.

I cried and demanded that he come back to me, to us.

But he didn't come.

No matter how hard I prayed and pled.

That was when my enchanted childhood ended.

My mother turned into a gray and listless woman, who outwardly lived—she was a good and capable nurse—and inwardly died.

And I was alone.

I read. And read. And read.

Books, books, books.

They became my life; they are still my life.

Why do I write?

I think I am searching. I am trying to find once again the enchantment, the glory, the magnificence.

I find it for a space, for the space of the lines that I write. Once again, then, the world is glorious, and I am both enchanted and an enchantress.

I go back in time to an era that answers my hunger for great emotion. It is not a simpler time. No. I go back to an era of passion and heartbreak, of triumph and despair. I go back to lives both magnified and diminished by the turbulence of events.

Books. My books. The books of others. In them, I have felt alive.

What does that containment of vitality mean to my everyday life, the life that is not compounded of words? Throughout the days and years I have moved like a ghost, there but not seen, not comprehended and surely not comprehending. This has cost me dearly. My first marriage ended in divorce. My children owe more to my housekeeper than to me for their upbringing. I think perhaps they have forgiven me. They dutifully return for holidays or invite me to their homes. But if they ever lived in an enchanted time, it was not of my making. I do not know that I can forgive myself.

And always, the words absorb me, redeem me, bless me.

But in recent years, I have begun to live beyond my books, and for this I thank my husband, Carl Kirby, whose gentle love and kindness and support have permitted me once again to feel that I live within enchantment.

I cannot help but wonder if I shall write books beyond my present imagining because of Carl.

Annie's nose wrinkled. Of course, to be fair, the woman obviously had been asked to discuss her life as a writer.

But talk about self-absorption city!

Yet the autobiographical piece answered one question for Annie. Yes, Leah Vixen Kirby had the ego necessary to kill.

Applause boomed from the meeting room. The doors opened and people streamed out.

Annie went against the tide.

Leah Kirby was the center of an admiring buzz of readers.

Annie wondered if she ever got tired of the adulation.

The author took a minute with each reader as she signed books. She made an effort to smile. But Annie felt it definitely was an effort.

As the last admirer reluctantly moved away, the writer saw Annie. Her face went quite blank for an instant, then smoothed into polite inquiry.

"Yes?"

Annie reminded herself of flies and honey and vinegar. She made her voice cheerful. "You are certainly a great favorite, Mrs. Kirby."

"Yes." There was no excitement in her answer. Not even pride. Simply acceptance, and a profound weariness. "Sometimes I feel''—she paused, pushed back a strand of that vivid hair—''as if I'm swarmed by piranhas, each wanting a piece of me, demanding more and more and more.''

There was an edge of desperation in her voice.

''If you feel that way, why did you come?''

Those huge green eyes glittered with sudden anger. ''Because I have to. If I didn't come, my sales would drop. And that's the death knell in publishing. No one would publish my books.''

Her books, her books, her books.

''But if you'd rather be left alone—''

''That's so stupid.'' Contempt flashed in Leah's eyes. ''You don't understand.'' Her voice was insultingly patient. ''I have to write. I *have* to. But then everyone wants to know more and more and more about you and they pick up little pieces of your life and carry them away and twist them and they come back ugly and deformed.''

''Is that how you saw the book Kenneth Hazlitt planned to write?''

Just for an instant, Leah's face twisted with fury, a witch's version of her immense beauty. Then she took a deep breath and managed a brittle smile. ''I'm sure Kenneth's novel would have been a wonderful tribute to authors for whom he had great reverence. I feel so honored—''

Annie forgot about flies and honey and vinegar. ''Oh, come off it. He was going to describe your sex life in lurid detail. Who's the young handsome author you're having an affair with?''

Leah glared at Annie. Then she snatched up her notes from the lectern and plunged down the platform steps.

Annie turned and kept pace.

Leah stopped midway up the aisle and faced Annie.

"Why are you harassing me? Why are you doing this?" Her voice trembled with fury.

"I'm sorry." And Annie was—sorry at this exchange, sorry to cause hurt, sorry to be involved at all in the dark passions of people she scarcely knew. But she had no choice. Brown drops of nicotine had taken her choice away. "All I want is the truth," Annie said quietly. "Someone poisoned Kenneth Hazlitt. I want you to help me find out who did it. And you can help, Leah. You know the authors. You know what was behind Kenneth's book proposal."

The author stared at Annie for a moment, then her lovely lips curved in a frigid smile. "But, my dear, there was *nothing* behind Kenneth's proposal. You sound as though this book would have been critical! Why, that would come as such a shock to me, and, I'm sure, to the other authors. I'm confident Kenneth's book would have been a celebration of our lives. You are simply misinformed."

Perhaps if Leah Kirby hadn't been quite so arrogant, so disdainful, Annie wouldn't have reacted as she did.

But as she watched the author stride toward the doors, Annie exploded.

"Then you'll be thrilled to know," Annie shouted, "that I'm going to write the book myself. I'm going to call a news conference tomorrow—right before the Medallions are awarded—to share with the world the fascinating background to a book that won't be stopped even by murder! The tabloids will *love* it!"

"Oh, yeah, yeah, I remember. The kid died in my arms." Officer MacDougal's voice was uninflected, but Max heard the pain. "No reason for an accident. Dry weather. Clear. Unobstructed view of the bus stop. Driver said a bee buzzed in the window, she lost control. Accidents happen.''

''Was it an accident?''

''Could have been. Jury would probably have believed her. The insurance company settled.''

''You didn't believe her.'' Max wished he could see Officer MacDougal. What would the policeman's face reveal? Intelligence, spite, prejudice, amiability, illness? All Max had was the voice, dry, even, weary.

''No. I didn't. Mister, I got nine kids. I know a liar when I hear one. But I don't know what she was lying about. I worked it. I never found any connection between her and the kid or the kid's family. Nothing. And she had her boss's permission to drive his car. She was on her way to the post office. Nothing there. Of course, she didn't stop after she hit the kid. But she went around the block and came back immediately. She claimed she was in such shock she didn't know what to do. She acted nervous, but not panicked like you'd think for somebody who'd just killed a seven-year-old. Somehow it wasn't right. But she wasn't drunk or on drugs. The next day I talked to her boss. A mean-eyed wimpy guy. He didn't give a damn about the dead girl, just wanted to be sure his secretary didn't have to miss work and demanded we give him back the car so he could get it fixed up. Snarled something about how his secretary would have to pay for the damage. I looked her over three ways to Sunday. No record. No previous accidents. Hell, she's never even had a ticket.'' A thoughtful pause. ''But I'll tell you one thing for dead certain: She's a liar.''

. . .

Annie glowered at the house telephone. Of course, it was perfectly reasonable that not a single one of her authors would be in their rooms. Why should they? There were readers to meet and booksellers to charm, although she rather doubted Jimmy Jay Crabtree was charming anyone at the moment. But he was no doubt swaggering among the festival-goers, Mr. Big Deal determined to be noticed. She turned, ready to plunge down the hall and hurry to the booths, then shook her head. She could dart all over the place and miss connecting with all of them by the space of a few feet or the passage of a few minutes. No. Running about willy-nilly made no sense.

She glanced at the red-and-yellow-spotted porcelain clock in the ceiling of the lobby. Almost noon. Twenty-four hours more and the Festival would be over. The Famous Five would be free to leave, and Annie would be left as Detective Wheeler's major suspect.

Annie felt a sudden breathlessness.

Left as Detective Wheeler's *only* suspect.

But there was some safety in numbers. During the party, the Hazlitt suite was crammed with people. Maybe not everyone could have added the poison to the whiskey bottle, but certainly it was possible someone had done so.

Annie intended to expand the suspect list to include the Famous Five, whether Wheeler agreed or not.

But her threat to write *Song of the South* hadn't dented Leah Kirby's determined revisionism. However, some of the others might not be as disciplined as Leah. Or they might be more willing to dish the dirt about their fellow Medallion honorees.

It was the best idea Annie had going.

But, dammit, how to share the great news about her

purported literary career with those who would appreciate it the most?

She glanced at the front desk and around the lobby.

The authors had to come through here to reach the elevators.

Annie nodded, and picked up a message pad from the shelf for the house phones. She chewed on the end of her pencil, then wrote rapidly. She stopped, shook her head, wadded up that sheet. Three tries later, she nodded in satisfaction:

> . . . *always wanted to be a writer.* (A lie in a good cause was a lie in a good cause.) *I am thrilled to report that interest is growing in the proposal Kenneth Hazlitt made for* Song of the South. *It now looks now as though there will be an auction among four publishing houses. I have obtained a great deal of background information that fleshes out Kenneth's view of the characters. I know you will be eager to talk with me about the future of the book.*

She gnawed again on the pencil, smiled grimly, and added *Sincerely yours, Annie Laurance Darling* with a dramatic flourish. She made copies and addressed envelopes to Leah Kirby, Emma Clyde, Jimmy Jay Crabtree, Alan Blake, and Melissa Sinclair. She marched straight to the front desk, all the while refusing to listen to the little inner voice that had risen from a murmur to a clamor, warning Annie that her future held a confrontation with a very handsome, usually equable blond man, aka her husband. Max was not going to be pleased.

She was turning away when the clerk said swiftly, "Oh, Mrs. Darling—I have a message for you."

.   .   .

The cellular phone faded in and out. "Listen, buddy, it's . . . Saturday morn . . . and I'm on the eighth hole. I've got a three-foot putt with a century note riding on it."

Max said, "I've got ten of those babies riding on your finding out—in the next hour—everything I ever wanted to know about Regina Perkins, age thirty-three. Her address is . . ."

Annie accepted the envelope, noting Henny's handwriting, and a large piece of white poster board. She slipped the folder from Max under one arm and moved away from the front desk, out of the traffic, to stare at the ink-smudged poster. It reminded her of the illustrations of atoms that decorated the walls in her high school chemistry class. However, instead of varicolored balls, these circles held numbers. Various colors traced the erratic paths of these balls. A note at the bottom of the poster instructed:

> *The guests who attended the cocktail party in the Mint Julep Press suite Friday are listed by number on the back of this poster with the exception of one Bill Smith, who was not registered at the Marriott as he claimed. However, through interviews with the rest of those attending, the movements of the guests have been charted. (See above.) Please read accompanying report.*

Annie lugged the poster, the note, and her folder to a comfortable easy chair with a good view of the front desk, the entrance, and the hallways that converged in the lobby.

She opened the note:

Dear Annie,

Through assiduous and insightful interviews, we three (Dora Brevard, Henrietta Brawley, and Laurel Darling Roethke, known hereinafter as the Attestors) affirm that the following information is accurate:

No one had an opportunity to poison the whiskey bottle with nicotine during the cocktail party. (See appendixes 4 and 11.)

Annie scanned the rest of the information. Which was not easy. Detail piled upon detail. Witness 1 corroborated Witness 4 who corroborated Witness 9 who . . .

It was clear-cut and irrefutable.

The overlapping observations by one person or another standing in the vicinity of the wet bar—all apparently of unimpeachable background and integrity (a rabbi, a social worker, a nun, Miss Georgia, the local president of the Daughters of the Confederacy)—proved that no one touched the bottle from five minutes to five, when the first guest arrived, to five-thirty-seven, when Kenneth poured the fatal drink.

In conclusion therefore, we, the Attestors, conclude that the poison was introduced into the whiskey bottle during the period that the suite was unoccupied from approximately ten A.M. to three P.M. One of our members (Cookbook Author Dora Brevard, Aunt Dora's Delectables, 87 pages) found the suite door open at shortly after eleven A.M. and took that opportunity to leave a wel-

coming tray of *Delectable Divinity* on the table. *Mr. William Hazlitt returned to the suite at approximately three P.M.*

Clearly, ALL PERSONS VISITING THE FIFTH FLOOR *during that period must be considered as having had Opportunity. May we respectfully suggest an effort to determine who among these were aware that Suite 500 was registered to Mr. Hazlitt.*

In the pursuit of justice,

HENRIETTA BRAWLEY

cc: Det. Clarence Wheeler

"Thanks," Annie said aloud, bitterly. "Thanks, pals. Serve me up on a platter. Hand the lieutenant a noose with my name on it."

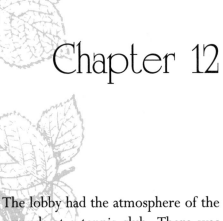

Chapter 12

The lobby had the atmosphere of the veranda at a tennis club. There was a great deal of coming and going, a parade of gorgeous sports attire, a comfortable, well-bred holiday air. Annie was impressed by the unobtrusiveness of the Buccaneer staff. They were there—if you looked— but you had to look. She must remember to compliment Jeff Garrett on the employees' guest awareness and attention to detail. A doorman promptly opened the glass doors. No sooner was a cigarette plunged into a receptacle than a young man in a crisp maroon uniform scooped it up, raked the sand, and impressed the hotel crest. One swift ring of the melodious bell at the front desk and bellmen came hurrying. The concierge, matronly and middle-aged, spoke four languages, including German-accented English. Annie wondered how life had led her to a sea island. The concierge was prepared to book a limousine or a tee time or a restaurant reservation. Brochures touted a backcountry exploration of Daufauskie, now both an enclave of enormous wealth and a remnant of the Gullah culture, a kayak odyssey in the wetlands, or a trip to Charleston, perhaps the most fascinating and without doubt the most charming historical site in America.

But Annie was not on a holiday.

She scanned the lobby once again, settled more comfortably in her chair, and opened the folder.

And looked into Emma's cornflower-blue eyes. So Emma did have clothes other than caftans. The famed mystery writer stood poised beside a palmetto in a navy linen jacket, an ivory silk blouse, and a slenderizing navy skirt. This was a recent photo because her hair was blue-gray and in crisp waves. Her square face was genial. Annie was impressed. This was photography by a wizard. Yes, Emma looked smart, but in this clever picture, there was no hint of her overpowering personality.

Emma Clyde: A stolen book started me on my career. Though its owner had no further use for it. He was only nineteen or twenty. I remember they'd been out in the field for several days, yet he had only the downiest fuzz of a beard beneath the dirt. He stepped on a mine. Both of his legs were blown off. He lost too much blood, though we tried. Perhaps I should say I salvaged his book. In those days, we salvaged anything and everything that could make a day a little better. I found the book on the floor of the operating room. Actually, the operating room was a tent, the floor swept sand, portable lights mounted at both ends of the table. I was an Army nurse.

After a battle, we'd operate for eighteen hours, twenty at a stretch. Buckets held the amputated limbs. Blood was everywhere. When I think back, it's always the blood that I remember.

I was young, too. Sometimes I find it hard to believe I was ever that young. But, if you lived, if you survived the sand and the bombs and the machine-gun fire and the fear, you didn't stay young for long. Not in North Africa. Day after day after day, the pain and suffering and the heat and the men—so many of them my age—looking up at you and knowing they were horribly maimed—or dying.

When I was off duty, I read that book and reread it and reread it. I must have read *Death on the Nile* a hundred times. I can still quote it by heart. When Hercule Poirot first speaks to Jacqueline de Bellefort, he pleads with her, ". . . Do not open your heart to evil."

To me, that sentence says everything there is to say about mysteries. People who don't read mysteries are puzzled by them. They want to know why any writer would focus on crime. They don't understand that crime isn't the point of a mystery. When Marigold Rembrandt sets out to solve a murder, she must find out what went wrong in the lives she is exploring. What fractured the relationships between these people? In everyday life, if John steals from his partner, is cruel to his wife, demeans his son, destroys a competitor's reputation, the result is anger, quarrels, confrontations—fractured relationships. Rarely, of course, in real life, does murder occur. The murder in a mystery is simply a magnification of the miseries that are so common when people open their hearts to evil. So mysteries are not about murder, they are about relationships.

Christie once said that the modern mystery was the equivalent of the medieval morality play. I agree absolutely. Mysteries serve as parables to readers. The reader can see what happens, the unhappiness and turmoil and despair that are created in lives dominated by evil.

My next Marigold Rembrandt, *Holiday for Harlots,* will be my eighty-third published novel. Recently, a fan wrote and asked if I intended to retire. My answer is swift and certain: Never.

Oh, of course, I understand—have understood since I was a battlefield nurse—that absolutes are absurd. Certainly, if I am incapacitated, I would have to retire. If my sales should plummet, if readers should tire of Marigold, I would be retired. You will note the distinction there. But to make that choice? Never.

You see, in the mystery, I found a structure I can hold to. Not predictability. That's the snide assessment of narrow-minded critics like Edmund Wilson. A good mystery—aside from its structure—is never predictable except for one absolute: Justice will be served.

What does that mean? In North Africa, I found no justice. The captain admired for his courage died on the operating table; the colonel despised for his stupidity survived. Greed, cruelty, viciousness, exploitation, and every vile motive can—and often do—triumph in the world.

But not in my mysteries.

I create that world, I control it, I am its master.

From the insanity of war to the clear, coolly reasoned creation of a world that responds to order, it has been a long and fascinating journey, a journey not yet concluded.

Annie looked again at that genial face and knew it reflected so little of the woman.

Emma Clyde. Complex, tough, unsentimental, courageous, determined—a woman to be reckoned with.

Emma didn't discuss her personal life in the essay. Annie knew that Emma had been married twice. Neither husband was mentioned. Of course, the first marriage ended in divorce many years ago, the second in death—his—only a few years before.

Annie frowned, grappled with memory. Oh, yes, Enrique Morales, that was the name of Emma's late second husband. Apparently he hadn't been pertinent to Emma's writing. Actually, Annie would be surprised if Enrique had been pertinent to anything other than Emma's quite vigorous appreciation of sex. Recently, there had been whispers on Broward's Rock about the frequent visits to Emma's home of a natty, retired librarian from Savannah.

Annie shook her head, dismissing gossip and considerations of why Emma had married—if only briefly—the much younger Enrique.

But, on second thought, perhaps Enrique and what happened to him on Emma's luxury yacht—*did he fall? was he pushed?*—was extremely pertinent.

Emma, from all accounts, discovered that neither her wealth nor their marriage controlled the amorous activities of Enrique.

Justice—or at least Emma's view of it—obtained only in her mysteries.

Would Kenneth Hazlitt's tell-all novel possibly have revealed such a cold, manipulative personality to the readers who idolized Marigold Rembrandt that Emma's dazzling reputation could have been jeopardized?

Fans are fickle.

What would Emma do to protect her writing career?

Whatever it took, Annie thought. Whatever it took.

And Emma was known throughout the southeast for her spectacular roses. She was, in fact, the creator of a sweet-scented rose of the palest pink tint, known, just like her yacht, as Marigold's Pleasure.

But would the cleverest, canniest writer of detective fiction in America, an admitted rose fancier, use a garden poison to commit murder?

Sure.

If she could get away with it.

Annie squared the sheets on Emma, slipped them in the back of the folder, and picked up another essay.

The photo here was definitely a soft focus. Melissa Sinclair's luminous eyes glowed with sly humor and curiosity. Her mouth curved in an enigmatic smile. She looked fey, amused, and slightly cruel.

Melissa Sinclair: Aren't all Southerners storytellers? Why, I recollect my grandmother sitting in a rocker on the front porch, the rocker squeaking back and forth, back and forth, as she told about the way Sherman's troops marched toward the sea, burning and pillaging, raping and killing, leaving blackened ruins and broken lives behind them. How her grandmother, Annalee, hid the silver in a dried patch of sweet potatoes, but the Yankees found it and stole every piece. How her grandfather came limping home, a musket ball lodged in his hip, to find three fresh graves in the family plot, his brothers, Sam and David and George. So he turned his back on the ruins and took Annalee and walked away. They went to a little community called Dixon, not far from Snellville. Fifty years later, he was the mayor of the town and owned a big white house on the hill, and to this day my momma and poppa live in Dixon and rock on the porch in the summertime and talk about their people and the glory days before Atlanta went up in flames.

I remember standing by the notions counter in the drugstore, pressing against the glass like a shadow so nobody would see me and say, "Child, you run on out and play now," and I'd listen to the men talk while they drank their morning coffee, and sometimes they talked about Verdun and sometimes about the price of tobacco and sometimes about the widow woman who shot the *revenooer* and sometimes about the ghost that opens the door on Christmas Eve at Tarleton Hall.

I heard stories about yellow dogs and gypsies, about once when Ava Gardner came through town and Mr. Forsythe claimed he knew her when he was a young man, about a gambler named Slim and the sack of gold dust in his pocket, about the farmhand who hung himself from a crosstie in the railroad bridge, about that little baby they found on the steps of the church and who might be her momma. And poppa.

I heard stories in the summer at the church socials, stories I remember every time I taste sweet, drippy red watermelon. I heard stories in the winter in front of an open fire as bacon hissed in a big iron skillet.

At night, I'd listen to the hound dogs bay at the moon and the faraway whistle of the train and the thunks on the roof that might be a squirrel but could be a ghost tap dancing in the moonlight. Can't you see that? A swirl of mist and the glint of the taps and the swift, sharp clatter? Oh, I can see it, right now I can see it.

I grew up with stories. I never knew there was another way to live.

Annie shrugged. It was a charming essay, notably more charming than the others. As an indicator to homicidal tendencies, it lacked pizzazz. But—Annie thumbed through her papers—yes, here was the fax of Kenneth Hazlitt's proposal.

Her eyes skipped down the sheet to the paragraph about "Lily St. Mair":

". . . *(Hanagin) reads her life story and thinks it sounds like fiction.*"

Annie frowned.

Hmm.

She carried the folder to the telephone alcove, but she left the poster propped in her chair.

It took four phone calls before she was referred to Miss Lavinia Boudreau of Snellville, retired librarian and full-time genealogist. Annie was barely launched on her quest when Miss Boudreau interrupted brusquely:

"Nonsense. There's no such place."

"Uh." Annie started over, tried to improve her diction. "Dixon," she repeated, raising her voice. "Just outside Snellville."

"Young lady, I heard you the first time. There's no such place."

Annie swiftly checked. ". . . little community of Dixon, not far from Snellville."

No such place.

Annie had an odd feeling, like a spiderweb brushing against her skin. "I see. Then, perhaps I could go at it another way, Miss Boudreau. I understand you are familiar with the family histories—"

Annie learned more than she'd ever wanted to know about genealogy, as a fine art and intellectual pursuit. At last, she gathered up her courage and interrupted Miss Boudreau's recitation of her accomplishments—they were apparently extensive and widely recognized and admired—in this arena as they pertained to Snellville and its environs.

"Then perhaps you know the Sinclair family, the descendants of Morgan Sinclair, who settled in the area shortly after the War?" Annie knew better than to designate which war. In Miss Boudreau's lexicon, there would only be one.

"Morgan Sinclair?"

Once again Annie increased her volume. "Yes, ma'am. Morgan Sinclair."

Miss Boudreau was a lady, so she didn't sniff. She remained polite. "Young lady, you have been given misinformation. There are only two Sinclair families in a six-county area, the descendants of Herrick Sinclair, who arrived in

1742, and the descendants of William Roger Sinclair, who arrived in 1811.''

"Morgan Sinclair," an amused voice drawled next to Annie. "Oh, I *love* it."

Annie turned and looked directly into the sloe eyes of Missy Sinclair.

The telephone crackled in her ear. "Mrs. Darling, are you there?"

Annie managed to keep her voice even. "Thank you, Miss Boudreau. I'm sorry to have bothered you. Thank you very much." She hung up the receiver.

Missy Sinclair stepped closer, peering down at the papers in Annie's folder.

Annie's nose wrinkled at the waft of musky perfume.

Missy's full lips curved into a sly, satisfied smile. "Why, Annie, honey, how sweet of you to want to know all about me." Crimson-tipped fingers snatched up the flimsy fax. The author scanned it, then dropped it onto Annie's papers. "You and Kenneth, too, spending so much time over little old me." Mocking eyes taunted Annie.

"Dixon," Annie said determinedly. "It doesn't exist."

"Oh, yes, it does. In my mind, it does."

Now Annie felt like she was caught in a gossamer web. "Who are you? Where did you grow up? What are you hiding?"

"Honey, I'm Melissa Sinclair. And who is that? A storyteller, honey, pure and simple. And I adore my little story about Morgan Sinclair. It makes me feel good. Don't you think it's nice?" She didn't wait for an answer. Instead, she held up Annie's note. "But you know what I don't think is nice?" Her voice was the same, the buttery, soft accent, the musical tone. "I don't think this is nice at all." Her smile widened. "Or wise. Sometimes bad things happen to people who go where they aren't invited."

Annie didn't sense fear or even anger. Instead, there was a flicker of exhilaration in those dark, taunting eyes.

A final sleek smile and Melissa turned away.

Annie had once walked into a thirty-foot banana spider-web and twisted and turned and flailed trying to shrug away the silky, sticky strands. Her skin had crawled then just as it did now.

Dammit, she wasn't going to be intimidated.

She glared at that plump retreating back, then punched the number to her suite.

"Max Darling."

"Max!" She burst into speech. ". . . so see if you can find out what's true about Missy's past. If anything. Max, what do you suppose her secret is?"

"Maybe that doesn't matter as much as our knowing there has to be a secret. Anyway, I'll get on it."

When Annie hung up the phone—Max promising to meet her for lunch in the restaurant in half an hour—she walked back to her chair in the lobby, ready to read about Jimmy Jay Crabtree. But she glanced toward the desk. And squared her shoulders.

Emma Clyde stood there, Annie's note in her hand. She finished reading it and turned toward the elevators. And saw Annie.

Annie had asked for it. She'd better be ready.

Today, Emma's caftan was russet and turquoise-striped. The celebrity was as imposing as always, her square-jawed face composed, her gaze sharp. She strode across the lobby.

They faced each other.

Annie looked defiantly into the writer's hostile blue eyes. "Hello, Emma."

Emma merely stared at her with the interest an entomologist might accord a rarely seen, environmentally threatened insect. Slowly she lifted the note and waggled it. "I wouldn't."

"It's too fascinating a project to be dropped." Annie was proud that she managed to speak without even a slight quaver, despite Emma's icy scrutiny.

"Kenneth died in a particularly unpleasant manner, Annie. Has that escaped your notice?"

"Emma, are you threatening me?"

"No." It was crisp, direct, untroubled. "I'm simply concerned for you."

Oh, sure. Their relationship had always been pleasant, but never close. Never. Who was close to Emma? Her editor? Her agent? Her stockbroker?

Annie put it on the table. "Concerned enough to help me find out who poisoned Kenneth?"

"I am not Marigold Rembrandt."

Annie stood a little straighter. "Emma, will you tell me something?"

"Perhaps."

"Marigold Rembrandt is so charming, so appealing." Annie stared into wary, cornflower-blue eyes. "Readers love her. She's the grandmother they recall with joy—or the grandmother they wished they'd had. Marigold's lovable and sweet and gently wise. Who is she?"

Emma got it, of course. Her square, tough face might have been chipped out of granite. She knew that Annie knew that Emma's success depended in large part—perhaps altogether—upon the public's adoration of her as the creator of

Marigold Rembrandt, and surely, those readers reasoned, as the epitome of all they most admired in Marigold.

What would happen if they learned that Emma Clyde was tough, hard, dangerous, and calculating?

Was Marigold Rembrandt what Emma might have been if she hadn't lost her youth in a dusty, hot theater of war?

Annie decided to gamble because she knew all too well that she was not dealing with Marigold Rembrandt.

"Emma, New York's hot for Kenneth's book. But I can modify it. *Song of the South* can be the story of four authors." Annie held up four fingers. "Not five."

Those cold eyes were thoughtful.

Marigold Rembrandt wouldn't dream of betraying her friends.

Emma Clyde's firm mouth spread in a slight smile. "Very wise of you, Annie. Too many major characters clutter a book. Perhaps I can be of some service to you in creating those four characters . . . and their pasts." She glanced at her diamond-encrusted watch. "I'll meet you here in the lobby. At three, after my panel." Her smile widened. "If you have time, you might want to come to my panel. It's a fascinating topic: 'Do People Get Away with Murder in Real Life?' Always a popular question. Of course"—and those blue eyes glittered—"I can't speak from personal experience." A brisk nod. "See you later."

Annie watched her walk away.

Was Emma chuckling?

Pretty damn funny.

Annie doubted if the late Enrique Morales would consider it hilarious.

Annie propped the poster up and threw herself back into the chair. She glanced at her watch, then flipped open her folder.

The squinty little eyes looked stupid, but Annie knew they lied. Jimmy Jay Crabtree might not be a charmer, but he had brains. His photograph showed him leaning against a bar, a glass raised high. He didn't smile for the camera, of course. Instead, his head jutted forward, his mouth was thin and straight. Probably trying to look tough. To Annie, he looked bilious.

Jimmy Jay Crabtree: The wimps want to pasteurize the world, suck all the guts out of it. I don't buy their program. I'll never buy their program. I'll smoke as much as I want to, drink as much as I want to, screw as much as I want to, and they can stuff it up their collective blue noses. That's what they are, bluenoses. They don't know how to scrap. All they can do is whine.

You add the wimp factor to the prig factor and what've you got? You've got a liberal. You know what a liberal reminds me of? The scum that sticks to the soap dish, soft and sticky and forever there. I hate them.

Hate's a nasty word with the PC scum. But there ought to be a lot of hate in this old world and I don't mind saying so. A lot of people agree with me. They're just too scared to say so. But I'm not scared, and I'll say it loud and clear and keep on saying it.

I learned all about hate when I was a kid. Who did the teachers handhold and pet? The prigs, always the prigs. So I complained, and they nicked my grades, so when it came scholarship time, who got the help? Anybody but a white American male.

Like me.

I had to work my way through college, doing

night shifts at a convenience store. There were special good classes for the geeks with the high test scores. Ordinary people like me, they shoved us into classes of two, three hundred.

But I fought every step of the way. Got kicked off the school newspaper because I told it the way it was.

If it wasn't a geek with special treatment, it was a WOMAN.

Women discriminated against?

Give me a break, buddy.

They've got you with a double barrel, and they unload it if you look at them crossways. A guy says a broad looks good, and he's pilloried for sexual harassment. If women kept to their places, this world would work a hell of a lot better.

You know what women are good for?

Sure you do.

Anything else is crap. After three wives, I know it for a fact. Trust me.

So yeah, I've been trying to fight the good fight for me and the rest of the guys, for the guys who make this country work, the everyday guys who want to have a beer after work and go home and find the goddamn dinner ready.

I'm a scrapper. On the page and off. And that's what writing is all about.

Annie resisted the impulse to shred the essay right there in the lobby and stuff the pieces into the nearest ash receptacle. She satisfied the temptation by muttering, ''But you don't sell in my store, buddy!''

She shoved Jimmy Jay's essay to the bottom of her pile. And picked up the essay by Alan Blake.

.   .   .

Eight phone calls later, Max decided Melissa Sinclair was a woman of parts. Many, many parts. Every time he thought he had a good lead on her past, he ran into another brick wall. Hmm. Okay, he'd try something different after lunch.

He was smiling as he stepped out into the hall. In just a few minutes, he'd see Annie, and that always made his day—any day—better in every way. Dear Annie. His stubborn, determined, serious wife. With the steady gray eyes and vivid smile. And absolutely impulsive nature. He shook his head. If she hadn't ducked into the Hazlitt suite yesterday . . . But she had. And somehow he had to extricate her from the resulting chaos, though the idea that Annie would poison anyone was ludicrous. Maybe Frank Saulter could talk to Detective Wheeler.

Max punched the button to the elevator.

A door at the end of the hall burst open, and two little girls in swimsuits, carrying beach towels, raced past him at a gallop.

"Last one down's a butthead!" the redhead screamed.

Her companion didn't say a word, but lowered her head and picked up speed.

They collided at the door to the stairs, struggled with the door, pushed and shoved at each other as they wormed through.

The door was closing behind them when they began to scream.

The elevator door opened, but Max was already down the hall and yanking open the door to the stairs.

The little girls spilled past him. "A body's down there!" the little redhead sobbed, her eyes huge and scared.

The second girl nodded. "She's just lying there. Not moving. I think she's dead."

Annie studied Alan Blake's picture. He wore tennis whites and stared quizzically into the camera. Annie noted how clean he looked. No sweat-dampened rings on this idol's tennis outfit. So how casual was this photo? But that wasn't fair, was it? Maybe not, but it made her feel better.

Her eyes dropped to the essay.

Alan Blake: When I was in the fifth grade, my English teacher, Miss Carey, decided to have a contest for the best essay about love.

"Annie." Winsome, beguiling, soulful.
"Annie." Crisp, straightforward, incisive.
"Annie." Clipped, imperious, regal.

Laurel radiated Simplicity in a simple white cotton blouse and powder-blue linen skirt. Her only jewelry was a pair of tiny gold dolphin earrings. She looked like a movie star version of Mother Teresa. She smiled beatifically, her hands folded together, her golden hair cupping her face with a halo effect. Annie wondered if at some appropriate moment she might suggest that the Mother Teresas of the world do not wear shell-pink fingernail polish. Nor do they carry self-advertising placards (CATCH A WAVE—*From* Simplicity *by Laurel Darling Roethke. Page 22.*)

Henny Brawley was the epitome of the well-dressed festival-goer in a pink knit cotton blouse and pastel plaid cotton skirt. Despite her casual attire, she had the confident air of an empire builder. However, Henny had obviously decided that Simplicity, either lowercase or capital, was not for her. She gave Annie an ebullient smile and held up a pink poster with twenty-four-point type in boldface:

A sound thinker gives equal consideration to the probable and the improbable.
Dr. John Thorndyke *in* The Red Thumb.
From The Quotable Sleuth *by Henrietta Brawley. Page 36.*

Miss Dora— Annie blinked. Surely that wasn't— It was. Miss Dora wore one of her usual dresses, long, black, distinctly funereal. Annie had often wondered if the old curmudgeon's attic held an inexhaustible supply of trunks replete with antebellum furnishings. But, instead of her customary head covering, Miss Dora's shaggy silver locks were topped by a tall chef's hat. Not, perhaps, that remarkable. Except this chef's hat was as black as ebony.

Miss Dora didn't have a placard or a poster. Instead, she held out toward Annie a tray—of course it was silver—with tiny crisp taco shells filled with—

Annie looked at the spidery handwriting on the card affixed to the tray:

Papaya-Accented Rice and Bean Salad in Shells.
From Miss Dora's Delectables *by Miss Dora Brevard.*
Page 63.

Annie gripped Alan Blake's essay. She would not succumb and reach for one of those delec—one of those damn salad shells. Even though she was starving. Of course, she was trying to solve a murder. Not, apparently, the main preoccupation of the Three Musketeers.

Perhaps Annie's face betrayed her thoughts.

"Hewing to the course," Miss Dora said firmly.

"Perfect for undercover activities," Henny announced.

"Our every thought has been with *you,* dear child."
Laurel's husky assurance throbbed with sincerity.

"You saw our poster." Henny beamed with pride.

"Yes." Annie reached out, took one of the miniature
shells. After all, it wouldn't help matters if she were faint
from hunger. Hmm. Papaya *and* avocado trimmings!

Miss Dora's reptilian expression softened. Annie
wouldn't have cared to wager whether it was from pleasure
in the consumption of the salad shell or fondness for
Annie.

Henny nudged the poster with a pink-and-green-striped,
ribbed-cotton sneaker. "An exhaustive survey. Rather proud
of it. We did keep crossing paths with the local constabu-
lary."

Annie wanted to point out this wasn't an Eve Gill adven-
ture, but Henny continued swiftly, "The deputies seem to
agree with our conclusion, which definitely restricts the circle of possible perps."

"*Qué será, será,*" Laurel offered. The smile was now not
so much beatific as philosophical.

Perhaps it was admirable to be philosophic about the
prospect of one's daughter-in-law being considered a prime
suspect in a capital murder case.

Annie didn't feel the least bit philosophical.

"The authorities are working quite hard." Miss Dora's
rusty voice was admiring.

"To put me in jail?" Annie demanded.

"Annie!"

"Annie!"

"Annie!"

She glared at each in turn. "Well, what else are they doing?"

Three voices—one throaty, one distinct, one raspy—spoke at once, then there was a pause.

It was a test of the *tres amigos.*

Annie waited with interest.

Who would prevail?

"Alphabetical," Henny suggested.

Raisin-dark eyes met Nordic-blue eyes met brown eyes.

Miss Dora nodded complacently. "The authorities have interviewed every member of the hotel staff on duty yesterday. A painter was working on the interior stairwells between the fourth and fifth floors. No guest walked up the stairs to the fifth floor."

Annie shrugged. "Elevators."

"Certainly, certainly," Henny boomed. "But it's reassuring to know the police are considering every possibility."

It sounded to Annie like the police were busy drawing a thick black arrow that pointed straight to her.

"Karma," Laurel murmured. "Annie, you simply exude darkness. We must lighten your load. Now, I had the great pleasure of talking with that lovely Captain Wheeler this morning. And he is quite actively looking at *everyone* residing on the fifth floor."

"That's nice," Annie said agreeably. "At least he admits there are others who *are* residing on that floor."

"Brown, brown, brown aura." Laurel's sigh was huskily regretful.

Annie could feel it growing browner by the instant.

But she made a heroic effort. "I do appreciate your hard work on my behalf. I wonder if—"

The wail of a siren shattered the tennis-club atmosphere of the lobby.

Chapter 13

Paramedics hustled the gurney past the front desk then wheeled to the left, following a grim-faced Jeff Garrett. The hotel assistant manager's carroty hair spiked in every direction. A bellman waited at the open door of a freight elevator.

As the door slid shut, Annie gave her companions a startled look.

They looked back at her, equally worried.

"I'd better see." Annie popped to her feet.

The young woman behind the desk was trying to field a dozen questions from hotel guests.

Annie listened intently, then rejoined the waiting trio.

"A maid's hurt. She's unconscious. They think she fell down some stairs. But nobody knows exactly." Annie and her companions watched the floor indicator. It stopped at IV.

Annie realized they were watching the same action that must have unfolded yesterday. Except yesterday, the elevator stopped at V. And yesterday was murder.

Miss Dora cleared her throat. "In the midst of life . . ."

There was a respectful silence.

Annie broke it. Whatever the emergency on the fourth floor, it had no connection to the demise of Kenneth Hazlitt, and she had her own emergency to deal with—avoiding a murder charge. She was confident that given time, she'd be able to come up with the right answer. No one matched her expertise in mysteries.

Oh, all right, Henny Brawley. Henny, however, had other interests at the moment.

But there were still so many questions. . . .

"Look." She gestured for her Dauntless Trio to come closer. Although she felt positive—okay, if not positive, at least confident—that the key to Kenneth Hazlitt's murder would be found in the lives of the Famous Five, she wasn't quite willing to dismiss Hercule Poirot's dictum that in the victim's life could be found the reason for his death. So— "Here's what I want you to do . . ."

They listened with flattering intensity.

Annie really felt good about their devotion to her cause.

She gazed after them fondly as they walked away.

Their voices carried with great clarity.

Crisp, straightforward, incisive: "We'll fan out. We can cover all the booths that way."

Winsome, beguiling, soulful: "And, of course, it's always such an advantage in life—for us, for dear Annie—to make connections."

Clipped, imperious, regal: "Before dispersing, I suggest we start as a unit with Peachtree Press. Certainly in the course of our visit there, I'm sure we will have an opportunity—"

The front doors closed behind them.

"What's wrong, Max?"

"I'm sorry I'm late. An accident upstairs. A maid fell down the fifth-floor stairs."

The door to the freight elevator opened, and the gurney was wheeled out into the lobby. It was occupied.

Annie glimpsed pale, slack features.

The front doors were opened wide, and the gurney was hustled outside. The assistant manager followed. His freckles were the only color in his pale face.

As Annie and Max settled at a table in the dining room, Max described his find. "She's unconscious. Of course, there's no telling how long she'd been lying there."

A sudden sharp wail marked the ambulance's departure.

"I heard the ambulance come." Annie looked toward the street. "It must have been almost the same thing yesterday. Just a different floor. Miss Dora always has the bon mot. As the paramedics hurried by, she muttered, 'In the midst of life . . .' "

"So how are our intrepid sleuths? Still banded together?"

"Sleuths? Fat chance. Max, they're out there shopping

their manuscripts! I mean, talk about first things first.'' She shook her head indignantly.

Max grinned.

Despite her sense of being an also-ran, she couldn't resist smiling in return. She loved Max's sexy grin and the way her fingers wanted to smooth his hair and the spark she always saw in his deep blue eyes when he looked at her. Maybe this afternoon—

And he could read her mind. The sudden light in his eyes was unmistakable.

''Max, we have to work.''

''Mmmm. But—''

''And eat. I think I'll order the pan-fried black-eyed pea cakes.'' Talk about *mmmm*. She wondered if Miss Dora had this recipe. Okay, so it was piggy to order hors d'oeuvres at lunch. So—

Max, of course, chose grilled salmon ribbons.

The food in the hotel restaurant was not only superb, but, despite the crush of Festival attendees, the service was splendid.

When the waitress brought the hors d'oeuvres, Annie reached over and speared one of Max's salmon ribbons, swiping it through the dill sauce. *Mmmm. Mmmm.* ''Okay,'' she said briskly and quite firmly, although she didn't meet his eyes. ''I'm stirring the pot.'' She kept her voice light and positive as she described her proposed venture into publishing.

Max didn't let her finish. ''Annie, that's crazy!''

She refused to be put on the defensive. ''Max, I had to do something! Detective Wheeler won't listen to me.''

''So you set yourself up to be the next victim!'' His face was stern. ''I'll talk to Wheeler, get permission for you to get out of here.''

"For starters, I don't drink bourbon." Annie knew that begged the question, so she continued hurriedly, "And I'll be around people all day," which hadn't helped Hazlitt, so she talked even faster, "and at night I'll be safe with you." She resisted clasping a hand to her heart and calling out, "My hero!" Even Max's sense of humor had its limits. "Besides, the murderer's not going to be dumb enough to simply take it for granted that I know something dangerous to him. Or her. I wouldn't try something that hokey." Annie said this piously, then continued her departure from the truth. "That wasn't why I did it. I did it because"—a little voice in her head murmured—"because Leah Kirby made you mad. Because," she said firmly, "I figured I could use the threat of publicity to get some information. And it worked! Emma Clyde's going to go around the Festival with me this afternoon and we'll talk to people and get the real skinny on the Medallion winners. I'll get more inside stuff than Wheeler—even if he's looking—could come up with in months. Emma knows *everybody*."

Max wasn't mollified. "Annie, look at me."

Reluctantly, she met his gaze.

"You march right around the Festival and tell each Medallion winner you've changed your mind."

"No." Surely that was a hint of sour cream in the cakes?

He sighed. "At the very least, promise me you won't—under any circumstances—go off alone with any of those people."

"Cross my heart."

"Annie, for God's sake!"

She laughed. "I mean it. I won't. And I won't eat or drink anything you haven't tasted first."

Their entrees arrived, fresh snapper for Max, oyster pie

with mushrooms for Annie. She gravely waited for him to take the first bite of her lunch, then with gusto plunged her fork into the baked dish.

Max squeezed lemon on his snapper. "Annie, seriously, you must be careful. Kenneth's murderer is as cold and cruel as killers come."

Annie looked at her husband thoughtfully. Max was right, of course. Because it was almost certain Kenneth's killer was at that cocktail party and saw the hideous result of those drops of nicotine. And watched without an apparent qualm.

Of course, they couldn't be absolutely sure of that. It seemed clear now that the bottle of whiskey had been poisoned between ten o'clock in the morning and Willie Hazlitt's return to the suite at three. So, the poisoner need not have been present.

All the Medallion winners were there.

If one of them was the poisoner, he or she certainly would have been present.

An absence would have been noted.

Annie tried to remember the faces of the Medallion winners at the cocktail party.

Leah Kirby had been deep in conversation with her blond friend. Leah was pleased about something. And not, Annie thought, pleased in a nice way. There was an unmistakable air of smugness in her good humor.

Missy Sinclair was slyly watchful, amused.

Alan Blake—Annie frowned—Alan Blake was furious. He'd been talking to someone, and he was scowling. Not the way to charm booksellers or readers.

Jimmy Jay Crabtree, his face arrogant and self-congratulatory, was spewing out his usual invective.

Emma Clyde was self-possessed and amused as she looked

speculatively at their host just after discussing methods of murder. Surely that was nothing more than a deadly coincidence!

Unfortunately, Annie hadn't looked at the authors after Kenneth downed that fatal drink.

Except for Emma, of course. Emma's face was composed as she moved toward the stricken man. Solemn. Not unaffected. And she had come forward. She need not have.

But Emma was never reluctant to take charge.

Would she have done so, if she were the poisoner?

Perhaps.

As for the rest of the authors, Annie was too caught up in the horror of the moment to notice their reactions.

She certainly had seen Willie, his face stricken with panic and helplessness, every vestige of his charm and easy humor erased.

"Max, that's what we have to find out. Which one of them is utterly cold and cruel." She put down her fork, reached for her purse, and lifted out a notepad. "All right, here are the people who could most easily have poisoned the bottle of bourbon." She wrote the names of the five Medallion winners and Willie Hazlitt. To be complete, she added:

Annie and Max Darling
Henny Brawley
Miss Dora Brevard
Laurel Darling Roethke

She paused. "Max, the woman who took that box out of the suite. She could have poisoned the bourbon."

Annie wrote down:

Unknown

Then, with a swoop, she put X's by the last five entries, and at the bottom of the page an asterisk with the notation: *X indicates no discernible motive.*

She paused, tapped the pen on the table, then printed a title:

ASSESSMENT OF CHARACTER

Leah Kirby—Completely self-absorbed, high-strung, passionate.

Missy Sinclair—Imperturbable, sly, willful, secretive, utterly unpredictable.

Jimmy Jay Crabtree—Arrogant, angry, jealous, hostile.

Alan Blake—Surface charm. A streak of ugliness. But ?????

Emma Clyde—Smart, tough, crafty, cold-blooded.

Annie handed the sheet to Max.

He pointed to the entry on Alan Blake. "Why the question marks?"

"I don't have any sense of who Blake is. He's good-looking and he knows it. He's got a great smile and a smooth voice. He writes romantic stuff about a sensitive guy who knows how to make a woman feel special. Of course, the guy —he's named Burke or Clint or Travis—anyway Burke/Clint/Travis makes Susan/Jane/Esther feel special, then he fades into the distance, sadly downcast that their love can't last, but he must move on and leave her to fulfill her obligations. Burke/Clint/Travis wears khakis and running shoes and smokes a pipe and makes soulful observations about Life."

"Do I detect a lack of enthusiasm?"

"You might. For all I know, Blake believes every word of

it. But I don't think so. He was awfully short on charm when I talked to him this morning.'' And she'd not felt exactly scared, but darned uncomfortable when he'd pressed her to say what she knew. ''He figured out really quick that the police were after me—and he thought it was funny in a slimy kind of way. That's what I think about him. He's slime.''

''But you went ahead and left him a note about the book proposal?''

Annie shrugged. ''I'll be honest. I don't think it will bother him a bit.'' She whisked through the papers in her folder, checked the paragraph on ''Lake Allen'' in Kenneth's proposal. Hollywood. She wished she'd seen this before she'd talked to Blake. But the afternoon wasn't over.

''. . . trying to find out more about Jimmy Jay's secretary,'' Max explained. ''She won't talk about the car wreck that killed that little girl. Crabtree's always a jerk. He loves being a jerk. Why didn't he dump his secretary when she caused him trouble? You know it caused trouble with his insurance company. But he kept her on. Why?''

Annie was pretty sure she could answer that one. ''I'll bet she's one sexy broad.''

''Could be,'' Max agreed. ''Anyway, I'm working on that.''

''Hi, Annie, Max.''

They looked up. Max stood and shook hands with Frank Saulter.

''Hi, Chief.'' Annie glowed. ''Thanks. Thanks for coming.''

''Oh, sure.'' Saulter sat down and glanced around the dining room. His weathered face had the hard-to-read composure cops acquire. His dark eyes moved slowly. They didn't miss anything. ''Pretty fancy hotel. You can bet they want this cleared up quick." He faced them. "Have you talked to the manager?"

"I will," Max promised. "What's the temperature at the sheriff's department, Frank?"

"Strictly between us?"

They both nodded.

"Puzzled. They've got Annie's prints on the glass that held the poison. And, so far, Annie's the only person they've come up with who'd fussed with Hazlitt. At least, fussed with him around here. They're digging around, trying to find a closer connection between Annie and Hazlitt."

"They won't." Annie was impatient. "Frank, are they doing anything about the authors, the ones Kenneth was going to write about?"

"Oh, yeah. But not because of that." His tone dismissed the importance of the novel. "They're on the list because they had access to the Hazlitt suite during the day."

At least she wasn't the only suspect, even if she headed the list.

The very short list. Barring Unknown, of course. Annie didn't consider Unknown to be a great possibility. Max was too careful and thorough to have missed anyone with a serious reason to do away with Kenneth. As for the blond woman who took the box, they'd have to find her.

But Annie was betting on one of the Famous Five. Or . . .

"Frank, what's the dope on Willie Hazlitt?"

The Broward's Rock police chief nodded when a waitress inquired if he wanted coffee. He waved away a menu. With the steaming cup in hand, he frowned at Annie. "No good. Been in trouble of one kind or another from the time he was a kid. Stole a car when he was fifteen. Suspended sentence.

Claimed it was a prank. Ever since, mostly stuff just this side of crooked. Kicked out of college for cheating. Accused of stealing jewelry from this rich gal in Boca Raton, charges dropped. Woman said she gave him the jewelry, told her husband it was stolen. Some question whether he was involved in some shady insurance claims in Florida, but nothing came of it. His latest almost landed him in jail, though. He was milking this old lady out of money to invest. The family dropped it when Kenneth paid them off. That's what brought Willie back to Atlanta.''

Max gave Annie an I-told-you-so look.

She shrugged. ''Nothing violent in any of it. Long on charm.'' She knew she was smiling indulgently and suspected that was always Willie's effect on those of her sex. ''Short on character, that's Willie.''

Frank added another packet of sugar to his coffee. ''Wheeler says Willie could have pushed Kenneth off his sailboat anytime. Dandy little accident. Why poison him here in front of a crowd of witnesses? Hell of a lot of trouble, and he's one of the suspects.''

Max was dogged. ''Sure, that's a natural assumption. But if Willie did it, it was brilliant to have it happen here. A push off a sailboat? Somebody could question that, given Willie's history. Here there are lots of suspects and nobody can be positive who did it. The only hard evidence is against Annie, but there's not enough to charge her. Unless something breaks, this will go down as the famous murder at the Festival. The famous unsolved murder.''

Annie strode briskly through the holiday crowds. It was another May-perfect day, a cloudless sky, a gentle sea breeze, the soothing warmth of the spring sun.

Kenneth Hazlitt's murder might be uppermost in the minds of a few, but it hadn't affected the temper of the festival-goers. Smiling faces—

"Hey, hey, you, hey, *bitch*!" With a guttural growl, Jimmy Jay Crabtree planted himself directly in her path. "Listen, I've been looking for you. You stay the goddamn hell out of my room." The words were carefully enunciated. Too carefully.

Annie looked at his flushed face. He reeked of whiskey. "Back off, buddy. I've never set foot in your room. Go have your DTs somewhere else."

He glowered at her, but something—uncertainty? fear? —flickered deep in those dulled eyes.

"Wait a minute, hey, wait a minute. You telling me you didn't get—didn't go through my stuff? It wasn't you?" His tone still blustered, but now there was an edge of panic. "It wasn't you?"

"Right the first time. I'd rather paw through a sack of rattlesnakes than touch anything of yours. You can put it in the bank, buddy."

"Christ."

He no longer looked at Annie.

He gave a swift, hunted glance around them and started to brush past her.

"Hey, *you* wait a minute," she ordered. "You're drunk. It's just past lunch, and you're drunk."

His eyes jerked back to her, dull, glazed, blank.

"That's why you didn't fire your secretary. *You* drove the car that killed the little girl. And *you* were drunk when you ran her down. Weren't you?"

"Car." He took a ragged breath. "What car, bitch? I don't know squat about any car." And then he pushed past her.

.   .   .

Every chair was taken and people stood twenty deep. Annie wormed her way around to one side until she had a clear view of Emma Clyde and her fellow panelists. Annie checked her program. Two authors she didn't know.

". . . one expert suggests as many as two out of every five accidents may not be accidents at all.'' The speaker had a fleshy moon face, a genial expression, and a cheery voice. "Most suspect, of course, are drownings, falls, and . . .''

Annie checked her watch. At least another ten minutes. She inched a few feet away, found a driftwood trunk, and sat down. Really, she would have to remember to compliment Blue Benedict. The outdoor panels were a stroke of genius. Certainly it provided a backdrop unlike that at any other book festival.

Annie opened her folder.

Alan Blake: When I was in the fifth grade, my English teacher, Miss Carey, decided to have a contest for the best essay about love. That was the first time I wrote about love. I've been writing about it ever since.

I remember the way that essay began:
Love is you.
And then—to me—it was.
Miss Carey.
Miss Carey with the midnight-black hair and the rosebud mouth and the brilliant blue eyes.
I don't know where she is now. If she were to read these words, I wonder if she would remember the quiet little guy with the freckles and the happy grin.

God yes, it was a happy grin.

Every day that I ran into her class, I felt like sunshine poured inside me.

I wrote that.

Every day that I looked to the front of the room and saw her face, I felt like the band struck up a march.

Every day—

Annie reached down and picked up a handful of sand. What tripe. Her eye slid down the printed page. It got worse.

. . . Miss Carey's voice made my heart sing.

But what idyll can survive betrayal?

That's how I saw it, of course, when she told us with great excitement that she would be marrying when school was out, and we were all invited to her wedding.

Perhaps it was then that I realized there are magical moments that can exist only for the space of a heartbeat, moments that are not intended to be forever but are no less precious for their evanescent nature.

Love. I've spent my life looking for it.

Just like my readers.

"Oh, gag," Annie said aloud.

She slapped the folder shut.

Applause erupted.

The crowd apparently enjoyed learning just how treacherous stairs, sailboats, and cliffs could be if explored in the wrong company.

Annie wondered that someone hadn't held dear little Alan's head under the water in the school pool when he was such a precious little bundle of prepubescent lust.

Of course, Alan Blake's essay was hogwash.

Actually, any self-respecting hog would gag on it, too.

But of all the essays, his seemed the most contrived, the least sincere.

It was almost as if he had sat down in front of his word processor, analyzed his readers (70 percent women over age fifty who listen to news/talk radio at 56 percent above the national average, read *Money* magazine at 54 percent above the national average, and the newspaper home news section at 29 percent above the national average) and plotted out the most appealing essay possible.

Which bespoke a carefully controlled, coolly cynical writer.

Who, according to Kenneth Hazlitt's book proposal, had a past in Hollywood that he very much didn't want to talk about.

Annie stood on tiptoe, keeping track of Emma as she talked to fans and signed books.

Okay, Alan Blake. If anybody can nose out the dirt, it's Emma.

Here we come.

Chapter 14

Annie hurried to keep up, slipping a little on the sand. It was amazing how fast Emma could move. And she had to be in her seventies!

"So who would know about Alan Blake and Hollywood?"

They reached the plaza. Emma shaded her eyes and gazed around the festival area. "I said I'd help, Annie, but I'm fresh out of miracles. Hollywood might as well be Zimbabwe or Mars as far as most people here are concerned. Let's see—yes, there are some people I know from Nashville. Let me handle this.'' She charged ahead.

Annie glared at her sturdy, rapidly retreating back, then broke into a trot. So Emma was her usual uncharming self. So what else was new?

Annie skidded to a stop in front of a booth. She noted that Emma could manage to make extremely nice when it suited her purposes. In fact, for Emma, she was downright charming.

''Louise, Wilma, it's wonderful to see you.'' Emma chattered on for a moment, then inclined her head toward Annie. ''My assistant, Annie.''

Gracious nods, then instant dismissal.

''. . . know you are so excited about Leah's Medallion.''

''And yours, Emma, and yours.'' Wilma twittered, pushing thick gold-rimmed glasses higher on a beaked nose.

Louise nodded vigorously, her long black hair rippling over her shoulders. ''Absolutely *thrilled* for you.''

Annie stood there like a lamppost. Or a parking meter. Or a book dump. It was quite interesting to be invisible. A new experience.

Emma edged closer to the two women and nodded her head confidentially. ''You know, I was so relieved to see that Leah was able to come. I'd heard that perhaps—oh, you know how rumors get around . . .'' She let her voice fade suggestively.

They took the bait. ''I just don't believe a word of it,'' Wilma snapped, but there was a squiggle of malicious excitement in the eyes behind their magnifying lenses. ''Why, that young man's twenty-five *years* younger than Leah. Of course, she swears she's simply his mentor. But a friend of mine in New Orleans saw them there together last month—at the *same* hotel—and it wasn't a conference.''

Louise wrapped long thin arms around her angular torso and giggled. ''Oh, but Wilma, Brett Farraday is wonderful.''

Wilma might be a nerd, but Annie agreed with her taste. Brett Farraday was indeed wonderful: tall, sandy-haired, lanky, with a sunny grin on a bony, likable face, and the author of wickedly funny satiric newspaper columns that didn't leave a single Southern stone unturned. Farraday regularly lampooned everybody from tobacco lobbyists *(They bring a tear to my eye in their struggle against government interference. I always knew I could count on the tobacco interests to keep America free.)* to the antiabortion activists *(Tote that barge, lift that bale, make that woman have that baby! After it's born? The government take care of it? That's socialism! Government has no responsibility for people's babies. If people can't do better than live in slums, why, that's their problem.)* to the insurance industry *(It's our God-given right to make money, so, of course, we have to drop sick people from coverage. Anything else would be a betrayal of our stockholders. The flag flutters in the breeze to the tune of "Stars and Stripes Forever," and the insurance company logo flashes across the screen. Change jobs, lose your health insurance? Tough cheese, old buddy.)*

Brett Farraday!

''Is Brett here this weekend?'' Emma asked.

Wilma shook her head. ''No. He isn't on the list of authors.''

Annie wondered if she could track Farraday down. And when she did? How far would she get opening a phone conversation with, ''I understand you're having an affair with Leah Kirby, Mr. Farraday?''

But maybe he wasn't the person to talk to.

Emma exhibited another burst of charm and disengaged from her admirers with great skill. Annie almost complimented her. Almost.

As they quickly skirted around the information booth to study the map of the exhibits, Annie whispered, "Did you know about Leah and Brett Farraday?"

"I'd heard she was involved with someone." Emma's tone was neutral.

Annie shot her a swift glance. The topic of unfaithful spouses might not be a popular one with Emma.

But the mystery writer's square face was untroubled. She stabbed a blunt finger toward the map. "Booth Twenty-three."

Once again Annie found herself introduced with the dismissive, "My assistant, Annie," and she felt the cloak of invisibility slide over her. It seemed to her that Emma was relishing Annie's subordinate role entirely too much.

". . . I heard there was some criticism of Jimmy Jay's selection as a Medallion winner."

A tall, birdlike man with bulging dark eyes clasped his hands and bent his head. "My dear, who can doubt it? Have you heard . . ."

Annie bent her head, too, to listen. But it was the same old, same old. It was easy as an observer to be casual about the litany of Jimmy Jay's lousy treatment of others, though Annie doubted that any of Jimmy Jay's ex-wives—still battling viciously for alimony and child support—considered it old hat.

". . . little boy had an operation for a defective heart valve, and do you know Jimmy Jay didn't even go! And they say he won't even call the little guy. And . . ."

Jimmy Jay had insulted a bookseller in Boca Raton, hit a television interviewer in Nashville, borrowed money and not repaid it to a current girlfriend, been cut off the air for obscene language in Pascagoula, skipped out on a hotel bill in New Orleans and the hotel was demanding that the bookstore make it good . . .

"Did you ever hear he was drunk as a skunk and driving —not his secretary—when his car killed that little girl?"

The bookseller and Emma both looked at Annie in surprise.

Of course it came as a surprise when an invisible creature spoke.

The bookseller's prominent eyes widened. "Lordy. Why, honey, I'll bet you're right as rain. Any way you cut it, that Jimmy Jay's a sorry piece of goods."

As they headed for their next booth—Number 14—Annie almost dismissed that interview as nonproductive, then she stopped short. "Wait a minute. Wait a *minute*. That bookseller—"

"Walt Hisell," Emma supplied.

"He said Jimmy Jay skipped out on a hotel bill and the hotel was going after the *bookseller*. Okay, that has to mean Jimmy Jay was in New Orleans to do a signing. Otherwise, the hotel wouldn't try to get money out of the bookseller. And if they tried to get the bookseller to pay for the hotel room, that has to mean Jimmy's publishing house wasn't paying for the trip. And if his publishing house wasn't paying for a book trip—"

Annie didn't have to finish because Emma knew what that meant.

If Walt Hisell had the story right.

To her credit, Emma was generous with her praise. "That's quite insightful, Annie. Let's see—" Her pale blue eyes scanned the crowd. "Over there. By the hot dog stand. Beau Kramer's a sales rep for Jimmy Jay's publisher."

Emma headed straight for Kramer. Annie stuck close behind. Sales reps know everything that's happening in a publishing house.

Cornered, Beau Kramer tried to be discreet, but Emma wasn't having any.

"As a favor to me, Beau. I swear I won't tell anyone."

Kramer, chunky and athletic, glanced doubtfully at Annie.

"Annie, my assistant," Emma announced.

The cloak descended.

"Okay, the story's true. We refused to pay for this last tour. He set it up himself. Emma, he's on the skids. His books aren't selling, as in no place, no way. And he's such a stupid jerk, he's trying to pressure us to pay for this tour anyway. He thinks it will embarrass us so much we'll cave in." Kramer took a huge bite from his hot dog, licked some relish from his chin. Annie decided not to tell him about the mustard on his lapel.

"Thanks, Beau," Emma said gruffly.

"You didn't hear it here."

"Right."

Annie waited until they were out of the sales rep's hearing. "Good going, Emma."

The mystery writer shrugged. "So Jimmy Jay needs money. How does that figure with Kenneth's murder?"

Annie's elation seeped away. But she held stubbornly to the thought that they had learned something they hadn't known: Jimmy Jay Crabtree might be desperately short on cash.

But, as Emma had pointed out, how could that tie in with Kenneth and his tell-all, sexy Southern novel? If anything, the free advertising of being part of Kenneth's novel might have been enough to jump-start Jimmy Jay's sales.

Annie sighed. Damn, it would be nice to hang the murder on the most hated Medallion winner.

Unfortunately, Emma's latest contribution simply seemed to make him the least likely suspect.

On their way to Booth 14, they passed the Mint Julep Press display.

Annie was surprised to see Willie Hazlitt on duty. But she had encouraged him to keep on keeping on. It was one way of handling grief.

Sunglasses hid his eyes. Despite the blazing colors of another Hawaiian-patterned sports shirt, Willie didn't have a holiday air. He looked tired, forlorn.

She lifted her hand in greeting.

He didn't respond, though she was certain he'd seen her.

In fact, his mouth drew down in a frown of—disapproval? disgust? dislike?

Annie reached out, tugged on Emma's billowy sleeve. ''I want to talk to Willie Hazlitt.''

But as she reached the booth, Willie crossed his arms. His body language couldn't have been clearer. He didn't want to speak with her.

The subtlety of John Marquand's Mr. Moto was not for Annie. ''So what's wrong with you?''

''I don't like vultures.''

She stared at him blankly.

''Picking at bones. That's what you're doing. Taking Ken's idea and trying to make a bundle with it. Blake told me all about it.''

''Alan Blake?'' Obviously, he'd picked up Annie's message at the hotel desk. ''And he came running right to you?''

''Not the way you mean,'' Willie shot back. ''Alan came because he was an old friend of Ken's. Ken published his first book, gave him his start. And Alan wanted me to know how much Ken—'' Willie stopped, bit his lip, took a shaky breath. ''He thought a lot of Ken. Wanted me to know that. That's when it came up. I wouldn't have thought you were that kind of person. But I guess it could make you a lot of dough. That's what I told Detective Wheeler.''

Despite the silky warmth of the sun, Annie felt a sudden chill. Oh, great, her effort to get the attention of the Famous Five might boomerang. What if Wheeler got the idea Annie might have killed Kenneth to take over his book idea? If so, it would be damned ironic. A lot more irony than she could appreciate. And infuriating if the investigator would believe someone might kill to write a book but that no one would kill to *keep* a book from being written!

She opened her mouth, then closed it. She couldn't tell Willie her threat to write the book was simply a ploy. Not with Emma standing beside her.

Besides, he wouldn't believe it.

So what could she say?

Emma thrust out her hand. ''Emma Clyde. Mr. Hazlitt, I want you to know I'm very sorry about Kenneth. But, believe me, Kenneth would be all in favor of Annie picking up his idea. He loved excitement. As for making money . . . writing books for most people is a labor of love, Mr. Hazlitt.''

But Willie continued to frown. ''I'm going to talk to my lawyer. I don't know much about this kind of stuff, but it looks to me like she's stealing Ken's idea. And I don't like it.''

''Your lawyer can talk to my lawyer,'' Annie told him stiffly. ''Come on, Emma.''

He stepped in front of Annie, blocking her. ''And I want that box back. The box you took from the suite!''

Annie held on to her temper. "I didn't take the box, Willie. I don't even know what's missing. What was in it, do you know?"

His eyes glinted with suspicion. "It was all about the book, the book you now say you're going to write. The hell you didn't take it—"

Annie interrupted sharply, "Detective Wheeler can search our suite anytime he wants to."

Willie folded his arms across his chest, glared at her. "I'm going to tell my lawyer about the box, too."

"Be my guest." Annie stepped past him. "Let's go, Emma."

This time Annie led the way. In front of Booth 14, she stopped. "That's the guy who's sponged off everybody all his life," Annie hissed at Emma. "Now he inherits a small press and he's suddenly proprietorial. Talk to his lawyer! Can you believe it? Talk to *Kenneth's* lawyer, he means. I'll bet the closest Willie ever got to an attorney was to hire one to keep him out of jail!"

Emma's firm mouth curved in amusement. "The transformation from ne'er-do-well to entrenched capitalist only takes long enough to change the name on the bank accounts," she said drily.

Annie almost explained that Mint Julep Press would probably be inherited by Kenneth's two children, at least according to what she'd learned from Willie, but that wasn't information Annie was supposed to have, and Emma would pick up on that immediately. It might be dangerous to Annie's health if Emma decided Annie was more interested in finding Kenneth's murderer than in getting background for the book.

But Emma didn't notice Annie's hesitation. The writer

moved closer to Booth 14. She boomed, "Craig, I haven't seen you since the conference down in the Keys. That *was* a weekend, wasn't it?"

The bookseller's narrow face crinkled in mock misery. "God, Emma, you put everybody under the table—and won the pot. But you always do. Next time I'm going to check the deck."

"That won't save you either." She waved a casual hand toward Annie. "Craig, my assistant, Annie."

Annie smiled and felt herself disappearing.

Emma looked positively benign.

Since she was invisible, Annie permitted herself a skeptical glance.

Emma's tone dripped the very best butter. "Craig, I heard you speak at SEBA on the importance of hand-selling books. As I recall, you used Alan Blake's first novel for an example."

Annie had missed that session at the annual conference of the Southeastern Booksellers Association. She knew the importance of booksellers telling customers about new books they liked. It made careers every year.

Craig beamed. "One of my assistant buyers, Arlene Counts, first spotted Blake's novel. Arlene's got an uncanny sense for what's going to hit it big. She was the first one in the store to go crazy over *Like Water for Chocolate,* too. And of course, Alan's a hometown boy, so that makes a big difference."

"Does his family still live in Birmingham?"

"His dad retired as principal of one of the high schools a couple of years ago. I think maybe his mom still teaches kindergarten."

"Sounds like an all-American family."

"No doubt about it, Emma."

"Didn't Alan spend some time in Hollywood?"

Craig grinned. "Oh, you ought to hear him tell it. He says he wrote dozens of scripts and only sold one. It was a Dracula movie, and he thinks it was distributed in Italy and maybe it made it to a few B houses here. You know how Alan is, so modest and down-home. Never tries to act like he was any kind of a big deal out there. Then he gets a little serious and tells the audience that Hollywood's a heartbreaker, just like they've always heard. And he's really so glad he was able to come home. He says you *can* come home again, and it's better than when you left."

Emma took time to look over the bookseller's display. She bought a Cajun cookbook. And handed it to Annie to carry as they moved away.

Annie snarled. "If I hear any more about how charming Alan Blake is, I'm going to gag. I can tell you he's not nearly as nice as everyone thinks."

"No one is," Emma responded serenely. "I'd say Alan knows how to sell books. That didn't sound like his Hollywood years were too exciting."

"No." Annie hurried to keep up. "But if there's something slimy in his Hollywood past, he's not going to share it at a book signing."

"True." Emma paused; her steel-blue eyes raked the row of booths. "I don't see anyone in the Dekalb bookstore booth." She glanced at her watch. "Four o'clock. Let's try the hotel bar."

Henny shaded her eyes from the westering sun. "The crowd seems to be thinning."

Laurel smoothed back a strand of golden hair. "I do believe," she murmured, "that perhaps we've exhausted the possibilities here."

Henny checked her program. "Actually, we've approached all but three publishers. And of those, only one looks promising."

Miss Dora thumped her cane. "Nonetheless, true to our promise to Annie, we must check with each of the publishers to be sure we've gathered all possible material about Mr. Hazlitt."

"Certainly, certainly," Henny said quickly. "I haven't forgotten our mission. Not at all. Never. But everyone seems to be departing." She glanced around the Festival area, suddenly much quieter and less congested.

Miss Dora pursed her lips. "I've overheard several of the booksellers and publishers making plans to meet for libations. Apparently, book gatherings are not devoted solely to a celebration of the Arts. It would be pleasant to join them. However"—she lifted her cane as if to arms—"duty requires us to make our report."

The private detective was brisk, but Max detected a note of pride. ". . . not easy to dig stuff up on a Saturday afternoon. Okay. Subject: Regina Perkins, age thirty-three, single, white, five-feet-four-inches tall, one hundred sixty-four pounds. Native of Marietta, Georgia. Associate degree in business from a junior college. Nobody much remembers her. Never caused any problems. Average grades. Worked her way through school. Part-time jobs at a local McDonald's. I found a woman who worked there when Perkins did. Said Perkins was nice enough, never said much. When she got out of school, she got a job with a temp agency. With them for six years. Worked as a temp for a writer named Crabtree. He took her on permanent about four years ago. That's when she moved into a fancy apartment in midtown and bought herself a shiny new Jaguar. According to a neighbor, she's 'nice enough, never says much.' Same song. So, same gal. Don't know what she does for this writer Crabtree, but he's paying her big time. She files her income tax electronically. It's easy to get into those files if you know how. Course you understand I wouldn't do a thing like that, but let's just say a little bird told me Perkins's income popped from temp wages, about fourteen thou a year, to a cool fifty grand. You want more? I can get on it Monday.''

''That's all I need.'' And Max gave the address of Confidential Commissions for the bill.

Four years ago. That's when Jimmy Jay Crabtree's car—ostensibly driven by one sober, unremarkable secretary named Regina—struck and killed a child at a school-bus stop.

And that's when Regina got a full-time, permanent, quite lucrative job.

Max scrawled a summary on his legal pad, ripped off the sheet, and slipped it into an envelope.

The bar was jammed with people shrieking at one another at full lung power.

It was hard to wedge through the packed bodies.

Emma had to stop every foot or so as booksellers recognized her.

''Emma, you're still my bestselling mystery writer!''

''Emma, I know this isn't the time of year you tour, but would you consider . . .''

''Emma, *The Case of the Purple Parrot* is absolutely . . .''

"Emma, congratulations on your . . ."

Annie would have yawned in total boredom, but she was afraid the thick cloud of cigarette smoke would asphyxiate her.

A bookseller popped up from a jammed table. "Here, Emma, take my seat."

Regally, like a queen among courtiers, Emma wedged herself in at the table. She waved her hand airily. "My assistant, Annie."

Perfunctory nods.

Annie wondered what she would have to do to regain visibility. Tap dance? Scream? Disrobe?

But, finally, Emma got cracking.

Annie draped herself around a fake palmetto and unabashedly listened. In her invisible state, no one at the table noticed.

"Ginger, didn't Missy Sinclair grow up not far from you?"

A bouncy redhead looked surprised. "No, Emma, Missy's from New Orleans."

"Wrong, Ginger." The portly man was firm. "She's from Mobile."

"No, no, no," a petite woman objected. "She grew up in Tallahassee."

A plump, motherly bookseller frowned. "You must have misunderstood, Margaret. Missy told me she was from Franklin."

An earnest woman with gooseberry eyes and prominent teeth smiled condescendingly. "You are all missing the point."

Emma's cool blue eyes studied the speaker.

Anyone else would have shriveled into a ball.

But the patronizing smile didn't waver.

"So where's she from?" Emma demanded.

"Yes, Fredericka, where's she from?"

"Yeah, Fredericka, clue us in."

Fredericka's pale eyes glistened. "I, of course, realized some time ago that Miss Sinclair had cited a number of cities as her birthplace. In fact, I attended several of her signings in Atlanta to confirm my observation. I overheard her at different times in conversation with individuals as she signed her books—I have quite acute hearing—mention Biloxi, Memphis, Lexington, and Savannah. It is quite significant, of course. Don't you see?"

"If we saw," Emma interjected sharply, "we wouldn't be asking."

"Well, it seems so *clear* to me. Melissa Sinclair is claiming *all* of the South as her birthplace. Not simply one town, one state. She is our spokeswoman. She speaks for *all* Southerners."

Despite the book background of those listening, Fredericka's highly literary interpretation of Missy's fabrications elicited no exclamations of awe.

In the flat silence that followed, a hawk-faced woman who'd had too much sun spoke for the first time. "Fredericka, I hope you don't go shopping alone when you're looking for a used car. The truth of the matter is, Missy Sinclair's from the wrong side of the tracks in Tupelo. We went to high school together. She was fat, unlovely, and came from a family that makes the Snopes sound aristocratic. So she has a lot of fantasies about how she might have grown up—if she'd been from a good family in Savannah or Franklin or Lexington. But it doesn't matter a damn. As far as I'm concerned, she can claim to be Scarlett O'Hara's oldest daughter if she wants. Her latest book is quite possibly the best Southern novel in twenty years, at least since—"

The battle was joined. Querulous, well-read voices rose to a screech.

Emma's eyes sought Annie. "You want a drink?"

Annie knew Emma was signing off.

"No, thanks. But thanks, Emma."

"Happy writing, my dear." Emma's canny blue eyes glittered with amusement, then she turned to the bookseller at her side.

Annie knew she was dismissed.

As she wormed her way out of the bar into the comparative quiet and much less-noxious air of the lobby, Annie knew she hadn't fooled Emma a bit.

So why had Emma agreed to probe the pasts of her fellow Medallion winners?

Perhaps Emma felt that one could never know too much when murder occurred.

Or perhaps Emma was making sure suspicion pointed away from herself.

Whatever the truth, Annie knew that Emma was not to be trusted.

But neither were her co-honorees.

The Medallion winners. Each one knew by now that Annie intended to carry on with Kenneth's literary endeavors. Perhaps tonight she could use that threat along with what she'd learned today to jostle loose enough information to make an impression on Detective Wheeler.

Annie glanced at her watch. The Low Country cookout started at seven on the terrace behind the hotel. Even though she'd certainly not charmed several of the honorees today, no one would be surprised to have her, as author liaison, arrange for them to meet together for the cookout.

It only took a few minutes to pen the invitations on hotel

notepaper in the telephone alcove, which was beginning to seem like a second home. Annie carried her missives to the front desk.

The clerk behind the desk was on the telephone. ". . . not conscious yet? Yes, sir, I'll tell Mr. Garrett. He's trying to get in touch with her husband, but he's a trucker, and they think he's in Montana. Yes, sir, thank you."

The clerk hung up and hurried to the counter. "Sorry to keep you waiting, ma'am. We're shorthanded this afternoon."

"Is she still unconscious? The maid who fell."

"Yes, ma'am. It's odd. There's no reason for her to go down those stairs. She's Five and Six. But maybe the staff elevator didn't come, and she needed to go upstairs."

"But she fell *down*. Right?"

"Yes." The clerk shook his head. "Anyway, she can tell us what happened when she comes to."

If, Annie thought grimly, she regains consciousness.

But a maid falling down steps couldn't have anything to do with the poisoning of Kenneth Hazlitt.

Unless the maid had seen someone going into the Hazlitt suite.

Someone in addition to the blonde who had stolen a big box?

Annie shuddered.

Wheeler was certain she was that blonde.

Annie wanted very much to talk to that maid, to find out what else she may have seen on the day of the Mint Julep cocktail party. She asked the clerk, "Are the police investigating her fall?"

"Why, no, ma'am. Why should they? She just fell. It's an accident."

Annie frowned. Certainly if anyone had pushed the maid —and who would and why?—they wouldn't stop with a push, not the malevolent person who'd decreed Kenneth Hazlitt's agonizing death. So, the fact that the maid lived, even though unconscious, argued against anything but accident.

"What's her name?"

The clerk hesitated, then shrugged. "Judy Fleet."

Annie nodded, then remembered her mission. She held out her envelopes. "I'd like to leave these, please. And do you have any messages for Mrs. Darling?"

While she waited, Annie glanced around the lobby.

And there was America's Most Adored Male Author.

This afternoon, Alan Blake was matching his image. He lounged against a pillar, a smile on his admittedly handsome features as he entertained a circle of admirers. He saw Annie looking at him and raised a hand in a casual hello. At one point, he broke into easy laughter.

"Ma'am?"

Annie turned back toward the desk.

"Here's a message for you."

Annie thanked the clerk, who nodded hastily as the phone began to ring and four people converged on the desk. Annie stepped to one side and ripped open the envelope. She scanned the sheet. Max had come up with the goods. At last she had some ammunition for her talk with Jimmy Jay tonight.

As for now—maybe Max would be upstairs. After all, she'd done all she could for the moment. And certainly she had some information to give to Detective Wheeler, and she might have more before the evening ended. She'd earned a respite.

The elevator seemed to take forever.

She sped up the hall toward their room, shoved in the card.

"Max—"

He was there.

But he wasn't alone.

Chapter 15

Four faces turned toward her.

Laurel could have posed for one of the mega-bestselling books on angel encounters. Her classically lovely features were serene, her ocean-blue eyes meditative, her mouth curved in an uplifting smile.

Henny radiated assurance; her brown eyes snapped with vigor, her expression was intent.

A faint flush touched Miss Dora's

parchment-pale skin with a hint of apricot. Her small, tight mouth budded in a satisfied smile. The black chef's cap tilted at a jaunty angle.

Max's eyes lighted up with relief. "Annie, we have company. I ordered tea. For you, too." He gestured at the individual teapots. "To accompany Miss Dora's assortment of delicious desserts."

"How nice." Annie was proud of herself. She managed to infuse her voice with a semblance of pleasure, even though her vision of afternoon delight most definitely hadn't included the Dauntless Trio.

Laurel beamed. "Annie, it's simply been *serendipitous.*"

"Have to agree." Miss Dora's nod made her shaggy silver hair ripple like cirrus clouds beneath the jet-black cap.

"I know you'll want to be the first to congratulate Miss Dora on the acceptance of her manuscript. Truffle Press of Savannah." Henny gestured toward two heaping platters on the coffee table. "Tasting is believing."

Annie stared at the beautifully arranged cookies, slices of cake, and candies. Silently, she vowed she was going to redirect her enthusiasm for sweets into more healthy channels, fresh fruit, gingersnaps, vanilla wafers. Still without exactly meaning to, she took one step, then another, toward the coffee table. It wouldn't hurt simply to look. . . . After all, it would be dreadful to hurt the old dear's feelings.

Miss Dora's flush heightened becomingly. "Certainly appreciate the support I've received. Success would not have come except for the stalwart efforts of my comrades. Now we must bend every sinew to secure acceptance of their manuscripts."

"Huzzah!" Henny exclaimed.

"I have faith." Laurel's husky voice floated in the air like a petal from a magnolia blossom. She held up a card:

Waltz And The World Waltzes With You.
From Simplicity *by Laurel Darling Roethke. Page 17.*

Annie's hand hovered over the platters.

Henny grinned. She snapped through her stack of cards and held up one:

"It's comparatively simple to renounce earthly delights when they're not available. It can be exhausting to deny yourself when they are."
Inspector Smith *in* Swift to Close *by Simon Troy.*
From The Quotable Sleuth *by Henrietta Brawley.*
Page 61.

Annie tried to turn her reach into an airy gesture of admiration.

It truly surprised her when she felt the warm (God, how had Miss Dora managed that!) crumbling stickiness of the delectably fragrant cookie—exuding the ineffable, unmistakable, glorious scent of chocolate—in her fingers.

Of course, it would be horrid manners to pick up a cookie and then replace it.

As the rich, dark chocolate melted on her tongue, Annie heard Miss Dora muttering. ". . . squares of Droste chocolate. No other will do. And unsalted butter, of course. Vanilla from freshly ground beans."

Annie floated to a seat next to Max and simply by happenstance found herself seated directly in front of the laden platters.

Miss Dora smiled benignly.

Annie's hand hovered over the slice of apple-studded cake saturated with a thick brown syrup—

"Apple Delight," Miss Dora murmured. "Rome or American Beauty."

—then darted down to pick up a praline chock-full of pecans.

The sugar jolted her system.

"Miss Dora," Annie said expansively, pouring a cup of tea, "you deserve fame and fortune." She immediately sensed a cooling of the bonhomie and added quickly, "As do Laurel and Henny, of course, with their marvelous manuscripts."

"We've had several expressions of interest," Henny announced proudly. "Both Laurel and I. However, our efforts to gain attention from publishers were quite secondary to our survey of those who knew Kenneth Hazlitt. At least"— Henny darted a swift glance at Miss Dora—"*some* of us concentrated on our duties, perhaps to the detriment of *our* personal goals."

Miss Dora's gaze was as solemn and dangerous as an alligator watching a golfer. "Jealousy is the little sister of envy."

Laurel clasped her hands and beamed first at Miss Dora, then Henny. "United we stand." Her sultry laugh rippled through the room. "Though, of course, not right at this moment. Since we are seated."

Annie studied the cookies. Surely they were flecked with peppermint? Dear Max edged that plate a little closer to her.

"We sallied forth this afternoon, together and apart, seeking a true portrait of the unfortunate Mr. Hazlitt." Laurel opened her purse, drew out a notepad. "I won't, of course, list everyone to whom I spoke. Suffice it to say that I interviewed"—she paused, a pink-nailed finger totted down the lines—"twenty-three individuals." She tapped the sheet. "I'm not certain how best to summarize my conclusions." Dark blue eyes regarded Annie and Max doubtfully. "Mr. Hazlitt, the deceased Mr. Hazlitt, was a—I believe it is fair to say that Mr. Hazlitt was"—a tiny breath—"Mr. Hazlitt," she concluded firmly, "was a creature of strong passions."

There was a moment of silence while each pictured whatever that delicate assessment evoked.

"Ate too much, drank too much—" Henny paused, her eyes swerved toward Miss Dora. "—enjoyed the company of many, many women."

Miss Dora was sorting through her recipe cards. "Satyr. Bacchant. Lecher."

Max reached over to refill Miss Dora's cup. "Was there any suggestion he was ever involved romantically with either Leah Kirby or Missy Sinclair?"

The Three Musketeers, each in her own fashion, gave him a withering look.

"We checked that first thing." Henny waved her hand dismissively. "But oddly enough—for a man who ended up being murdered—everyone seemed to be very fond of him. The people I talked to went on and on about how much fun Kenneth was, a laugh a minute. They said he always planned a great practical joke for every book conference, something that really got everyone's attention."

Miss Dora cackled, and the chef's cap waggled. "One year, a big book was all about ghosts in South Carolina. Kenneth arranged for the lights to go off halfway through the author's talk, and then there were *whooooo* noises and a misty figure appeared near the ceiling." In anyone less dignified, Miss Dora's laughter would almost have been considered a snort. "Scared the poor author half to death!"

Annie glanced at the old lady in surprise. Miss Dora had always evinced strong interest in ghosts. Perhaps she objected to their commercialization.

"I doubt if the author appreciated it," Annie observed.

Miss Dora continued to cackle.

"One of his competitors' books, actually." Henny selected a luscious-looking ball of candy, a combination of orange peel and pecans. "Perhaps not coincidentally, Kenneth had just published a book debunking haunted houses that year."

Somehow Annie found a piece of the orange peel candy in her hand.

"He wasn't universally beloved. There was that appearance of a belly dancer, at Kenneth's instigation, two years ago. The *very* underclothed young woman appeared right in the middle of the banquet." Laurel's eyes sparkled. "The director of the Festival that year, an antiquarian bookseller from Mobile, was not pleased. But I checked, and that gentleman isn't in attendance this year."

"Did Mint Julep Press happen to have a book out on belly dancing?" Annie licked her fingers. The orange peel candy was superb.

But Laurel's reply was lost as a sharp knock sounded on the door.

Annie felt both soporific and edgy from her consumption of fats and sugar.

Until Max opened the door.

Then she felt edgy.

Detective Wheeler gave Max a crisp nod. "I'm sorry to interrupt, Mr. Darling. But I'd like to have a word with Mrs. Darling."

Annie attempted a flurry of introductions.

Wheeler nodded patiently. "I've met these ladies." He stood in front of the coffee table, ignoring Miss Dora's delicacies, feet apart, eyes glinting. "I understand they've been asking questions about Kenneth Hazlitt."

A trio of voices spoke at once.

Crusty and incisive, Miss Dora nodded emphatically, and the black chef's hat wobbled. "Boyish, one might say. However, indulging a grown man's passions with youthful gusto can be most unattractive. And perhaps dangerous."

Contemplative and otherworldly, Laurel's voice lilted seductively. "A very vigorous personality. Famed for his bonhomie." Those ocean-blue eyes fastened on Detective Wheeler with admiration.

Analytical and confident, Henny's tone was pleasantly assured. "A fascinating afternoon, Mr. Wheeler. And the most astonishing fact is that everyone I spoke with claimed to be on the best of terms with the late and, I must say, apparently most genuinely lamented Kenneth Hazlitt. I couldn't find anyone who'd quarreled with him. Except Annie, of course. Is that true for you, Miss Dora? Laurel?"

Silence.

Annie's eyes widened in amazement as she stared at the greatest mystery reader she'd ever known.

Henny clapped her hands to her mouth.

Miss Dora cleared her throat. "Detective Wheeler, won't you please have some refreshment?"

Laurel tilted her head. "Although our afternoon's survey reflected a general sense of loss at Mr. Hazlitt's demise, we must remember"—a winning smile—"that our efforts didn't encompass the Medallion winners. And clearly, they had reason not to be pleased with Mr. Hazlitt."

Something flickered in Detective Wheeler's slate-gray eyes.

Annie feared it was satisfaction.

"Actually, Mrs. Roethke," the detective told Laurel and damned if his eyes didn't warm as they rested on her, "I have had detailed conversations with each Medallion winner. To the contrary, I have been assured that inclusion in Mr. Hazlitt's book pleased them." Now his eyes turned, lost their warmth, and challenged Annie, who immediately felt like Miss Marple facing Inspector Slack.

But she didn't employ Miss Marple's adroitness. "Pleased them!" Annie's voice rose. "Mr. Wheeler, they were *furious*. Furious! Every one of them. They called me— even before the conference began—and left angry messages. They're lying! Ask them how pleased they are that I'm going to go ahead and write *Song of the South*."

Annie knew she'd made a terrible mistake the instant the words were uttered. And she knew exactly how Henny had felt moments before.

But worse.

Because Wheeler wasn't eyeing *Henny* like a copperhead spotting a plump mouse.

The cookies, cake, and candy began to churn in Annie's stomach.

"That's exactly what I wanted to talk to you about, Mrs. Darling. The book. You've appropriated Mr. Hazlitt's idea, haven't you?"

"Yes, but—"

"If Mr. Hazlitt were alive, you couldn't write this book. Is that correct?"

"Yes, but—"

"Is that what you and Hazlitt quarreled about on Friday?"

"Absolutely not. Detective Wheeler, I need to explain—"

"The book was under discussion. We have witnesses who can testify to that."

Annie scrabbled frantically to remember her hot exchange with Hazlitt. What exactly had she said?

"Detective Wheeler, I was asking him not to write the book—"

"Because *you* wanted to write it? Did you have the idea it could make you rich?"

"Detective Wheeler, my wife is in no need of money."

The policeman didn't even bother to look toward Max. "I have been led to believe"—and those cold eyes bored grimly into Annie's—"that money isn't always the reason for writing. Do you want to be famous, Mrs. Darling? Is that what attracted you to Hazlitt's idea?"

"No." Annie pushed up from the couch. She wasn't tall enough to be on his eye level, but she faced him defiantly. "Detective Wheeler, hear me out. I quarreled with Kenneth Hazlitt because he was upsetting the Medallion winners. That is fact. I didn't know someone was going to poison him. But someone did.

"Now you know and I know that the whiskey was poisoned sometime between nine A.M. and the start of the party. We know it could easily have been done by anyone staying on the fifth floor. That list includes me, my husband, the five Medallion winners, and Kenneth's brother, Willie. And," she spoke with great deliberation, "the blond woman who was observed carrying a box out of that suite." Her eyes locked with Wheeler's. "The thing is, I know Max didn't do it and I didn't do it.

"Now, Detective Wheeler, here is something you don't know."

Annie had to give the detective full marks. His gaze sharpened. He listened.

"I decided this morning to pretend—do you hear me, Detective Wheeler?—to *pretend* to take up Kenneth's book idea. I'm trying to find out whether one of the Medallion winners is the poisoner. That's the truth. That's all there is to it."

Detective Wheeler studied Annie for a long moment. Then he said, "Mrs. Darling, that's an ingenious explanation. But I suppose anyone who plans to write a book can come up with some pretty fancy ideas."

"Right." Annie spit it out. "I have another fancy idea, Detective Wheeler. You told me the fifth-floor maid told you she saw a blond woman take the box from Suite 500. Was that maid named Judy Fleet?"

He pulled a small notebook from his pocket, flipped it open. His eyes scanned the pages, then he looked up at Annie. "Yes."

"Well, then, Detective Wheeler, what do you think about her accident?"

For the first time, Wheeler looked utterly blank. "Her accident?"

He listened as Max and Annie took turns. And he made notes. Then he clapped the notebook shut. "I'll check into it."

But Annie didn't like the thoughtful, suspicious look in his eyes.

"Thank you for your time, Mrs. Darling, Mr. Darling. I'll get back to you." He opened the door. "Mrs. Darling, in regard to your quarrel with Mr. Hazlitt. Like the lady said"—he nodded toward Henny, who flushed—"nobody else had any trouble with him. Did they?"

As the door closed behind him, Max said, "Don't worry,

Annie. He's just frustrated.'' But his eyes were dark with concern.

"Oh, dear.'' Laurel's breathy sigh sounded like a dove's mournful cry.

Miss Dora mutely held up a tray of desserts.

Henny, her face stricken, proffered a card:

⚜

"Bang my head on the floor, eat slime."
Rex Travers in Murder's Little Sister *by Pamela Branch.*
From The Quotable Sleuth *by Henrietta Brawley. Page 69.*

"Apologizing for suspecting his sister of murder,'' Henny explained, her voice choked. "Just a slip of the tongue—Rex. Me. Annie, you know I didn't mean it the way it sounded.''

"Oh, Henny, don't worry. It will all come right.''

Annie hoped her voice didn't sound as hollow—and queasy—as she felt.

"You know''—Annie's eyes glinted, and one sandal-shod foot tapped against the boardwalk—"I do not like being brushed off.'' She almost had to yell to be heard over the whanging electric guitars of the Bubba Band.

"Annie, I wouldn't take it personally.'' Max somehow managed to make his voice soothing, even in a partial shout. He bent close to her. "It's just that they're feeling at home at the Festival by this point. And this is a big party''—he waved his hand at the huge crowd filling the terrace behind the hotel and spilling out over the boardwalk onto the beach—"and there are plenty of people for them to talk to. Everybody's excited to talk to the Medallion winners. They don't need an author liaison tonight.''

''They may not need it,'' she said grimly. ''But they're going to get it.'' She planted her hands on her hips.

Dusk was falling. The crowd eddied and surged around the buffet tables with the scrumptious Low Country cookout, fried chicken, shrimp, oysters, clams, and catfish, grilled swordfish, steamed snapper, crab cakes, baked grits with wild mushrooms and a Parmesan sauce, fried green tomatoes, black-eyed peas and rice, sweet potatoes, oyster pie, and stuffed artichokes.

Feeling virtuous, Annie had limited her plate to crab cakes and stuffed artichokes. If not a balanced diet, it was on the lighter side of the food available. Certainly she could come to a buffet and not pig out. She'd nibbled daintily at her portion and declined seconds. But most people were still eating.

Annie scanned the crowded patio. The varicolored lights strung around the terrace provided a festive air. She spotted Leah Kirby's flaming red hair, over by the swimming-pool bar.

She hesitated. Would it be better to attack together, she and Max? That had its attractions. But she had a strong sense they'd better strike early. If she knew Jimmy Jay Crabtree, it would be a miracle if he were still sober. Annie nodded decisively.

''Okay, Max, let's split them up.'' She'd already tried to face down Emma Clyde and Jimmy Jay Crabtree. Maybe Max would have better luck. ''You take Emma and Jimmy Jay. I'll do Leah and Missy and Alan. Let's meet here at the board-walk by eleven.''

.   .   .

Annie stopped a few feet from Leah Kirby.

". . . you're so wonderful. I can't tell you how much I *love* your books. Please, would you mind *very* much—" The dark-haired woman hesitantly held out a book.

Leah Kirby took the book, propped it against the end of the bar. "How would you like for me to inscribe it?"

"Oh, just your signature, please."

Annie lifted an eyebrow. It sounded more like a collector than a mesmerized reader. Collectors know that autographed books have greater resale value if they aren't personalized.

But Leah Kirby merely nodded and wrote her name.

"Thank you *so* much." The dark-haired woman flashed an unexpectedly appealing smile and turned away.

For an instant, Leah Kirby stood alone. A swath of orange light spilled over her. Her face was unguarded. Weariness—sadness?—tugged down the corners of her lovely mouth. Her face was utterly pensive, her eyes mournful. She could not have looked more lost and forlorn trudging across an endless tundra, adrift on a rudderless raft, cast ashore on a barren beach.

Annie wanted to walk away.

Leah lifted her glass.

The orange light suffused the amber liquid with gold.

Kenneth Hazlitt lifted a glass.

And he died.

In agony.

Annie took a deep breath.

Before she could move, Leah's blond friend from the cocktail party came around the end of the bar.

Annie could see her better now. She was tall and thin with an oval face. Her white pique polo dress emphasized her slenderness. The woman lifted her chin, looked as if she were steeling herself. In the light, her hair was a pale yellow. She reached out, touched Leah's arm, spoke hurriedly.

Annie moved closer.

When Leah's companion saw Annie, she broke off.

"Hello, Mrs. Kirby." Annie glanced at the second woman.

After a moment's pause, Leah inclined her head. "Annie, this is my publicist, Sherry Felton. Sherry, Annie Darling is the author liaison with the Festival."

Annie didn't hesitate. "Sherry, what did you do with the box you took from the Mint Julep Press suite?"

The publicist shot an anguished look at Leah.

The author stood very straight and spoke fast, her words clipped. "Sherry has no idea what you're talking about, Annie. No idea at all. And if you don't mind, we're rather busy—"

"Why don't you let Sherry speak for herself?" Annie faced the publicist. "Or perhaps you'd rather explain to the police? I can easily arrange that."

Leah's hand gripped her publicist's arm. "Annie, Sherry has nothing to say to you. And no reason to speak with the police. As for that box, I don't imagine it will ever be found." Like a cobra, the author stared at her publicist.

"The police will find it." Annie spoke with more confidence than she felt. Between the ocean and the lagoons, the likelihood of ever finding the missing box was next to nothing. But she wasn't ready to roll over and play dead for Leah Kirby.

Annie said confidently, "Look, you might as well know I have a copy of Kenneth's book outline from his secretary. So it doesn't matter that the box is gone. Did you think that would take care of it? It won't. I know what that book is all about and I'm going to write it. So the fact that you asked Sherry to steal the box—did you rip it open when you visited the suite, but it was too heavy for you to carry? I'll bet that's what happened—anyway, you found Sherry at the Festival and you ordered her to get that box and get rid of it."

"You do have a talent for fiction." Leah's tone was mocking.

The author seemed absolutely certain that Annie could prove nothing.

With a sinking heart, Annie knew she was right. Ignoring Leah, Annie pounced on the publicist. "Sherry, there was a witness who saw you leave the suite."

Sherry Felton drew her breath in sharply. Her anxious eyes widened in fear.

But Leah had to be a poker player, just like Emma. "Obviously, this witness hasn't identified Sherry. Or the police would have spoken with her already. So, there is nothing to discuss." Those expressive green eyes focused on the publicist. "Good night, Sherry. I'll see you in the morning. Have a good swim."

Sherry Felton finally spoke. "Good night, Leah. Mrs. Darling." She had a well-modulated voice; normally, Annie was sure, a pleasant voice. Tonight, however, it was thin and tight.

As the publicist hurriedly walked away, Annie demanded of Leah: "Do you know what the penalty is for concealing evidence?"

Leah sipped from her glass. She gave Annie a faintly insolent look. Her face was once again a mask of success—smooth, impervious, faultlessly lovely—and more than a little inhuman. "No. I neither know. Nor do I care."

"I think you do care. Very much. Does Carl know about Brett Farraday?"

Slowly, painfully, the haughty mask dissolved. Leah Kirby's lovely face flattened into despair. She looked her age. And older. "How did you—" Leah broke off. She took a greedy gulp of her drink. Her lips trembled. The brazen antagonist was gone. "What do I have to do? Please, please, don't tell him. Don't."

"Mrs. Kirby, were you afraid that your husband would find out about your affair with Brett Farraday if Kenneth wrote that book?"

"Carl wouldn't have read it. If I asked him not to. But if he did—" Tears trickled down those smooth, lovely cheeks. "Carl's sick. He has cancer. He has a chance. I know he does. But not if he gives up. And if he ever knew—" She stared at Annie, heartbreak in those huge green eyes. "You won't understand. I love Carl."

Jimmy Jay Crabtree was in the bar.

Slumped against the shiny mahogany, he stared sullenly at an empty shot glass. He gestured brusquely for the bartender.

Max slid onto the stool next to him.

Jimmy Jay took his fresh drink, downed it in one gulp, shuddered.

"Jimmy Jay, listen, man, you really pulled off a good one." Max nodded toward the bartender. "Scotch and water."

The writer's head swiveled slowly around. His squinty eyes blinked. "Who're you?" He wiped his mouth with the back of his hand. "Oh, yeah. Husband. Yeah." A snicker ended in a hiccup. "Never gave a damn for husbands. Shitload of trouble. Been one myself. Three goddamn times. Three times too goddamn many."

"But you know how to handle trouble. Like you did with Regina Perkins."

Jimmy Jay sat too still. He took too long to answer. But when he did, his glazed eyes flickered with cunning. "Don't know what you're talking about, buddy." He slid to his feet, staggered slightly, then sneered, "Been nice talking to you."

Max put down a bill and swung off his stool, blocking Jimmy Jay. "I'm not sure exactly where you got out of the car. It was someplace around the block, of course. Was it in front of that cleaners?" The Atlanta private eye had faxed the list of local businesses near the scene of the hit-and-run. "Or maybe in front of the grocery store. Once the cops start to look, they'll find somebody who saw you that day. Or it may get easier than that. If they offer Regina a plea bargain—"

Jimmy Jay shoved ineffectually against Max, cursed, and lurched toward the exit.

"Annie, how about a dance?"

Alan Blake reached out and grabbed her hand.

Before she knew it, they were on the dimly lit dance floor, doing a rowdy two-step. The band was so loud there was no point in trying to talk, and when they careened off the floor into a banana shrub, Annie was breathless and laughing.

"Hey, great." Alan Blake grinned at her as if they were the oldest of friends. There was no trace of his earlier anger. "Having a good time?"

And, belatedly, she remembered that he was one of her suspects and that she wasn't at the party to have fun.

But he was certainly attractive when he made the effort. "Sure. You?"

"I *always* have fun." Even in the dim light, she could see the flash of white teeth in a broad smile. "This is one of the best book meetings around. There must have been a hundred people lined up at my signing this afternoon. God, what a great weekend."

His rich tenor voice surged with vitality and satisfaction.

Annie stared at him. "A great weekend? How about Kenneth Hazlitt?"

Alan's face froze. "Oh, yeah. A hell of a bad deal. Poor old Kenneth." His tone was appropriately somber. "Hard to believe. I wonder if something got in his drink by accident. Some cleaning stuff or bug poison. I mean, why would anybody deliberately kill poor old Kenneth? Nobody ever kills the clown."

"You'd known him for a long time?"

"Mint Julep Press published my first book. And it just took off."

"You didn't stay with Mint Julep Press?"

His mobile face changed again. He tilted his head. "Honey, friends are friends, but you don't stay with a small press when your book gets listed as a *New York Times* Notable Book of the Year."

"How did Kenneth feel about that?"

Alan turned up his hands. "Unhappy. Sure, he hated to lose me. But he understood. We parted friends." He shook his head. "Poor old Kenneth."

Annie hoped Kenneth Hazlitt had some mourners who really cared. Because, in her estimation, Alan Blake was amiably sorry but far from grieved.

But if she didn't sense any real sorrow in him, she certainly didn't sense any emotional response deeper than casual notice.

Surely a murderer would emanate more emotion than that.

"Alan, tell me about Hollywood."

Those white teeth flashed again. "Honey, it would take longer than you've got. Come on, let's dance." And his vibrant grin was back in place. He was having a hell of a time.

Kenneth Hazlitt, R.I.P., Annie thought, as they swung around the floor.

Max ordered another crème de cacao.

Emma Clyde accepted it with pleasure.

Max sipped at his drink—definitely not crème de cacao—and wondered how to begin.

Emma saved him the effort. "I've been thinking about it, Max." Her brusque voice was coldly thoughtful and, despite the hubbub in the bar, very easy to hear. "These questions need to be answered: One. Why was Kenneth killed *now*? Why this particular weekend? Two. Why poison? In particular, why nicotine? Why not an overdose of a barbiturate, which would clearly be less brutal? Almost anyone can get that kind of drug, one way or another. Three. Why at the cocktail party?"

Emma sipped at the liqueur.

Max used a cocktail napkin to write the questions down. Whatever Emma considered important, he was quite willing to pursue.

"And there's the matter of character." Her face was in shadow. "I'd give a good deal of thought to that. Who among the suspects either hated Kenneth or is so completely self-absorbed that the kind of suffering Kenneth endured didn't matter? Yes, the importance of character cannot be overemphasized.''

Max tapped his pen on the napkin. "Perhaps nicotine was used because it is so quick. A barbiturate or tranquilizer could take hours, and if he had been discovered unconscious, he could possibly have been saved. And perhaps the murderer wanted it to occur at the party because Hazlitt was likely to gulp down a drink there." Max folded the napkin, tucked it in his jacket pocket. "Maybe the poisoner didn't realize how awful the actual poisoning would be."

"Hmm. I would think that if one were to plan to kill with a particular poison that one would thoroughly read up on it. I know I would." A dry, cold laugh. "But, of course, I already know a great deal about many kinds of poisons." Emma finished her second glass of liqueur. "As a mystery writer."

"As a mystery writer," Max said carefully, "what kind of character would you create who would poison with nicotine?"

Emma licked the last drop from the edge of her glass. "Narcissistic. Cruel. Craven. Manipulative." She put down the glass. "Unless, of course, my murderer were a writer. Then all bets would be off."

"Why, Emma?"

"Don't you see? It's like a box within a box within a box. That's how writers think."

Max frowned.

Emma wiped her fingers with a cocktail napkin. "Look at it this way, Max. Suppose the murderer is strong, forceful, direct, a person most unlikely to use poison." Her eyes glittered with amusement. "A person who might—oh, just for an example—a person who might push a victim from a high place. How clever then to utilize poison. Don't you agree?''

Even in the gloom, Max could see Emma's dry, cold smile.

"Just the most gorgeous night, isn't it, honey?'' Missy Sinclair's soft drawl made Annie feel like a fly stuck on a sticky sheet dangling on a country porch in August. "Let's stroll over and look at the water.''

They were at the edge of the boardwalk that crossed over the dunes. Into the darkness.

Annie stood quite still.

Missy's languorous eyes studied Annie. "My, my, my. First time anybody's ever been scared to walk with little old me. But you know something, honey, that's plain good sense on your part. You're a smart little lady. I'll tell you what, we'll just sashay into the lobby instead. Why, you'll feel safe as houses.'' Missy slipped a plump arm firmly through Annie's.

In the lobby, they settled into cane chairs near the terra-cotta vase with its magnificent profusion of bougainvillea. Occasional whoops of laughter sounded from the bar. Each time the doors to the terrace swung open, the music thrummed louder than surf.

Annie sat stiffly, facing Missy. Annie knew her face was flaming.

Missy Sinclair reached over and patted Annie's knee. "Honey, it's all right. At least it tells me you didn't poison the whiskey. Not that I ever thought you did. Poor old Kenneth. He always had such a good time.'' Her limpid gaze brightened as she spotted an ashtray. "Thank God. A Smoking Section.'' Her voice was derisive. "It makes you feel like a pariah. I declare, it's just marvelous to have the government keeping me healthy.'' She lit a cigarette and inhaled deeply.

The fly tried to shake free from the treacle. ''What did Kenneth know about Tupelo?''

''Tupelo.'' Missy's soft voice was enigmatic, as unrevealing as rain-muddied water, as indefinable as April sunlight shining through Spanish moss. ''Tupelo's a mighty old town, honey. I suppose Kenneth might have thought that's where I grew up. Tupelo might be a nice place to grow up in.'' Those languorous, hypnotic eyes lazily moved toward Annie. ''Or it might not be.''

''Missy,'' Annie's query was sharp, ''what are you hiding?''

''Hiding?'' That soft voice quivered with amusement. ''Everything. Nothing.'' The words hung in the air like spun sugar. ''I told Kenneth that he could write what he pleased. And so can you. I don't have anything to say about it.'' Her face was placid, untroubled. ''But I might give you a little piece of advice.'' Smoke drifted lazily upward.

Annie bent closer despite the tobacco-laden air.

''You know, in the South, when you go out in the woods on a spring day—''

Annie nodded, her eyes held by Missy's dark, brooding gaze.

''—and everything looks so pretty, the mosses and the wildflowers and the ferns, oh, ferns everywhere, bracken and cinnamon and ebony spleenwort—''

Annie waited.

''—it's best to stay right on the path, honey, and not be going off in the brush or reaching into dark places. Those dark places, that's where the snakes dwell.'' The pupils of Missy's eyes were huge; the irises glistened a yellow-gold.

"Poor old Kenneth, I do believe, maybe he stuck his hand in the wrong place. Don't you, honey?"

"Annie! Hey, Annie!" Jeff Garrett came around the desk.

Annie was struck by how tired he looked. Still, he managed a friendly smile.

"Hi, Jeff. How's everything going?"

"Better." Without the smile, he looked exhausted, his eyes red-rimmed, the freckles standing out on his pale face. "Everything's almost back to normal. At least the cops aren't swarming all over the place. It was hell trying to keep things going for a while there."

"How's the maid who fell down the stairs?"

"Better. She's conscious. Her only bad injury's a broken shoulder."

"Has she said how she happened to fall?"

The assistant manager frowned. "She doesn't know. She doesn't even remember being on the stairs. The last thing she remembers is cleaning a room. But the doctor said head trauma can cause people to forget things."

"I'm glad she's going to be okay."

"Thanks, Annie." He started to turn away, then swung back with an embarrassed laugh. "I don't even have head trauma as an excuse. Here. I almost forgot to give it to you. Your husband just called down. Here's the message."

Annie moved away from the desk. Jeff's printing was easy to read:

Annie, please meet me at your car as soon as possible.
Thanks, Max

She stared at it, frowning. Why on earth? She started for the long hall leading to the parking lot, then swerved into the telephone alcove. She dialed their room number.

The phone rang once, twice, a third time.

Annie plopped the receiver in its cradle.

She hurried out of the alcove and into the hall, picking up speed as she passed the White Ibis Room. Mint Julep Press was still drawing customers. She glimpsed Willie Hazlitt behind a table just inside the door, busily accepting checks. He didn't look up.

Annie was just as glad.

She'd exchanged enough hostile glances with handsome Willie.

Meet Max at her car. Why? She pushed through the side door, not exactly worried. But very puzzled.

The banana-sweet scent of the pittisporum bush mingled with the less savory stench of car fumes. Shrubs masked the parking lot from the hotel lawn. Annie plunged down the shadowy path, lighted every ten feet or so by globed lamps. Oyster shells crackled underfoot.

Faintly, she could hear the throb of the band from the raucous party on the terrace. But here it was very quiet. The crunch of her footsteps seemed quite loud. More distantly, car motors signaled traffic in the street. But another line of huge shrubs blocked the street from view.

Several women, their voices high and cheerful, turned up the path, passed her.

It made the parking lot seem even emptier when she reached it.

Her Volvo was parked about twenty yards to the left. She stepped out past the row of cars, turned left.

The Volvo was parked midway between lampposts in a shadowy pocket.

Annie reached the back of the car.

Oh, Max was already in the car, waiting for her, sitting in the passenger—

Pop.

Such a small sound.

Annie heard it and heard, too, the breaking of glass.

The nearest lamp shattered.

Now it was very dark.

Pop.

Annie heard the skitter of oyster shells close to her.

Her heart raced as she dropped to the ground, scrabbling desperately to get to the side of the Volvo. The sharp-edged shells scraped against her hands and legs.

Running footsteps thudded nearer.

Annie scrunched next to the car, rolling beneath the chassis. She scrabbled to open her purse. She had Mace— Then she realized she'd left her car keys in the room.

She clutched the purse, listened to the running steps.

And knew she'd made a mistake.

Now she was trapped.

Somehow she had to get away from the car, hide, get away—

The running steps slewed nearer, nearer.

Annie struggled to crawl out from beneath the Volvo on the other side. And Max! She had to warn Max! He mustn't open the door—

The footsteps crunched to a stop. A cloud of oyster shell dust roiled over her. A sharp, hard pain flamed as something hard struck her shoulder.

Oyster shells crackled. Running footsteps thudded away.

Chapter 16

Darkness and pain.

The running steps faded.

Annie's shoulder throbbed. Something hard, something unyielding—
She reached out, touched metal. Her fingers closed around the barrel of a gun.

A gun.

She fumbled, gripped it, wondered if it was loaded, if this was a way of tricking her, drawing her out from beneath the car.

Her finger squeezed the trigger.

Pop.

So she was armed.

She inched forward.

That was when she realized how silent it was, just the sound of her breathing and the crackle of the shells and the rattle of breeze-stirred palm fronds.

Oh, God, it was so quiet.

The wind rustled the magnolia leaves.

Terribly, frightfully, achingly quiet.

Fear turned her body to ice, numbed her mind.

She felt that she was falling into a void of darkness, a hideous emptiness.

Fear roared in her mind, like winds rushing through a cavern, tearing, destructive, violent winds.

She was on her hands and knees beside the car, struggling to her feet.

That slumped figure in the passenger seat was just as she'd glimpsed it earlier.

Inert, unmoving.

"Max . . ." Her lips moved, but no sound came.

Nausea welled in her throat. She couldn't breathe.

She dropped the gun, yanked at the door.

It opened.

The figure began to topple.

Annie reached out, tried to catch the heavy falling body, staggered backward, unable to bear its weight, unable to stop its slow, dreadful slide.

The interior car light spilled down.

Dark hair.

Dark hair. Blood.

Annie clutched the car door, clung to it. She stared down at the dead man.

In death, the muscles were slack, but his features had been bold, a sharp, bony nose, a prominent forehead, a pointed chin. His skin was swarthy. Dark eyes stared vacantly into the night. A single bullet wound marked his left temple. Blood trickled down his cheek. There was no exit wound. The bullet was embedded in his brain.

She'd never seen him before.

Slowly, she backed away.

Headlights flashed as a car turned into the lot.

Annie swung to face the lights.

She hesitated. But she had no choice. Whirling around, she began to run.

Behind her, a woman screamed.

Annie's heart thudded, her lungs ached.

This was dangerous. What if the driver in the car had a gun? What if it was a pickup truck with a gun rack?

She shouldn't run.

But she must run. God, she must run.

She bent low, swerved behind a hibiscus shrub.

Somewhere at the end of the lot, there was a path to the terrace. She was sure of it.

Almost sure.

Footsteps sounded behind her.

Annie ran faster.

Her side ached, her lungs burned.

There was light here. She could see better, but she could also be seen. She crouched low. Just in time, she saw a decorative row of boulders.

Annie jumped, slid on shells, found a gap in the hedges, and turned right. She skidded to a stop, gasping for breath, and listened.

Shouts rose in the parking lot.

"That way. I think she went that way."

"What's happened? What's going on?"

But the sounds grew fainter.

This must be how the fox felt when the hounds followed the wrong scent, loped away.

Annie hurried up the path. She came out on the terrace.

People milled about, talking, laughing. The dance floor was packed. The music blared.

No one on the terrace had heard the shouts in the parking lot. And the gunshot? It was just a pop, a little pop that destroyed a life.

Annie pushed through the crowd, reached the edge of the terrace.

And there, standing by the boardwalk, was Max.

She ran and flung herself in his arms and clung to him, tighter and tighter until she could feel the beating of his heart against her own.

Annie shivered.

Max shoved back his chair so abruptly it toppled behind him. He strode to the door, yanked it open.

A uniformed officer barred the way.

"My wife is suffering from shock. I demand that we be permitted to go up to our suite."

"Sorry, sir. You can't leave until Detective Wheeler interviews you."

"Then get a blanket for my wife. Get it *now*," Max's voice thundered.

The patrolman peered past Max.

Annie huddled in her chair, her arms tightly crossed. In the mirrored wall opposite, she could see herself, her hair snarled, her eyes bleary, her face splotched and pale. She couldn't stop trembling.

It wasn't simply that she was cold, though she was indeed. This little-used conference room was achingly cold. An air-conditioning vent rattled from the unending flow. She couldn't stop shaking, and she couldn't stop the pictures in her mind, disjointed and fragmented but freighted with horror, the dark shape in the passenger seat, the shattering of the lamp globe, the bloodied circle in the murdered man's temple.

"Yes, sir. I'll get a blanket. And maybe some coffee."

The door closed.

Max pulled a chair close, slipped an arm around her shoulders. "It's okay, Annie, it's okay."

She managed a wan smile and forced herself to sit straight to reassure Max. But she was grateful when the patrolman returned with a blanket and coffee.

Max tucked the blanket around her. She winced when the harsh wool touched the scratches on her arms and legs.

The coffee helped.

Annie cradled the cup in her hands, welcoming the heat against her palms. She no longer felt sheathed in ice.

But she couldn't stop shaking, and the shell cuts stung like fury.

She was almost too tired to care when the door opened and—finally!—Detective Wheeler walked in.

Max stood.

Wheeler nodded, strode to the table, and sank into a chair across from Annie. He didn't look starched tonight. His cotton suit was wrinkled. Patches of oyster shell dust clung to his jacket. He needed a shave. He gestured for Max to sit.

Max leaned forward, his palms on the table. "My wife has been through a harrowing experience. To help the police, she's willing to describe what happened. Then, Detective, I'm going to take her upstairs. Any further discussion will have to wait until tomorrow.''

''A man's been shot, Mr. Darling. In your wife's car. And we found the gun she's admitted dropping—''

Annie looked directly at Wheeler. ''I didn't shoot anyone with it.''

''But you admit dropping it by your car?''

''Yes. I'll—''

Wheeler held up his hand. ''We'll get to it, Mrs. Darling. But first, Mr. Darling, I understand your concerns. I can see that your wife is upset. But I'm not going to put any limits on my investigation. I will keep in mind your wife's condition.'' His voice wasn't unpleasant. But it was frigidly impersonal.

''I will insist upon it.'' Max sat down next to Annie, his face grim.

Annie looked at Detective Wheeler, who regarded her without expression.

What else, Annie thought, could she expect? She put down her cup, sat up straight, hugged the blanket a little tighter. ''Who is he, Detective Wheeler?'' She had to know the answer to that. She had to know.

His gun-metal eyes probed her face. ''You don't know him?''

''I have never,'' she replied steadily, ''seen that man before. Never.''

''You didn't go out to your car with him?''

''No.''

''Did he assault you? Did he climb into your car and did you shoot him in self-defense?''

''Detective Wheeler, I didn't shoot anyone. Not for any reason. Here's what happened . . .''

He listened without interrupting. When she had finished,

he pressed his fingertips together, looked at her over their arc. "Why did you run away?"

"I didn't know if Max was all right. I didn't know. I had to find him." She met the policeman's gaze squarely. "Nothing else mattered."

Wheeler's face remained stolid. "To run was a very unwise act on your part, Mrs. Darling."

Annie shook her head. "Detective Wheeler, it isn't always possible to love—and be wise."

For an instant, Annie felt she saw a flash of understanding in the detective's eyes. Then his gaze was once again cold and bleak.

"Mr. Darling, did you leave a message at the front desk asking your wife to meet you at her car?"

"No. I was expecting to meet her at the boardwalk at eleven."

Wheeler nodded. He pushed back his chair, walked to the door, stepped out into the hall. In a moment he returned.

He eyed Annie. "You didn't question the message?"

"Why should I? Jeff—Jeff Garrett—said my husband called the desk and left a message for me. I went by the house phones and dialed our room—I thought I might catch him, ask why—but there wasn't any answer."

Max leaned forward. "I didn't return to the suite at any time after Annie and I went downstairs to the terrace."

The questions came thick and fast.

"Are you sure you've never seen this man before?" Wheeler opened a folder, pulled out a Polaroid photo, and placed it on the table.

Annie carefully studied the dead face. Lank black hair, overlong for her taste. Bushy eyebrows. The stubble of a beard. Not especially attractive, but memorable, with strong, sharp features. Somber, of course, in death. She tried to imagine him smiling, laughing. But there was nothing about that face that stirred in her memory. ''Detective Wheeler, that man is a complete stranger to me.''

Max picked up the photograph. ''What's his name? Where's he from?''

''We're working on that.''

Max's gaze sharpened. ''Do you mean you don't have *any* ID?''

''Not yet.''

''Was his billfold gone?'' Annie demanded.

The detective nodded.

''There's no identification on him at all?''

''Not that we've found yet,'' Wheeler admitted. ''At the morgue, they'll be thorough. And I've got men looking over the parking lot, the trash barrels, the hotel.''

Annie took the picture from Max. ''Who he is must be important. That or where he came from. It must be very important.'' She placed the photo on the table in front of her.

''We'll find out.'' Wheeler was confident. ''Sooner or later, we'll find out. Now, Mrs. Darling, did you see anyone in the lot?''

''Not in the lot itself. Some women passed me on the path going toward the hotel.''

''In the lot, what did you see?''

''Cars. Just cars. I walked up behind my car. I saw someone sitting in it. I thought it was Max.'' Her hands clutched the blanket. ''It all happened so fast. There was a pop and the sound of glass breaking and suddenly it was much darker. I looked up and the nearest lamp was broken. There was another pop. Someone was shooting at me! I ran around the back of my car and dropped down on the ground and crawled underneath the car''—her voice quavered—"then I knew that was stupid. I could hear someone running—"

"A man? A woman?"

Annie pressed fingers against her temples, struggling to remember the sound. Wearily, she shook her head. "I don't know. It was just a crunch, crunch. Fast." She knotted her fingers together. "It was so dark. I was trying to get out on the other side of the car, then the person was there and he—she—kicked dust under the car and I was choking. Something hard hit me. Whoever it was ran away. I felt around, and that's when I found the gun."

They went over that. And over it.

"All of a sudden"—Annie shuddered—"I panicked. Because I believed it was Max inside the car. I believed it was Max." Her voice was a thin reed of sound.

Max took her hands in his. She gave him a grateful glance.

Wheeler rubbed his bristly jaw. "And then, Mrs. Darling?"

Annie squeezed Max's hands, released them, and drew the blanket tighter around her shoulders. "I scrambled out from beneath the car and pulled open the door—"

Wheeler's expression changed. "The door opened immediately?"

"Oh, yes, it opened." Annie's tone was thoughtful. "I locked the car when I left it there. How did they get it open?"

"They, Mrs. Darling?"

"The man who was killed and whoever was with him."

"Why do you think someone was with him?"

She waved her hand impatiently. The blanket slipped from her shoulders. "Because he didn't shoot himself. Not if the gun that was thrown under the car is the one that killed him. Do you know that yet?"

"No. We won't be certain until the autopsy is done. But the coroner thought the entry wound looked like it was made by a small-caliber gun, and the gun you dropped was a .22."

A gun's caliber, measured in hundredths of an inch, was determined by the diameter of the barrel. So, a bullet shot from a .22 would leave a much smaller wound than a shot from a .45. Annie wondered how many wounds a coroner must have seen to be able to make a judgment from sight.

It was good to think in general terms, to distance herself from that dreadful moment when a heavy body slid from her desperate grasp.

"Okay. Okay." Color seeped back into Annie's face. "Let's figure it out, Mr. Wheeler. To begin with, that's the only gun at the scene, so far as we know. Right?"

Wheeler nodded.

"So, not a suicide. Now, the murdered man was sitting in the passenger seat. Can the pathologist figure out if the wound would be consistent with someone sitting beside the victim having shot him?"

"I imagine he can. Mrs. Darling, I—"

Annie swept on. "But the most important question is, how did they get into my car? And why *my* car?"

"Exactly, Mrs. Darling." His dispassionate eyes bored into hers.

Annie folded her arms. "Not *with* me. Or *by* me, Detective Wheeler. I left my car locked. What's more, I left the keys upstairs in our suite."

Max nodded emphatically. "I can swear to that. Annie dropped her keys on top of the television set. I saw them there before we went downstairs."

"You and Mrs. Darling weren't together for the entire evening. She could easily have returned to the room and picked up the keys."

"Let's be sure we know what we're talking about," Max said briskly. "I can go upstairs and—"

A knock sounded on the door. The uniformed officer stepped inside. "Mr. Garrett is here, sir."

"Thank you, Travis."

Jeff Garrett no longer looked merely weary. He was haggard. He gave Annie and Max a brief nod, then demanded, "Detective Wheeler, how long is the parking lot going to be blocked? I've got some furious people who want to get to their cars."

"The lot will be open when we've finished that portion of our investigation, Mr. Garrett. I apologize if it causes any inconvenience."

"But people can't get out, and they're mad."

Wheeler gave a small shrug.

Garrett shook his head wearily, then sighed. "All right. You wanted me?"

"Yes, Mr. Garrett. I understand you took a message from Mr. Darling for—"

Max broke in swiftly. "Detective Wheeler, that's known as leading the witness, and it's just as unfair here as it would be in court."

A wintry smile touched the detective's lips. "All right, Mr. Darling. Let me rephrase it. Mr. Garrett, please tell us about the message you received for Mrs. Darling tonight."

Garrett's eyes widened as he looked at Annie. "Is that *your* car? Did that guy get killed in *your* car?"

"Answer my question, please." The detective was crisp.

"I was working the switchboard." Garrett glanced uneasily at Max. "You asked me to give Mrs. Darling a message to meet you as soon as possible at her car."

"No." Max shook his head.

Garrett said doggedly, "The call was placed from your suite."

"I didn't place it." Max spoke firmly, pleasantly.

"Okay, okay." Annie slapped her hand on the table. "Don't you see what that means?"

The detective cocked his head. "Why don't you tell us what that means, Mrs. Darling?"

"Someone—and it had to be a man"—she paused—"Jeff, did it really sound like Max?"

The assistant manager glanced warily at Max. "I don't know. Yeah. Kind of. But, maybe not."

"Could it have been a woman?"

"I don't think so. But the call definitely came from your room."

"Yes, I'm sure it did." Annie's face was composed.

Wheeler looked surprised.

"Because," she continued quietly, "my keys were upstairs. So, someone got into our suite, picked up my keys, called down to the desk."

"Why?" Wheeler crossed his arms across his chest.

Max's gaze was challenging. "That should be obvious. Here we are. Here *you* are, focusing on Annie. The murderer must be very pleased."

But Annie wasn't looking at Wheeler. Instead, she stared gravely at the assistant manager. "Jeff, how long have you known that Janet Fleet's keys are missing?"

Jeff Garrett gripped the back of a chair. "Oh, Christ—"

"They are, aren't they?" Annie pressed.

"I thought"—he swallowed—"I thought maybe they got lost. Between here and the hospital. They should have been on a ring on her belt. They could be lost." His hands tightened on the chair. "We have extra sets. I got one late yesterday for the maid who took over the floor. But I figured we'd get the keys back from the hospital. I didn't have any idea they might have been taken."

"Were they?" Wheeler demanded.

Garrett lifted his hands in surrender. "I don't know. I went by the hospital tonight. Before all this stuff happened. The hospital didn't have them. I talked to Janet just for a minute. She says they were on her belt the last she remembers. And when I got back here, all hell was breaking loose."

"Turn a little more to your right, please." The technician's voice was perfunctory.

Annie obeyed, squinting against the harsh brilliance of the lights. A half-dozen spotlights mounted on tripods turned this portion of the parking lot into an oasis of sharp, white light.

"Now hold up your arms. Yeah, that's right."

A close-up of the scratches on her arms.

The camera lens zoomed down.

And her legs.

Wheeler was thorough, very thorough.

The bright light hurt her eyes. Through slitted lids, Annie looked toward her car, the car she'd had so long, shabby and safe. She knew she would never drive it again.

The passenger door was still open, but the body was gone.

Abruptly, the light in her eyes flicked off.

Annie blinked.

"All right, Mrs. Darling. Now, if you'll describe what you did, step by step."

As she went through it, Wheeler dropped to one knee a few feet from the Volvo. He played a flashlight carefully over the shells. The light stopped on a narrow scuff that ran for about three inches next to the back door of the driver's side.

He motioned to a stocky officer. "Crenshaw. Photograph that, then bag up those shells."

Annie nodded. Yes, yes, yes. That was where the runner had kicked the shells, sending a cloud of dust beneath the car to make certain she couldn't see his feet. With the wonders of a microscope, something might be found. A trace of oil. A shred of leather or cloth or rubber from a shoe.

Some of the coldness began to seep away from Annie. Wheeler was looking, really looking. He might suspect her, but he was willing to look.

It was long past midnight when they reached their suite. When the door closed behind them, Annie moved into Max's arms. There was a way to expunge the dreadful memory of the fear that had shaken her when she saw that inert body in her car.

A wonderful way.

Her lips sought his, found them, and there was no other world.

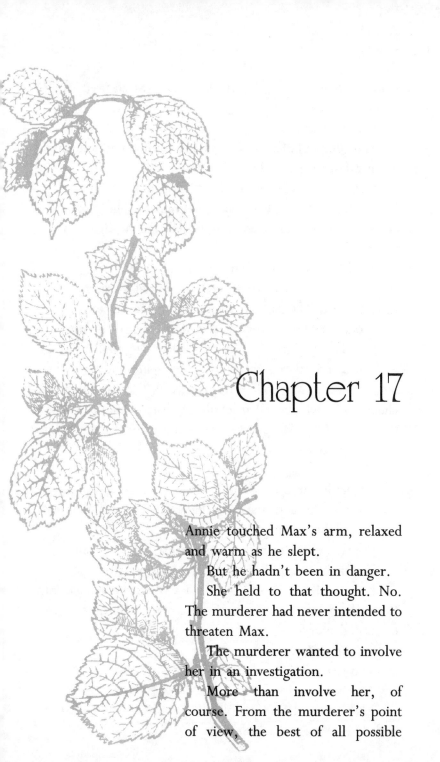

Chapter 17

Annie touched Max's arm, relaxed and warm as he slept.

But he hadn't been in danger.

She held to that thought. No. The murderer had never intended to threaten Max.

The murderer wanted to involve her in an investigation.

More than involve her, of course. From the murderer's point of view, the best of all possible worlds would be one in which Annie was accused of the crime.

Misdirection.

Thoughts and images flickered in her mind with the rapidity of a fast-forward film.

Carefully, Annie eased out of the bed.

She slipped into her robe and slippers. She closed the bedroom door behind her and turned on the lights in the living room.

She'd never felt more determined.

She made a small pot of coffee, poured a brimful mug, turned out the lights, and stepped onto the balcony.

Clouds scudded across the sky. She couldn't see the water, but she heard it, the continuing, unending thunder of the surf. A wind stirred the tops of the pines, a high, fine, delicate rustle. Magnolia leaves clattered. Cicadas buzzed. A chuck-will's-widow called loudly. A sharp whine revealed a mosquito. Annie flapped her hand and stood by the railing and sipped coffee.

Max wasn't at risk.

Anger flickered deep inside.

Because for a devastating, hideous, dreadful moment, she'd thought the magic in her life was over.

She was going to make someone pay for that pain.

The night was full of sound, yet terribly still.

It was quiet, as it had been quiet when she walked into the parking lot that evening to discover a silent, secretive, calculated murder.

Two murders.

Two sharply different murders.

Two wildly opposed scenes.

An exuberant, noisy, rollicking party ended with Kenneth Hazlitt's agonizing death.

The quiet, isolated parking lot provided very private surroundings for the swift death of an unknown man.

A man, Annie felt sure, who had not expected to die on a warm spring evening.

She sipped at the coffee. No, the man so soon to die had walked to the car with a companion. That companion was faceless in Annie's thoughts, but she imagined two figures strolling over the crushed oyster shells, a hand unlocking her car, pressing the button to open the doors. The faceless figure slid into the driver's seat—her seat, her car—and the man so soon to die ducked into the passenger seat.

The doors closed.

The driver's hand—right hand?—moved swiftly, and the little gun quietly exploded. The unknown man slumped to his right. The gunman got out of the car and walked rapidly away. It would have been quick, final, and not as noisy as the rattle of a falling palm frond or the crunch of a footstep.

That was when the murderer returned upstairs to Annie and Max's suite, reentered with the maid's master key, and placed the call directing Annie to come to her car.

Yes, that made sense.

Perhaps she'd never be able to prove it, but Annie felt certain this was what had happened.

The murderer had to shoot his quarry, be certain it was done, before the message was left for Annie.

But it would take only a few minutes to leave the corpse, go upstairs, call down the message, and return to the lot to find a shadowy place to watch and wait.

If Annie didn't come within twenty minutes, perhaps thirty, the murderer would simply walk away. It wouldn't be perfect, but she would still face suspicion from the police because the dead man would be found in her car.

But, thanks to the hotel's efficient staff, Annie got the message and came.

The rest had been easy.

Yes, a brilliant plan brilliantly achieved.

But the murderer, caught up in cleverness and cruelty, made a huge mistake.

Stealing her car keys, enticing the victim to her car, announced without doubt and without question that the murderer not only knew Annie but knew her car.

Annie swung around, hurried back inside. She flicked on the light.

The door to the bedroom opened. "Annie, what's wrong?"

"My car. Max, my car!"

He blinked, shook his head. "Your car?"

"Max, how did they know it was *my* car?"

Max padded to the wet bar, opened the refrigerator, and pulled out a carton of juice. He yawned. "The key chain—"

"No. My keys are on a chain attached to a sand-dollar shell." They'd found the shells the summer before, dead and empty, taken them home, and put them in a mixture of bleach and water, then set them out to dry. His-and-her keyrings, courtesy of the ocean. "There's nothing to indicate which car."

Annie grabbed a legal pad from the coffee table. They settled on the couch, Annie scribbling furiously as she and Max worked it out. Annie's eyes glinted with satisfaction when they finished.

FAMILIAR WITH ANNIE'S CAR:
Emma Clyde fellow islander
Leah and Carl Kirby airport pickup
Jimmy Jay Crabtree airport pickup (and drop)

Alan Blake airport pickup
Missy Sinclair airport pickup

"Okay, Max, we're getting somewhere. Obviously, the person who lured that man to my car *knew* it was my car."

It wasn't elegant phraseology, but Max understood. "It was deliberate, Annie. I've never doubted that. But why your car?"

Annie frowned in thought. "Because the police already suspected me in the death of Kenneth Hazlitt?"

Max grabbed the pad, took the pencil. "All right, who knew that?"

This list was just a little different.

DEFINITELY AWARE OF ANNIE'S INVOLVEMENT
IN THE HAZLITT MURDER:
Willie Hazlitt
Emma Clyde
Alan Blake

Annie took the pen and paper and made a third list.

PROBABLY AWARE OF ANNIE'S INVOLVEMENT
IN THE HAZLITT MURDER:
Missy Sinclair
Leah Kirby   (Carl, if she told him)
Jimmy Jay Crabtree

Annie chewed on the pencil.

"Okay, Max, we can strike Willie Hazlitt as a suspect in the second murder."

Max looked mulish. "Why?" His jaw jutted aggressively.

"He never rode in my car, never saw my car."

"Maybe he asked somebody."

"We'll check it." But she had lost interest in Willie. She put down the pad and shook her head. "Max, we're not looking at the big picture. Okay, so it's important who knew the Volvo was mine. Very important. But much more important is the link with Kenneth's murder. That's what counts. So we have to find out *how* this man who was shot in my car threatened Kenneth's murderer. Did he—let's call him X— did X see something Friday that would link someone to the poisoned bottle of whiskey?"

"Maybe it wasn't the poisoning that X saw," Max suggested. "Maybe Kenneth said something to X about one of the authors. Or maybe X was in the fifth-floor hall when someone went into the Hazlitt suite. Or maybe X saw someone talk to Kenneth at the party."

"The party." Annie looked eagerly at Max. "Do you suppose X was at the cocktail party? If we could only—" She clapped her hands. "The *party*! Laurel and Henny and Miss Dora contacted everyone who was on the list of those who were there when Kenneth died. Maybe one of them even talked to X!"

Laurel picked up the telephone on the third ring, emerging reluctantly from a most charming dream. The handsomest young man, gazing at her with such adoration . . . She murmured a throaty, distant greeting and opened one eye. Opened it wider. Yes, indeed, the clock said five A.M.

"Annie, my sweet, always such a pleasure to hear your dulcet tone."

Laurel listened, nodded. "Of course, my dear. You can count on me."

.   .   .

Miss Dora watched the arc of lights from a passing car sweep across the room. Would it be offensive to include some tactful directions for outlanders in her cookbook? Although it was galling indeed to think a cook might have the temerity to attempt cornbread and greens without the proper equipment. Surely it would not be unseemly to point out—firmly —that these foods must be cooked *only* in a well-seasoned cast-iron skillet on a gas stove. Of course, it should go without saying. However, it had, most unfortunately, often been her experience that when one assumed a matter could go without saying—

The phone rang.

Miss Dora's obsidian eyes noted the time.

"Good morning." She listened without comment. "Certainly. I shall be there directly."

Henny Brawley woke in an instant, alert and poised for action. She picked up the receiver.

"Annie." She nodded several times. "Good thinking. I'll be right there."

They clustered around the wet bar.

Laurel's lake-blue eyes were thoughtful. "Not a very handsome fellow. Something about his mouth. Unpleasant, don't you think?"

Annie stared down at the flyer. Was there a suggestion of insolence in that slack face? She could envision a taunting smile on it.

"So I wouldn't have warmed to him." Laurel's husky voice was dismissive. She pressed her hands delicately against her temples. "But I do believe I saw him at the party." Her hands fell away. She turned them palms up. "I simply can't be sure. I know he wasn't one of the partygoers I later interviewed."

Miss Dora brushed back a shaggy lock of silver hair. "I've never seen him before. If he was at the party, I didn't notice him." A pause, then the crusty voice continued with a minuscule hint of embarrassment. "I was concentrating on the green ribbons."

Annie wasn't surprised. The name tags Festival participants wore were distinguished by occupation: red ribbons for authors, blue for booksellers, green for publishers. But she admired Miss Dora's honesty.

Annie looked at Henny, her last hope.

Henny lifted her eyes from the flyer. "Quite interesting. No, Annie, I'm afraid I didn't talk to this fellow either."

Annie's shoulders slumped. She'd counted on her trio. And she'd been so certain that X had to have been at the party, that X had some connection, some way, to Kenneth Hazlitt.

"But," Henny's voice quivered with eagerness, "you're on the right track." Henny yanked her shoulder bag closer, opened it, went straight to a back compartment, and lifted out folded sheets. She scanned the first page, turned to the second. Her finger stopped. "I knew it. Look at this—"

Henny slapped the paper down on the wet bar on top of the dead man's picture.

Her carnelian-red nail pointed to Number 43 on the list: *Bill Smith, Room 503, Marriott.*

"That name was on my list to check. There was no Bill

Smith registered at the Marriott.'' Henny pointed to the neat check marks in the margins. There was no check mark by Number 43. ''This was the only name on the entire list that we were unable to find. So——''

It was tenuous. Detective Wheeler could easily shrug it away. They had no proof the fake name had belonged to X. But there was a false name, and Laurel thought she remembered seeing the dead man at the fateful party.

If he had been there, someone would have noticed him.

They all spoke at once.

Annie pointed at Henny's neat list. ''The people you talked to, we've still got their names——''

Max said briskly, ''Someone will remember him. And if we can find anyone X talked to——''

Laurel slid the list aside, picked up the photo. ''We can easily copy this, make as many flyers——''

Miss Dora produced a thick black pen. ''We can add this question to the flyers: HAVE YOU SEEN THIS MAN? and show——''

Henny picked up her purse. ''We've no time to lose. Laurel, Miss Dora, let's go down to the hotel business center. We just have time to get the flyers made before the Author Breakfast begins. Everyone will be there. And so will we.''

Annie's hand hovered over the basket of breakfast breads.

Of course, she was aware that the body finds it harder to extract fat from bagels—or at least this was the propaganda happily shared by bagel makers.

Did she believe it?

Did she, this morning, *care*?

Her fingers plucked the warm, buttery, flaky croissant

from the basket. But, healthy eater that she was, she ignored the rosettes of butter and plopped a mound of marmalade atop the roll.

Max poured fragrant, fresh coffee.

She smiled at him, her eyes warm. And aching with fatigue. But she was on a roll—not just the croissant—and determined to continue her struggle to solve two crimes.

Two very different crimes.

She'd always pegged a poisoner as weak but vicious, unwilling to face down the victim.

It took a kind of courage to lift a gun and shoot. Certainly the victim knew the identity of his murderer.

Poison—indirect, hidden, a deadly trap.

A gunshot—brutal, swift, direct.

Why two such different means of death?

There had to be a reason, a good one.

But maybe they wouldn't have to learn the reason why. Not if their plan with Laurel and Henny and Miss Dora worked. Even now, the intrepid threesome should be taking their places downstairs at the Author Breakfast, flyers in hand.

And as soon as possible, Annie needed to talk to Detective Wheeler, find out if the police had made any progress in identifying the dead man. She finished the croissant, licked her fingers, and looked at Max. "Here's what I want to do." But before she could explain, a knock rattled their door.

Annie's sense of comfort fled. It came as no surprise when Max opened the door and she saw Detective Wheeler's somber face.

Annie put down her coffee cup and stood. After all, she couldn't be in any worse pickle than she'd been in last night, and she did want to talk to him.

But why did Wheeler look even more grim?

He refused the offer of coffee. In fact, he remained standing, his feet braced, his muscular body at parade rest.

Annie and Max remained standing, too.

Wheeler once again held out the photograph of the dead man. ''Mrs. Darling, do you continue to claim you never met the victim?'' The detective's stare was hard and skeptical.

''It is a fact,'' Annie said steadily, ''that I have never met, spoken to, or seen this man. But, Mr. Wheeler, we think—''

He interrupted. ''First, I'd like for you to look at another set of photographs.'' He stepped to the wet bar, spread out several color photographs.

Obviously, they'd been shot in sequence.

The first showed the corpse resting on a gurney. It was still fully clothed. Annie hated seeing that small, deadly wound again.

The second was a close-up of the victim's light blue sports shirt.

The third was a close-up of the pocket on the left side of the shirt. The cloth was thin enough that an oblong shape in the pocket was visible.

The fourth photo showed a hand holding tweezers poised above the pocket.

Two more photos showed the oblong of white cardboard being slipped out.

The seventh photo showed the card, resting above the pocket. The legend, in crimson ink, was quite legible:

DEATH ON DEMAND
109 HARBOR, BROWARD'S ROCK ISLAND, S.C. 29900
The finest mystery bookstore east of Atlanta.
Prop. *Annie Laurance Darling*   Ph. *(310) 225-BOOK*

A dagger, in equally brilliant ink, pointed at the bookstore's name.

Annie swallowed. For an instant, she had difficulty breathing. Wheeler's stare was piercing.

"When the killer was in our suite—" Max began.

Annie shook her head. "No. Max, my card case was in my purse. My purse was with me." She continued to stare at the dreadful, damning photograph.

Max jammed his hands in his pockets. "Did you put out some cards at the information booth?"

"No."

And still Wheeler stared at her.

Business cards. Her business cards. Of course, they were available at the store. But that was a ferryboat ride away. How could anyone—certainly anyone here at the hotel—have gone to Death on Demand?

Emma?

Oh, yes, Emma could have one of her cards.

"Fingerprints?" Annie asked Wheeler. She wished her voice wasn't so high and thin.

"Yours. The dead man's. Some unidentified prints."

What an overwhelming, shocking, damning piece of evidence: her card, with her fingerprints.

And the dead man's.

Annie cleared her throat. "The murderer could have taken one of my cards, put it in the dead man's hand, pressed his fingers against it. Put the card in his pocket."

"That's possible." Detective Wheeler's tone was arctic. "And how did the murderer get your card?"

Her cards, she showered them about like confetti, always tucking one in a gift basket—

"Oh. Oh! OH." Annie felt like dancing a jig, turning a cartwheel, throwing a party. Well, maybe not a party. Not for a long time. And she never wanted to see a bottle of bourbon again. "Detective Wheeler"—her eyes were shining—"I know what happened. A third set of prints! Of course! Look, here's how we can prove it . . ."

Wheeler stood, arms crossed. His impassive face never changed.

Finally, she concluded, "I want to bring all the suspects together at eleven o'clock. All I'm asking you to do is check those prints against the prints of the authors. Will you do that, Detective Wheeler?"

"I can do that." He didn't sound impressed. He reached out, swept the photos into a pile. "All right, I will do that. But your fingerprints are on the weapon, Mrs. Darling. You held that gun, palm around the stock, finger around the trigger."

Annie opened her mouth.

He held up a hand. "I know. You explained it. You were trying to defend yourself." He slipped the photos into an envelope, neatly bent the clasp. With no change in inflection, he continued brusquely, "Your fingerprints are on the handle to the driver's door—but they're smeared. Lab thinks the last person to open that door wore a glove. The car keys also hold your prints—smeared." Those steady gray eyes bored into hers. "And on the card, there's a smear from a glove on one edge. Take it all together, what have we got? A possibility you're telling the truth."

Annie began to smile.

His next words wiped it right off her face.

"But you're not in charge of this investigation. I am. And there isn't going to be a gathering of the suspects for you to interrogate. That may fly in the books you sell. It won't fly here."

The door closed behind him with grim finality.

Annie squared her shoulders.

Okay. That's the way it was. Detective Wheeler had turned down her invitation.

But there was no law that she couldn't call a meeting of the Medallion honorees in her capacity as author liaison.

And call it she would.

As for the gathering, she'd better come up with more than the provenance of the card in the dead man's pocket.

She'd better come up with a murderer.

The problem was, she didn't have a clue.

And only an hour to figure it out.

Annie and Max reached the Green Room, where authors gathered prior to events, at a quarter to eleven.

It was an unremarkable room with an oval conference table, beige drapes, and too much air-conditioning.

Max arranged glasses around the table.

Annie paced.

All right. She was a mystery reader. A world-class mystery reader, right up there in the ranks with Jon L. Breen and Janet Rudolph and Marvin Lachman.

But the inexorable swing of the minute hand of the clock on the wall made it difficult to marshal her thoughts with logic and precision.

Tick. Tick. Tick.

Answers. She needed answers. Now.

She reached the end of the room, turned, head down, hands clasped behind her back.

Thoughts darted like undisciplined goldfish. Headstrong, mercurial goldfish.

Kenneth Hazlitt loved to be the center of attention.

Jimmy Jay Crabtree needed money.

Poison.

A gunshot.

Public.

Private.

Willie Hazlitt left the suite door unlocked for his convenience.

Alan Blake thought it was amusing that the police suspected Annie of Kenneth's murder.

Jimmy Jay accused Annie of being in his room. What was missing from his room?

The bourbon bottle was poisoned before the Mint Julep party began.

The maid's master keys made it easy to get into any room on the fifth floor.

The tell-all novel was based on the lives of the five Medallion winners.

The Death on Demand card was found in the victim's pocket.

Kenneth was murdered at the Dixie Book Festival.

An unidentified man died in Annie's car.

Annie stumbled to a stop.

She'd received the message, never questioned it, gone straight to her car.

The murderer had the gun, actually shot twice as she came near.

But didn't shoot *her*.

The murderer had an opportunity and didn't take it. The murderer was satisfied to see Annie embroiled in the second murder, suspected of it as she was a suspect in the death of Kenneth Hazlitt.

Annie was the link between the two slayings.

"Max . . ." There was wonder and excitement in her voice.

Then the door opened.

In came the Dauntless Trio. Henny triumphantly waggled a note card before handing it to Annie. Laurel hugged her warmly. Miss Dora raised her cane in a victory gesture.

Detective Wheeler followed right on their heels. Wheeler's face was a dull red. "Mrs. Darling, I told you—"

"And I'm telling you, I have to do this. So, be my guest, Detective Wheeler." Annie faced him squarely. "Or leave."

Wheeler's jaw ridged with anger.

Annie knew it hung in the balance. She could read in his eyes the temptation to arrest her. He could do it, of course, arrest her for murder. Certainly, he had enough evidence to justify it. And he was furious at her meddling in his investigation.

"This"—and it was close to a snarl—"this better be good, Mrs. Darling." He strode past her and slammed into a chair, then stared stonily toward her.

Annie glanced down at the note card.

By God, it *was* going to be good.

The conference room was like a morgue, silent and chilly, the vents whooshing out icy air.

Annie shivered and faced her audience.

Willie Hazlitt slumped back in his chair, his arms folded. His color was better today, but deep lines bracketed his mouth and his eyes darted from face to face.

Annie was surprised he'd come. But her call had made it clear she suspected one of the authors. And even if Willie didn't like her, he certainly would want to know if one of the Famous Five turned out to be his brother's killer.

Annie cleared her throat and ran a hand through her hair. "I appreciate everyone coming. I know all of you are eager to help the authorities in their search for Kenneth Hazlitt's murderer.''

Leah Kirby's silk dress rustled. ''I beg your pardon! You called and asked me to come to the Green Room prior to the Festival luncheon program. What does that have to do with Kenneth?''

''Yes, Mrs. Kirby. I did. As I invited each Medallion winner and others who have a special interest in Kenneth Hazlitt's death.'' She paused, then said firmly, ''But especially the Medallion winners.''

Leah Kirby cupped her chin in one hand, her camellia-perfect face watchful. An ornate emerald ring glistened in a gold mounting. This morning her silk dress was a bright Kelly green.

Carl Kirby's brown eyes were glazed with pain and worry. He sat stiffly as if braced against his chair. His jacket hung from too-thin shoulders.

Jimmy Jay Crabtree rubbed his head as if it hurt. His sallow face was puffy. Annie had the fleeting thought that Agatha often dragged in dead mice that looked healthier. And —her nose wrinkled at the odor of stale alcohol—smelled better.

Missy Sinclair's enigmatic smile never wavered, but her eyes glittered with fury. She looked like an alligator wakened from sleep, dangerous and lethally unpredictable.

Alan Blake lounged in his chair. His chestnut curls were attractively tousled, his diffident smile in place, but his eyes were arrogant and amused.

Emma Clyde glanced from Annie to Detective Wheeler, her gaze cold and measuring.

Max and the Dauntless Trio watched her appreciatively, a nice change from the other hostile faces.

The five authors might have been carved from stone.

"Kenneth threatened each of you, your lives, your happiness, or your success. His novel, if published, could cause great unhappiness. The characters were so clearly delineated: the elegant redhead involved with a much younger writer, America's sweetheart novelist with a shady past in Hollywood, the author of psychological novels whose own past is marked by lies and deception, the tell-it-like-it-is writer who dumps on everybody around him except the secretary who runs over a child, and America's greatest detective-story writer who may have committed her own real-life perfect murder."

"It was all a lie." Leah Kirby's voice shook.

Carl Kirby rested a hand on his wife's arm. "Of course, it was all a lie, Leah. I know that." His gaze challenged Annie. "This kind of innuendo is something a writer like Leah has to deal with. She has always been extremely generous in her support of new authors, and Brett Farraday is an exceptionally gifted young man. I have been delighted that Leah is willing to share her great expertise with him. So you see, Leah had no reason to poison Kenneth, although, of course, a cheap book such as he proposed would have been distasteful."

Leah's lips parted. Her emerald-green eyes widened.

It was sharply clear to Annie that Leah had no idea her husband had heard rumors linking her to the young writer.

It was equally clear that Carl was lying. And that, in his wife's defense, he would continue to lie.

Leah slowly, timidly reached out toward him.

Carl took her hand in a hard, tight grip.

Leah's eyes filled with tears.

Missy Sinclair's voice was soft, but her eyes glittered. "Annie, honey, you just have the most old-fashioned ideas. I don't think Oprah or Geraldo would be even a teeny bit interested in Kenneth's silly little book. Why, honey, if you can't offer incest or black magic or stolen babies or something special, you don't have diddly-squat.''

''Maybe not enough for Oprah or Geraldo,'' Annie agreed. ''But it could be enough to break a heart''—she carefully did not look toward Leah and Carl—''or ruin a career or send someone to jail. But Kenneth's book may not be the reason for his murder.'' She looked coolly at Willie Hazlitt. ''There's always Kenneth's little brother, the little brother he bailed out so many times. Until this last time, when he ordered Willie to come home and go to work.''

''And I did,'' Willie said angrily.

''Yes. You did. And Kenneth died.''

''But not at home.'' Willie's voice was rough. ''He died here—where all these people hated him.'' He gestured disdainfully at the authors.

''Yes. Kenneth died here. But not only Kenneth. So did another man. Last night. In the parking lot of the hotel. In my car.'' She held the note card tightly.

Willie Hazlitt gaped at Annie, his face blank with surprise. ''Somebody else got killed? Who? What did he have to do with Kenneth?''

''Nothing. And that's what makes it so very, very interesting.'' In her mind, Annie could hear the echo of those words: . . . *so very, very interesting.* Now she understood quite well what they meant when Mr. Moto uttered them in the old John Marquand thrillers. Yes, it was so very, very interesting. . . .

''You see,'' Annie said, ''no one knows yet who this man was. Or why he was killed. But now we know enough to find out all about him. And the person who shot him is in this room.''

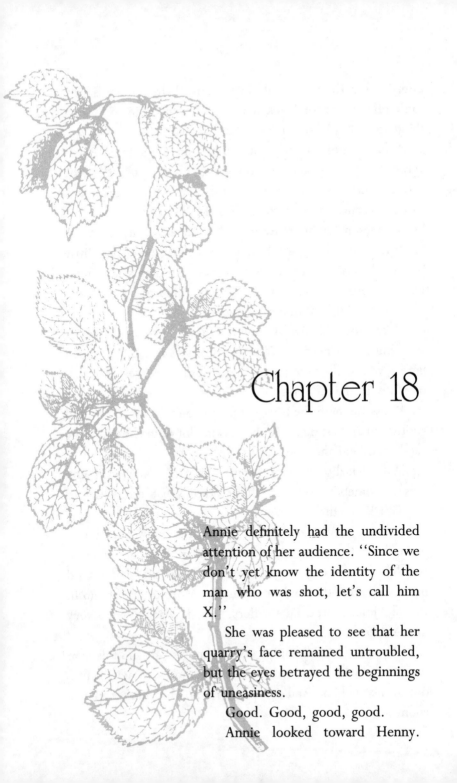

Chapter 18

Annie definitely had the undivided attention of her audience. "Since we don't yet know the identity of the man who was shot, let's call him X."

She was pleased to see that her quarry's face remained untroubled, but the eyes betrayed the beginnings of uneasiness.

Good. Good, good, good.

Annie looked toward Henny.

"Please make sure everyone has a copy of the flyer with X's photograph."

Henny slipped from her seat, moved around the table.

"Dreadful," Leah Kirby murmured.

Missy Sinclair clasped her plump hands together and looked up from the photo. "I suspect this man had a brutal nature."

Jimmy Jay Crabtree barely glanced at the flyer.

Alan Blake shook his head. "Don't know him."

Emma Clyde's eyes narrowed. "No exit wound."

"At the morgue, the technician found one of my business cards in the dead man's shirt pocket."

"And how do you explain that?" Missy's voice was silky.

"Quite easily. I see that each Medallion winner has brought his author packet as I requested. Will each of you please open your packet and turn it toward the middle of the table?"

Alan Blake flashed a bemused smile. "Isn't it a little early in the day for parlor games?"

"This is no game, Mr. Blake."

He shrugged, flipped open his packet, pushed it toward the center of the table, then once again lounged comfortably in his chair.

Leah Kirby opened her packet, studied it for a moment. The huge emerald on her right hand glittered as she turned the folder toward Annie.

Jimmy Jay Crabtree heaved a long-suffering sigh. "Jesus, I need a drink. Let's get this over with. Okay?" He yanked the folder open, shoved it forward without looking at it.

Missy Sinclair pursed her plump lips. She straightened her author photo, then placed the folder on the table.

Emma Clyde's cornflower-blue eyes were puzzled. She lifted out the contents of her folder, glanced at each item as she replaced it. Then one stubby finger pushed the open folder forward.

"As you will see," Annie continued, "every packet—but one—contains my business card in the slot on the right-hand—"

Jimmy Jay jolted forward like his thin rump had been poked by a pitchfork.

"Just a goddamn minute," he bellowed. "You setting me up?" He looked wildly around the room. His stringy hair straggled down in his face.

"I'm not setting you up." Annie's voice was equable. "But somebody did, Jimmy Jay. Because my card—the card found in the dead man's pocket—contained three sets of fingerprints." She looked toward the back of the room, at the stony-faced detective. "Can you tell us, please, Mr. Wheeler, whose fingerprints were on that card?"

Wheeler might not be happy with Annie's efforts, but he kept his promises and he was a truthful man. "Yours. The victim's. Mr. Crabtree's."

"Somebody got in my room!" Crabtree glared at Wheeler, then at Annie. "Somebody came in my room. They—" His thin lips snapped shut.

Annie honed in. "They did what, Jimmy Jay? What did they take?"

He stared at her sullenly, his mouth closed tight.

"Saturday you accused me of getting in your room."

He wouldn't meet her eyes.

"You were scared? What scared you?" Annie spoke swiftly. "Obviously, you didn't know my business card had been taken from your folder. So what else was taken? And why did the theft frighten you?"

Emma Clyde thrummed her blunt fingers on the table.

"The gun that killed the man in your car—was it a .22 caliber?"

"Yes," Annie answered.

Emma's square face creased in a grim smile. "You know, Jimmy Jay, you made quite a spectacle of yourself in the bar at the last Wynnewood conference. And we were all there, Leah, Missy, Alan, and I. All of us know you carry that little Saturday night special. You made quite a point of how easy it was to take a gun when you flew. You put it in your checked luggage. No metal detectors."

Annie's quarry was sitting tensely now.

Crabtree nodded vigorously. "Yeah, somebody took it. One of you bastards took it." He glared around the room.

"The Medallion winners," Annie said quietly. "It started with the five of you, and that's how this ugly affair's going to end. Our story—the story of two murders—opens on Friday, when you authors arrived. There had been quite a bit of publicity about the Medallion winners. Kenneth decided to take advantage of your celebrity to attract people to his book exhibit, starting with a cocktail party on Friday afternoon to hype his Saturday open house. How to get lots of people interested? Kenneth had a great idea. He announced his intention of writing a tell-all novel about the writers who had won this year's Medallions.

"Kenneth certainly succeeded in attracting attention, especially that of you authors. You were all worried about what Kenneth might write. But one of you had a further worry—the unexpected arrival of someone from the past, our Mr. X. Mr. X came to this Festival precisely to see one particular Medallion winner and, I'm sure, to ask for money in exchange for silence about something in the author's past.

"So, on Friday afternoon, Kenneth dies after drinking

poisoned bourbon. On Saturday morning, the fifth-floor **maid** is knocked unconscious and her passkeys are taken. The **pass**-key was used to enter Jimmy Jay's suite. Jimmy Jay's gun **was** stolen, along with my business card from Jimmy Jay's packet. Then the passkey was used again last night to enter our **suite** and my car keys were taken. An appointment was made to meet Mr. X in the parking lot. I suspect it was casual. 'Let's take my car and go get a drink. I know a neat bar.' Maybe there was to be talk of how future payments would be made. Mr. X and his companion walked to my Volvo, the author unlocked the car doors, they got in, and Mr. X was shot. The author returned to my room, called down to the front desk, and left a message for me to come to my car to meet Max. The author then returned to the parking lot. When I arrived, there were shots to frighten me. I hid beneath the car, and the gun was thrown under it and hit me.''

''A nice plan.'' Emma's tone was quite approving.

''But why? It was so elaborate. The effort to link me to the crime was so intense. That made me wonder. And that's when the murderer of Mr. X made a huge mistake. Yes, the police considered me a suspect in Kenneth's death, but I knew I was innocent. I decided to investigate on my own, so I informed all the writers that I intended to write Kenneth's tell-all novel myself.

''If one of the authors murdered Kenneth to stop the writing of the novel, then I should be next.

''But when I was in the parking lot, the killer made no attempt to shoot me. The shots were to frighten me, to make me run. But the murderer didn't try to kill me.

''So, Kenneth's book wasn't the reason for his death. Therefore, Kenneth's book could have nothing to do with Mr. X's murder.

"So the linkage between Kenneth's murder and Mr. X's murder was artificial.

"And for the first time, everything made sense. One death by poison. One by gunshot. One at a party. One in a secluded parking lot. Suddenly, I knew what mattered. Who was Mr. X? Where was he from? And, most important, who was it that he came to the Festival to see? Once the investigation focused on that, once these flyers were shown to enough people, the end was in sight." She glanced down at the note card, courtesy of the Dauntless Trio. "We have four witnesses who connect Mr. X quite definitely with his killer."

Annie looked at her quarry. "Would you like to tell us more about Mr. X?"

Alan Blake pushed back his chair.

Annie's voice was hard. "Kenneth's book may not have been a problem for you, but his fictionalized versions of the authors' lives reflected a lot of truth. So, exactly what did you do in Hollywood, Mr. Blake? Would it have something to do with pornographic films? Like the ones your friend Mr. X had delivered to your room, the videos that made you so furious? That kind of revelation could kill your nice-guy career. True nastiness could turn your reputation to slime, and then who would want to read your sweetly touching novels?"

Blake no longer looked pleasant. Or diffident. His face was tense and angry. "You can't prove anything. I may have talked to that fellow at a cocktail party. That doesn't mean anything."

"Oh, you talked to him. I saw it happen. But I never saw his face. I saw your face. You were very angry, not exuding your usual charm, were you? But linking you to the dead man is just the beginning. When Detective Wheeler arrests you and obtains a search warrant for your room, what are the odds he's going to find the maid's keys? And perhaps he'll find more, perhaps the keys to a rental car that will turn out to hold Mr. X's luggage. And what will happen when Detective Wheeler submits the dead man's fingerprints to the Automated Fingerprint Identification System in Southern California? You see, Mr. Blake, once the police know where to look, it's terribly easy to find answers.''

Detective Wheeler got to his feet. He took time to give Annie a brief nod, as if to say, *Okay, lady.* Then he moved toward Alan Blake. ''Mr. Blake, I'm taking you into custody as a material witness in the murders of—''

Annie broke in. ''Not murders, Detective Wheeler. Murder. The murder of the unidentified man. Kenneth Hazlitt's poisoner is in this room, but it isn't Alan Blake.

''We have two crimes. And two murderers.''

Chapter 19

Blake's departure under guard didn't cut the tension in the room.

Every eye was fixed on Annie.

"Kenneth Hazlitt's murder provided camouflage for Alan Blake. Blake knew he had a chance to kill a dangerous blackmailer and make it look as though that death was an outgrowth of Kenneth's murder.

"So who *did* poison Kenneth Hazlitt? At first, I was sure it had to do with Kenneth's plans for his novel, that one of the authors was willing to kill to avoid public revelations about the past.

''I knew the murderer wasn't Jimmy Jay Crabtree. Jimmy Jay needs money. Jimmy Jay could use any kind of publicity to sell his books. He's not likable, he doesn't try to be likable. And I think he'll do whatever he can to get attention. Like send letter bombs threatening himself.''

Jimmy Jay's mouth opened.

Annie nodded. ''Yeah. I figured it out, Jimmy Jay. You swaggered around, giving press conferences, one tough dude. No way were letter bombs going to stop you. Huh-un. But Saturday, you're scared witless when somebody's been in your room and filched your gun. So, you aren't a big, brave hero. That meant your swagger over the letter bombs was phony. Which meant the letter bombs were phony. And who would that benefit?

''So I scratched Jimmy Jay. Then I looked at Missy. So Kenneth threatens to unveil part of her past. So what? She refuses to live in any past other than one she's created. Why would she care what Kenneth might write? It wouldn't budge her out of the world she makes up.

''As for Emma—''

Cornflower-blue eyes dared Annie.

''—she's lived down ugly rumors for years. Why should she get nervous now?

''And Leah? She knew Carl wouldn't read Kenneth's novel if she asked him not to. She didn't want any discussion of a possible affair, but it wasn't a matter that could ruin her.

''And that left Alan Blake. Yes, he would kill to hide his past. But he made no effort to shoot me. So I knew that it wasn't the book that Alan feared. And why didn't he?

''Because, of all the authors, Alan knew Kenneth best.

Kenneth published Alan's first book. Alan had known him for many years, and obviously Alan felt sure Kenneth didn't really have a handle on his past in Hollywood, however sordid it might be. But more important, Alan knew Kenneth's character.

"And that is the most crucial point of all. What do we know about Kenneth Hazlitt? Kenneth craved excitement. He loved a good party. He was a cheapskate. What could be more fun than to announce plans to write a very damaging novel? It would fascinate book people, attract everybody to the party. It didn't matter that Kenneth never had any intention of writing that book."

A chair squeaked.

Annie looked into guilty eyes.

"Kenneth made it so easy for his killer."

Detective Wheeler was poised to move.

"Yes, I thought Kenneth was poisoned at the book festival because that was where the Medallion winners were. I was absolutely right. That's exactly why he was poisoned here.

"Wasn't it, Willie?"

Willie Hazlitt no longer looked handsome. Or youthful.

"Your big bud, Willie. The man who'd always bullied you, the man who controlled the income from your mother's estate, the man who was fed up with your ne'er-do-well, lazy, irresponsible life. Kenneth ordered you to come home and go to work, and a few weeks later he's dead. In a particularly nasty, vicious, hidden way.

"Who left the door to the suite unlocked?

"Willie.

"Who gets control of his trust fund because of Kenneth's death?

"Willie.

"And who egged Kenneth on with the plans for the big party, lots of laughter back there in the office in Atlanta? There never was going to be a book, was there, Willie? And you knew that all along. The hype about a big, gossipy novel was just a great way to kick off a party.

"A party to die for."

Chapter 20

Annie tucked the cordless phone between her chin and shoulder and
considered which books she might
choose for a classic mystery display.
As she wandered down the aisle,
stopping occasionally to pluck a
volume from a shelf, she made non-
committal murmurs into the receiver. She carried her choices to the
coffee bar and ranged them face-up.
She poured a mug of cookies-

and-cream-flavored coffee. "Henny, really, June's such a busy month—"

Trent's Last Case by E. C. Bentley certainly would please many readers.

Henny's voice sharpened.

Annie held the receiver away.

Yes, *The Amateur Cracksman* by E. W. Hornung was a superb selection.

Henny ended with almost a plaintive note.

Annie capitulated. "Okay, Henny. I know. Yes, of course." Annie glanced up at the calendar behind the coffee bar. "How about June eleventh?"

Henny was mannerly enough not to chortle. "Excellent, Annie. You won't regret it. Oh, I've got a bit more to do with the manuscript before I mail it off, but I'll be in this afternoon. Has anyone won the book contest yet?"

"No. Not yet."

Annie'd no more than hung up, nodding at her choice of *The Red Thumb Mark* by R. Austin Freeman, when the phone rang again.

This time Annie didn't even pretend to resist. "June eleventh, Miss Dora. It will be a lot of fun."

Annie hung up and balanced the Father Brown omnibus in her hand. No. She'd do a clerical mystery display next month—

The phone rang.

Annie answered. "Death on Demand. How are you, Laurel?"

Her mother-in-law, of course, wasn't fazed. "So clever of you, my dear. I know it's simply because you have been in my thoughts, if not my dreams." A light waft of laughter.

Diverted, Annie pondered the question of Laurel's dreams. She'd be willing to bet they'd make Max's ears burn.

But, of course, this was not a topic one could pursue, not even *en famille*.

". . . know you'll be happy to provide a forum for us as the newest authors on Broward's Rock, and I was wondering if we could determine when would be most convenient for—"

"June eleventh." Annie traced Francis Iles's name on the dust jacket of *Before the Fact*. What a wonderful book.

"My dear, it is so sweet of you. I am touched."

They parted with mutual protestations of affection, regard, and lack of candor.

Annie hung up, sighed, and looked at the books arrayed on the coffee bar.

A sleek black shadow landed lightly on the fourth title. Agatha immediately lifted a paw and began to scrub behind one ear. She ignored Annie.

"Agatha, I was only gone for two days." Annie reached down to stroke the glistening fur.

Agatha's head whipped to her left and her canine teeth lightly pricked Annie's wrist.

Annie sighed again. Abused by her cat, bullied by the Dauntless Trio. Why should Annie host a party to celebrate the sale of their books when the titles wouldn't be out for at least a year? Why couldn't they wait until publication?

The bell at the front door rattled.

Just for an instant, when Annie saw the two men, her heart thudded.

But Detective Wheeler was gazing around Death on Demand with evident interest as Chief Saulter proudly displayed its glories: the glossy black stuffed raven (Edgar) just inside the door, the bookshelves devoted to various kinds of mysteries—the English mystery, espionage thriller, caper comedy, psychological, romantic suspense, horror-sci-fi, and one full wall of traditional American mysteries. Agatha Christie had her own section, of course.

Wheeler was casual this Saturday morning in a red-and-orange-striped rugby shirt and faded jeans. He looked rather like a good-guy soccer coach. And his smile was friendly. So, he didn't hold grudges.

Annie invited them to the coffee bar and poured out mugs. She listened intently to Wheeler's report on his investigations.

". . . we've got hard evidence against Alan Blake—the maid's passkeys in his room, the keys to the dead man's rental car—and we've traced the dead man, Jack Lesseg, to Hollywood. It's going to be more difficult with Willie Hazlitt, but, as you said, Annie, when you know where to look, there's plenty to find. For example, we found a trace of nicotine on the right leg of the pants he wore on Friday, and . . ."

Finally, Wheeler finished his tale and his coffee. He looked up and saw the display of paintings. A puzzled look crossed his face. He pushed back his chair, walked to the fireplace wall to study them.

"It's a contest," Annie began.

Chief Saulter chimed in. "The first person who can identify the author and title each painting represents wins a free book and—"

"Any book at all?"

"Any book published this calendar year," Annie said quickly. You had to have rules or collectors would eat you up alive. And sometimes, even that could get sticky. Like the year Nevada Barr's first book sold out and collectors were anteing up bucketloads of dollars to get one.

"How about Annette Meyers's new book?"

"Sure."

Wheeler pointed at each painting and said without hesitation: "*Edwin of the Iron Shoes* by Marcia Muller, *Karma* by Susan Dunlap, *Indemnity Only* by Sara Paretsky, *"A" Is for Alibi* by Sue Grafton, and *Katwalk* by Karen Kijewski."

Annie clapped in sheer delight.

This would surely teach Henny to be so cavalier about her visits to Death on Demand.

About the Author

Carolyn G. Hart is the author of nine "Death On Demand" mysteries, including *Something Wicked,* for which she won an Agatha and Anthony; *Honeymoon with Murder,* which won an Anthony; and *A Little Class on Murder,* which won a Macavity. She is also the author of two Henrie O mysteries, including *Dead Man's Island,* which won an Agatha. With her husband, Phil, she lives in Oklahoma City, where she is at work on her third Henrie O mystery, *Death in Lover's Lane.*